CHINESE PUZZLE

CHINESE PUZZLE

Elizabeth Darrell

Severn House Large Print
London & New York

This first large print edition pu[blished 2008]
in Great Britain and the USA b[y]
SEVERN HOUSE PUBLISHE⌐ᵣₛ ₒᵣ
9-15 High Street, Sutton, Surrey, SM1 1DF.
First world regular print edition published 2006 by
Severn House Publishers, London and New York.

British Library Cataloguing in Publication Data

Darrell, Elizabeth
  Chinese puzzle. - Large print ed. - (A Max Rydal mystery)
  (Severn House mystery)
  1. Great Britain. Army - Germany - Fiction 2. Great
  Britain. Army. Corps of Royal Military Police - Fiction
  3. Rydal, Max (Fictitious character) - Fiction 4. Murder -
  Investigation - Germany - Fiction 5. Detective and mystery
  stories 6. Large type books
  I. Title
  823.9'14[F]

  ISBN-13: 978-0-7278-7662-1

Except where actual historical events and characters are being described
for the storyline of this novel, all situations in this publication are
fictitious and any resemblance to living persons is purely coincidental.

Printed and bound in Great Britain by
MPG Books Ltd, Bodmin, Cornwall.

Acknowledgements

The author wishes to thank various military sources for research information for this novel, in particular, Lieutenant Colonel (Retd) John Nelson, late of the Royal Military Police.

One

When a socially conscious Chinese student made to rouse his dozing neighbour as the Star Ferry *Wandering Star* docked at Tsimshatsui, he discovered the passenger was dead. The corpse had crossed and recrossed Hong Kong harbour eight times, unnoticed by the evening rush hour flow of humanity.

The young Chinese gazed with fascination at the body propped against the ship's rail. Of western origin, the man wore a lightweight fawn suit, tan shoes and a cream shirt with a club-style tie. He looked very peaceful. Death must have come like a cloud stealing over the sun. Understandable in the elderly, but this man looked to be in his thirties. Clearly, the gods had an urgent task for him in the next life.

The two policemen who questioned the youth shared this belief. They arranged for the removal of the body so the ferry could go back into service, then set about identifying the deceased. In his jacket pocket there was no wallet, therefore no credit or business cards, no club membership documents, no driving licence to aid recognition. His trouser pockets held loose change and a handkerchief. No keys. Curious for so well-dressed a man to be out and about carrying so little!

His suit and shirt had been made by a reputable Kowloon tailor. His shoes and underpants bore labels of international brands available anywhere. He could be a resident who had taken a taxi to the ferry terminal, and who carried no house keys because a servant would let him in to his home on his return. Any visitor to Hong Kong would surely carry the plastic room key used by most hotels. On the other hand, he could be staying with friends in Kowloon. Whoever he was, someone would miss him before long and start asking questions of hospitals and the police.

The next morning, Constable John Chew visited the premises of the tailor, Freddie Yau, in the Star House shopping complex near the ferry terminal, taking with him a photograph of the dead man and the jacket of his suit. The morning rush was underway, although there was scarcely an hour of the day when the streets of Kowloon were not filled with the urgency of people going places. Every few minutes the ferries spewed out a stream of passengers. Liners docked alongside them offloaded several thousands more every day. Buses, taxis, bicycles made crossing the road a feat for the brave or foolhardy. Noise, dust, bustle. The offshoots of commerce.

Yau's premises were on a corner of one of the cramped walkways between goldsmiths, silk merchants, bargain shoe shops, vendors of spices, acupuncture practitioners, racks of handbags cleverly copied from top designers and too many booths offering Oriental souvenirs for tourists.

Yau was measuring a customer's inside leg when Constable Chew arrived. One glance at the immaculate starched uniform told the tailor he was there on police business, not to order clothes. A swift word to his assistant to take over left him free to invite discussion in the busy walkway out of earshot of his customer.

Chew saw no hint of concern on Yau's broad face, which suggested he had nothing to fear from the police. But Chinese were past masters at hiding their thoughts. In this instance, however, the tailor's personal affairs were not at issue. The jacket and photograph were shown and his initial response was eager.

'That cloth! The finest wool gabardine anywhere in Hong Kong. In the entire East. You could not find better in Saville Row.'

'I am not a customer,' Chew reminded him, cutting off the sales patter, 'but do you remember this one?'

After barely a glance at the photograph, Yau shook his head. 'It is too long ago.'

'How can you know that?'

Yau grinned showing yellowed teeth. 'I have not used that cloth for nine, ten years. Su Yong Company went out of business. You won't remember. You are too young. Their

9

warehouses burned down one dry, windless night. Nothing was saved. The old man killed himself after his baby great-grandson was taken from the family home on the Peak and returned piece by piece.'

Constable Chew did not have to wonder at this. New to his job he nevertheless had always been aware of Triad take-overs that continued unchecked because, like the Mafia, their influence was far-reaching.

'So this suit was made before 1997?'

'Give me the customer's name. I look in my books and tell you the exact date.'

'We don't have his name. We want it from you.'

Glancing back impatiently to where an American couple were showing great interest in the tailored items on display, Freddie Yau said, 'I keep records at least ten years. If I have a name I can tell you date and address, how the customer paid, if he was recommended by previous customer – all about him. No use to show me faces.'

'So you don't remember ever seeing this man before?'

'I just tell you, no. What has he done, anyway?'

'Passed on to the next life.'

Yau shrugged and turned away, losing interest. 'Then he won't be wanting any more suits.'

Several days passed, but no one reported a friend or relative missing. When John Chew was on the brink of inserting the photograph of the dead man in the *South China Post* asking if anyone recognized him, pure chance stepped in. The corpse's few personal effects, along with his clothes, bagged and tagged, sat in the store housing other unclaimed items. A constable returning to duty after a spell of fever noticed the new addition and asked his colleague about them.

'Mystery man. Died on the Star Ferry after being mugged. A heart attack. That's all we know about him, there in that bag.'

'I can tell you a bit more, then. The last time I saw a tie like that my cousin's husband was wearing it. Royal Cumberland Rifles. It's a British Army regiment.'

Within forty-eight hours the Hong Kong Police had the identity of their corpse. Harry Barker, former captain in the RCR, on terminal leave after deciding against signing on for a further term of service. A check of his landing card told Chew when he had arrived in Hong Kong and where he proposed to stay. He immediately searched the hotel room that had been occupied by Barker for the past three weeks. The wardrobe contained another suit by Yau, two formal shirts and four casual ones to go with two pairs of slacks. The usual socks and underpants were in a drawer with a handful of brochures and a large-scale map of the New Territories. There was a holdall bearing a Heathrow to Hong Kong flight tag (business class) and a well-worn empty brief-case.

Chew called the hotel's service manager to

11

open the room safe. It held a British Airways ticket for a return flight dated a week hence, and a new passport in the name of Harold Barker which bore just the one entry stamp. The photograph was of the dead man. The spaces the holder should fill with details of who should be informed in the case of an accident or emergency had been left blank. Some travellers' cheques to the value of nine thousand dollars suggested Barker was not a man to stint himself on holiday. Sad that a heart attack should so soon put an end to his pleasure in life.

The sergeant handling the case concluded that Barker had been relieved of his wallet prior to boarding the ferry, maybe already feeling the onset of the coronary spasm leading to his death. A general notice was issued to report evidence of attempts to use any credit cards in Barker's name. His belongings were then packed in his holdall, including the regimental tie, and stored to await the shipping home of the body.

Vera watched him appreciatively as he threaded his way between tables mostly occupied by local Germans. Tall, muscular, confident; a good-looking man with a direct gaze. He was what she had been looking for since Peter walked out of her life. He had not so far angled for sex, but she was not going to push him in to something she wanted that he was not ready for. Curious. Men were mostly up for it on the first date.

'Sorry I wasn't here when you arrived,' he said, sitting opposite her at a small corner table.

'I got here very early. I guessed you'd have made a reservation, so I started on the vino,' she told him with a warm smile. 'Helga altered her plan at the last minute. Good thing I'd showered and changed as soon as I came off duty or I wouldn't have been ready. She did stretch a point to drop me right outside as it's such a foul evening.'

'I was more than willing to pick you up,' he reminded her.

'There was no need when a lift was on offer, Brian. It's bad enough that you have to drive all the way back to my digs at the end of the evening.'

It was the perfect opportunity for him to suggest they spend the night together, but he instead asked what she would like to eat. He added to their order a beer for himself and another glass of the Mosel wine she was drinking. Only then did he appear to appreciate the trouble she had taken with her appearance: tan suede jacket and skirt, patterned silk top with a single gold chain necklet.

'I'm sitting with the loveliest woman in the room.'

'It's taken you long enough to notice,' she teased.

'Uh-uh, you stood out as drop-dead gorgeous the moment I came in.' A rueful smile. 'Only just plucked up the necessary to say it.'

'I don't bite, Brian.'

'Oh no? You were damn starchy at our first encounter.'

'That was my professional self. Experience has taught me that wounded sergeants need to be shown who's boss right from the start. They tend to expect nurses to jump to their bidding like squaddies do.'

'Rot! We're totally at your mercy. Get out of line and we either have something jabbed in our arm or up our backside.'

The banter continued over their drinks until the food arrived. Both hungry after professionally hectic days, they ate with enthusiasm. Yet there was an unspoken message each time their eyes met that told Vera tonight was special. Brian was geared up for something. By the time they reached the coffee stage the dining area was crowded and noisy with conversation, mostly in German. No one was interested in the sergeant and the Englishwoman in the corner with eyes only for each other.

Pushing the last chocolate mint across to Vera, Brian said out of the blue, 'I was stationed in Hong Kong just prior to the handover.'

'Oh?' Why break the intimacy with service talk, she thought irritably.

'An interesting place. A successful mix of East and West, on the whole. I suppose the residents have integrated Brit methods and attitudes into their own and have the advantages of both worlds. Most of us wondered what would happen to them when we left. Felt rather guilty about it, although we had no choice but to go.'

Into the pause Vera said woodenly, 'It's turned out all right, hasn't it? Nothing's changed.'

'Oh, there have been changes. Nothing too drastic, but give it time.'

Another longish pause, so Vera took the bull by the horns. 'Where's all this leading, Brian?'

His gaze remained steady. 'To the fact that I married a Chinese girl while I was there.'

It was so devastatingly unexpected Vera was unsure what she felt. Anger? Disappointment? Pain? Disgust at allowing herself to be so taken in? 'How nice for you,' she said icily. 'A successful mix of East and West, as you said.'

'If it had been, I wouldn't be sitting here now. I've not been double dealing you, Vera.'

Totally confused, still hurt by the revelation, she asked stiffly, 'So where is she?'

'In Hong Kong.' He sighed heavily. 'Everything was working fine until nine months before my tour was due to end. I got a home posting at short notice. Some yarn about reinforcements being sent to trouble spots leaving UK strengths dangerously low, but as I was the only one listed I appealed against it. My company commander simply said his hands were tied.' He gave a shrug of resignation. 'Jacki refused to go. Said she couldn't leave her mother and sisters to face what they were sure would happen when the Chinese

15

took over. She claimed they were her responsibility.' He frowned at Vera, remembering. 'We had row after row, but she was pig headed. Said she would only leave if they came with us. It was bloody ridiculous. She knew the bottom line. Had known it right from the start. Captain Blakey pointed that out when I then applied for deferment on compassionate grounds. He said my wife had been aware the regiment would leave after the take over, so she had had eighteen months in which to accept separation from her family. In his opinion there were no compassionate grounds. He told me to put my foot down and start wearing the trousers. He was a right bastard. Very racist. Had no time for the Chinese.'

Vera fought her jealousy at the thought of this man she had come to love going to bed night after night with another women. 'Go on,' she prompted.

'I flew home alone. Blakey's attitude made sense once I was able to think straight. A few months back with family and friends put the whole business into perspective.' His mouth twisted. 'Oriental girls can be very alluring. They've an underlying demureness that appeals to Western men. Lots of the lads had business arrangements with girls out there, but Jacki was a respectable girl. Cashier in a good class restaurant. I was bowled over, so there was only one solution.'

Vera said nothing. His desire for sex with that girl had been so strong he had had to marry her to get it. Maybe she, herself, was not 'alluring' enough.

Brian broke the silence with gentle words. 'I divorced her a year later. The only possible end to a period of madness.' His brown eyes appealed to her. 'There's no madness behind what I feel for you, Vera. I think this is the sanest I've ever been. I knew from that first day you were special and I wanted to be with you all the time. Marry, settle down, have kids. But I couldn't go on seeing you, making my feelings clear, until I'd told you all this.' He let silence fall and, when she failed to fill it, added, 'I can see it's come as ... well, as a bit of a shock.' He laid a tentative hand over hers. 'I hoped you felt as drawn to me as I was to you that day we met. Nothing you've done since then changed that impression. I wanted you to be aware of the shadow in my past before I asked you to share my future, but if my marriage to Jacki is something you can't accept there's no point in this relationship.'

Vera did not withdraw her hand, but she had no idea what to say to him. It would be madness on her own part to throw away the chance of a life with this man, yet he had become a different person now. Struggling to come to terms with what he had revealed, she realized she had not told him about her hot affair with Peter. A shadow in her own past. Maybe everyone had that. Her gaze searched his features and saw sincerity, strength and present anxiety as he waited for her response. This man would not walk away from her as

17

Peter had.

'I think there's every point to this relationship, Brian.'

His fingers gripped hers; brown eyes grew warm. 'Are you saying you'll take me on?'

'On one condition.'

'What's that?'

'Opposite the hospital there's a small *Gasthof*. I'm on duty at six a.m., but if we booked a room there I'd make it on time. Before I say yes, I need to know how good you are in bed.'

He laughed loudly enough to make heads turn. Then he leaned toward her and whispered, 'I'll make bells ring, the earth move and summer come early.'

It was still raining hard when they left the restaurant, so they put their heads down and ran for Brian's car. They had almost reached it when Brian collided with someone threading his way between the closely parked vehicles.

'Sorry, mate,' Brian grunted.

Laughing, shaking the rain from their hair, they kissed with exuberance before Brian started up and drove from the car park. They were soon out on the road heading towards the cosy room where they would seal their future in each other's arms.

Death overtook Brian very swiftly. The car swerved on the dark road, then smashed head-on in to a stand of oaks. A truck driver passing shortly afterwards stopped, saw he could do nothing, then called an ambulance. The German police, on seeing the car's

18

registration, informed their British military counterparts of the disaster involving army personnel, and handed over responsibility. The Redcaps waited for the female passenger to give details of what had happened, but she died without recovering consciousness twelve hours later.

Pathologists soon rejected the idea of a drink-drive accident. Brian New's alcohol level was too low. Preliminary examination showed evidence of coronary spasm leading to cardiac arrest.

Cliff Busby was two-fingering his computer keyboard when Simon Kington came from one of the inner offices, locking the door. 'Still at it, Sar'nt Major? Not planning to burn midnight oil, are you?'

Busby grinned. 'Mother-in-law's here for the week. Good time to catch up on the back-log.'

'Refuge is always available in the Sergeants' Mess.'

'Oh, aye, sir, I'm going there soon as I've finished this.'

'Wise man. Goodnight to you.'

Busby heard the officer's heavy tread on the wooden steps and, soon afterwards, the sound of his car backing out before turning on to the perimeter road. Fortunate man. *His* wife's mother alternated between New York and Geneva, with exotic locations between. An interpreter with the UK Mission to the United Nations, she mingled with ambassadors and heads of state and seldom visited her daughter in an officer's married quarter in Germany.

Tara Kington was said to be as talented as her mother. She had that gloss of class and privilege that produces a serene type of beauty. A Cambridge graduate in European history, she had taught at a girls' private school until the birth of her twins. She now wrote educational books on the subject. She also owned and rode a horse, played championship golf and tennis, and gave talks on art appreciation to anyone on-base who was interested.

Her husband was also a Cambridge graduate, in modern languages and European politics. His sporting activities centred on speed. He rode at point-to-points, owned a Ferrari he gunned along the autobahns, and had a quarter share in a Learjet. Son of Sir Chetwin Kington, the pharmaceuticals giant, his army salary would be no more than pocket money. Silver spoon notwithstanding, Kington was an inspired leader who valued his career above almost anything else in his life, and he was fiercely proud of the Royal Cumberland Rifles.

As was Sergeant Major Busby. This shared regimental loyalty bridged the social gap, allowing respect and understanding between the wealthy major and the working-class man. Which was why Busby could share a mother-in-law joke with his commander at the end of a hectic day.

★ ★ ★

Ben Steele had just checked out the armoury and climbed back in the Land Rover when his phone rang. He cursed. It had started raining half an hour ago and it was now thundering down. He was wet, chilled and fed up. What he bloody did not need right now was a punch up between young bloods so rat-arsed they would hit out at anyone trying to come between them. Swallowing a sigh, he took up the phone.

'Duty Officer, Lieutenant Steele.'

'Ben, it's Tara Kington,' said a tense voice. 'Could you come to the house?'

Surprised, he checked the time. Just past midnight. 'Do you have a problem, Mrs Kington?'

'I think so.' She sounded hesitant.

'Is your husband away?' he asked, knowing he was not but always wary about visiting women in the middle of the night. Tara Kington did not seem the type to try it on, but one never knew with women.

'No ... well, not in the sense you mean.'

'I see.' Not that he did, but the underlying tone of her voice was anxious rather than sexy. 'I'm actually not far from your quarter. Be there in ten.'

Putting the vehicle in gear, he drove off along the deserted road where rain bounced up off a surface glistening beneath his full beams. He was still soaked to the skin, chilled and fed up, but he was intrigued. Whatever was going on here would be better than

21

sorting out aggressive squaddies, and he was sure to be offered a welcome cup of coffee. He pondered her answer regarding Simon being away. *Not in the sense you mean.* What the hell...?

Lights were on in the three downstairs windows at the front of the large, square house. Ben pulled in to the short driveway, noting Simon's cars and also his wife's beneath the double-width carport. Hunching his shoulders against the driving rain, he ran to the shelter of the enclosed porch and rang the doorbell. Tara was fully dressed, which Ben found reassuring, and she appeared composed, if rather pale, as she thanked him for responding so promptly.

He smiled. 'I was on rounds and glad of the chance to escape the rain. It's bucketing down out here.'

'I've made coffee. You'd like some, I expect.'

'Thanks.' He shrugged off his dripping parka, unlaced and removed his muddy boots to leave in the porch before following her along the hall to the pale-carpeted sitting-room. Ben had not been in the Kington home before. Wealth and good taste were evident in the paintings, ornaments and fittings he studied as he waited for her to pour from a cafetière. The glow from four elegant table lamps created such an aura of serenity, Ben had almost forgotten his reason for being there when the slender, auburn-haired woman offered him a bone china mug filled with coffee.

'I'm dreadfully afraid something bad has happened to Simon.'

Startled, he simply repeated her words. 'Something bad?'

'I thought it best to contact the Duty Officer before making too much of it. Simon would hate a big fuss.'

A big fuss about what? thought Ben, then recalled her enigmatic telephone statement. 'Your husband has gone missing?'

She nodded. 'It's all a bit weird.'

The hot mug was burning his fingers so he put it on a low table as he tried to get to grips with this situation. Drunken squaddies would have been simpler. Marital upsets were the very devil to deal with. She needed the Padre, not an unmarried twenty-four-year-old whose temperature rose every time he caught sight of her in jodhpurs.

'When did you last see him?' he ventured in true detective fiction style. It was the best he could come up with.

She perched on the edge of a settee, gazing up at him with worried eyes. 'I last *saw* him at breakfast this morning. But I heard him arrive a little before six tonight. You saw the four by four he calls his workhorse drawn up outside?'

He nodded.

'When I heard him drive in I poured two G and Ts in readiness. We'd planned a quiet evening in, listening to our favourite CDs. No guests, or invitations to dinner tonight.'

'I see.' He felt awkward standing there in his

socks, wet trousers clinging to his legs, listening to the intimacies of her life in this house.

'When he didn't come straight in I thought he must be checking over the Ferrari ready for the weekend rally. He fusses over it like a mother with a new baby, you know.'

Ben gave a nervous gurgle meant to be an expression of understanding of a Ferrari owner's foibles.

'After ten minutes I went out to chivvy him, but he wasn't there. I called out several times and got no reply.' Her brow furrowed as she explained to him. 'I couldn't understand what was going on. The keys were in the ignition and his cap and gloves were on the seat. His laptop was missing, and he was nowhere around.'

Feeling even more awkward, Ben asked, 'Haven't you any idea where he might be?'

'That's why I called you. Simon couldn't have vanished, yet that's what seems to have happened. Initially, I thought he must have gone next door to see Jim Ferguson about something. Or to our other neighbours, although we see little of them. After another half hour I called Jim, then the Mostyns. They hadn't seen Simon.'

Wondering what man in his right mind would two-time this gorgeous woman, Ben said carefully, 'Have you tried his mobile?'

Tara waved an elegant hand at a top-of-the-range model lying on the coffee table. 'I brought it in with his cap, gloves and the ignition keys. Look, Ben, I've contacted all our friends, the Mess, the Ferrari Club, the stables and the Corporal of the Guard. No one has seen him and he hasn't officially left the base through either gate. Perhaps you now understand why I think something bad has happened to him.'

Ben's thoughts were starting to take wing. Simon Kington's fluency in French, German and Spanish made him the ideal Defence Liaison Officer for the Cumberlands. He frequently attended meetings at other EU military bases, and was co-opted on to committees planning multi-national exercises. Had he stumbled upon evidence of something...? No, there had to be a simpler explanation. Men did not just vanish from outside their front door.

'What should I do, Ben?'

His attention returned to the woman needing support and expecting him to provide it. 'Leave it with me,' he offered with as much assurance as he could muster. 'I'll speak to the guys on the gates. If they're certain he's still on home ground, I'll send out search parties. I'll also check with the perimeter patrols, see if they've had sight of him tonight. After that, I'll drive around to look in the less obvious places.' He had a bright idea. 'Maybe he's suffering from delayed concussion. Didn't he have a hefty fall at the point-to-point at the weekend? Could be he got out of his car, couldn't think where he was, and wandered off in a confused state. When the rain started he would have holed up somewhere.' He forced a smile. 'We'll find him, Mrs Kington.'

She did not look convinced as she got to her feet and followed him from the room. 'He would have been checked over by the doc after that fall; but I suppose you could be right. It's the only sensible explanation for this. Sorry to lumber you with it, Ben.'

He glanced up from pulling on his mud-caked boots. 'Duty Officer's function to sort out problems, day or night.' Shrugging on his jacket, he added, 'If he turns up, call me pronto.'

Max Rydal was doodling on his notepad wondering whether to get something basic from the canteen or to drive in to the pretty suburb five kilometres away for a more delicious lunch. He had time on his hands. Three current cases being handled by his SIB section of the Royal Military Police were low-key: petty theft, insubordination with threats, and alleged sexual harassment. The team members were dealing with them all. As Commanding Officer he was burdened with the paperwork. A mountain of it. More than enough to urge him out to his car and his favourite eating place a short drive away. Spring had finally arrived after three grey days of pouring rain. That alone tempted him outdoors.

He slid from behind his desk and reached for his soft leather jacket, already mentally choosing his lunch menu. There was a sharp rap on the door before it was opened by Sergeant Major Black, the only member of the team who did not wait for permission to enter. Max and Tom Black understood each other; were as close as their respective ranks allowed. They had worked together many times, fostering loyalty, trust and respect on both sides.

'We've got a nasty one on our hands, sir.'

Max left his jacket on the hook. 'How nasty?'

'Two suspicious deaths.'

'Not another messy domestic triangle.'

'Messier than that. A sergeant of the Cumberlands and a British civilian, a nurse, in a car that left the road and concertinaed against a massive oak night before last. *Polizei* called out our traffic boys to what they thought was a drink-drive incident. No witnesses, no other vehicle involved. The NCO was dead when a lorry driver found the wreckage: passenger died of her injuries without regaining consciousness. Just as well, maybe. Severe brain damage. Could have been a vegetable for the rest of her life.'

'Why is SIB being brought in on a traffic accident?'

'Alcohol content disproved the drink-drive theory. A preliminary forensic examination suggested cardiac arrest while at the wheel but, as the victim was only thirty and extremely fit, the pathologist decided to probe further. His report states that cardiac arrest resulted from an as yet unidentified

27

poison being administered intravenously. We're looking at murder by lethal injection.'

Max whistled through his teeth. 'Double murder if the killer knew the victim was about to drive off with a passenger in the car. This "as yet unidentified" toxin suggests some fearful substance created by the boys at Porton Down, or a similar establishment. Has there been a major breach of security at one of those places?' He frowned at the other man. 'Poisonous jabs are an unusual m.o. Why not a bullet or knife in the chest?'

'Too obvious? Easier to approach the victim and stick a needle in him when passing. The killer would have to know how to give an injection correctly. Might narrow the field. It wasn't an impulse job: no one walks around with a hypo filled with poison in case someone gets stroppy. And it's no defence weapon. In sudden armed confrontation you'd be dead before you could put your opponent away. This had to be premeditated by someone who knew the victim's plans.'

They walked through to the Operations Room where dark-suited military detectives were checking facts on computers, or by telephone. Several were conferring, getting input from their colleagues. Most of them had some years of policing behind them; all were bright, intelligent and keen as mustard on their work.

Tom's sharp command caught their attention. They gathered in a half circle as he outlined the facts he had been given. Then he addressed the two women sergeants.

'Bush and Johnson, get over to the local *Krankenhaus*. Find out why an English nurse was working there, and what kind of relationship she had with Brian New. Question her friends about her off-duty activities. Had she close associations with Germans. Most importantly, did anyone know where she and New went that evening? We need to pinpoint where the assault was carried out.'

'Near the scene of the crash, I'd guess. He wouldn't have driven far once poison was in his bloodstream,' put in Max thoughtfully.

'Sergeant Meeker, start in-depth enquiries into identifying the toxin. Mr Fennemore will have a list of all experimental labs working on poisons. Don't be fobbed off by scientists. This is a case of murder.'

Lunch was just coffee and a baguette in a roadside cafe en route to the base housing the 2nd Battalion Royal Cumberland Rifles, thirty-five kilometres from their Section Headquarters. Max was quiet during the journey. Tom made no attempt to break the silence, guessing the cause of his commander's introspection.

A little over two years ago Susan Rydal, pregnant with her first child, had been killed when a car driven by a corporal crashed during a severe thunderstorm. The official story was that the good-looking NCO had offered Mrs Rydal a lift out of the torrential rain, but rumour had it they were lovers. Gossip had been buried with the bodies, and

Tom knew the question of paternity of the lost child had never been pursued by Max although it undoubtedly still haunted him. Vehicle crashes revived his pain.

At the main gate the guard directed them to B Company offices. 'I'll patch through to warn them you're coming, sir.'

As they drove through the extensive establishment, Max murmured, 'They never inform of our arrival, they *warn* of it. What do these people need to hide from our sight?'

Tom grinned. 'It's an instinctive urge to appear as white as the proverbial driven, when the constabulary comes calling. They're on the defensive before we say a word.'

'My housemaster at school was a sadistic bastard who could find even a saint guilty of wrongdoing. He only had to appear to have us all protesting our innocence.'

'You have the same effect.'

'Not in the least,' he countered, pointing to the left. 'That's B Company HQ. There aren't any signs of feverish concealment.'

As Tom brought the vehicle to a halt in the space reserved for official visitors, a tall, dark-haired young man wearing subaltern's rank emerged to stand expectantly on the veranda fronting the two-storey building.

'Good afternoon. Ben Steele, Acting Company Commander,' he said, shaking hands and ushering them through to his office. 'One of the clerks is making tea. Take a seat while we chat.' He remained standing while they settled on two hard wooden chairs. 'The CO

30

is presently on leave, and the 2IC is hosting a posse of French arms manufacturers keen to demonstrate their wares on our ranges.' He gave a faint smile. 'We're all keeping our heads well down.'

A female Lance Corporal came in with a tray bearing three mugs and a plate of un-interesting biscuits. 'There's no choc diges-tives left, sir,' she apologized.

'What a terrible state of affairs,' Steele said. 'How will we all survive?' Once the grinning girl had gone, he grew more serious. 'Major Kennedy's sorry he's tied up with the Frogs, but he thought I was the best sub having been the guy on the spot. Duty Officer last night,' he explained. 'His wife called me just after midnight and asked me to go to the house. I was totally unprepared for what she told me.'

He perched on the edge of his desk, mug of tea in his hand as yet untasted. 'The vehicle was there, all right. Keys in the ignition, mobile phone on the seat with his hat and gloves. But the laptop was missing,' he added darkly. 'She said she'd heard him drive up to the carport, then nothing more.' He frowned. 'It's a damned peculiar business. I set up im-mediate searches of the whole base. Bloody rain hampered that considerably, but there was no sign of him.

'Major Kennedy stepped up the search this morning. Sent out guys with dogs. Nothing. Crazy though it seems, he appears to have vanished into thin air.' He pursed his lips. 'The 2IC instructed me to give you whatever

31

help I can but, apart from concluding that he's suffering from delayed concussion after a bad fall from his horse at the weekend, there's no more I can tell you.'

Max leaned back in his chair and said quietly, 'We've no idea what you're talking about, I'm afraid.'

Steele looked from one to the other of his visitors. 'You're here to find out what happened last night, aren't you?'

'We're here to investigate the death of Sergeant Brian New two nights ago. We have evidence to suggest he was dead before the car left the road.'

Steele looked stricken as he put two and two together. 'Oh God, I've made a balls-up of this! The 2IC nominated me then because I'm Sergeant New's company commander. I completely misread his ... He simply said two plods ... *you* were coming and I was the best man to liaise with you. I naturally thought...' He paused to assess what had been said. 'New was already dead? How could...?'

Tom broke in to his confusion. 'You said someone on this base *vanished into thin air* last night. Who was that, sir?'

Still looking culpable, the young officer said reluctantly, 'Major Simon Kington, our Defence Liaison Officer.'

Max read Tom's raised eyebrows correctly. An NCO is murdered and an officer of the same regiment goes missing. Killer identified?

Two

Lieutenant Steele conducted them to a temporarily unused office in which to interview Brian New's close friends and colleagues, whom he undertook to send along in a steady stream. The room was cramped, no more than functional and sited near a cookhouse. From its windows came rattling, clattering and uninhibited loud comments from those preparing supper. *Offered every facility* was a glib phrase often trotted out by host regiments who resented the intrusion of Special Investigation Branch.

Left to themselves, Tom immediately voiced his thoughts. 'Why wasn't this major's disappearance reported to Connie Bush when she called to tell them we were on our way? It's too much of a bloody coincidence him vanishing the night after one of the regiment's sergeants is murdered.'

Max opened a small ventilator to allow in fresh air to combat the stale atmosphere. 'Steele naturally assumed we'd been called in to assist the search, not then being aware of the true nature of New's death. He's now very worried. Our being kept in ignorance of the disappearance indicates a closing of senior ranks, so he's aware of putting his hefty boot

33

right in it. That's why he clammed up when you pursued the subject.'

'I'll continue to pursue it. It's an obvious lead.'

Max frowned in thought. 'Too obvious? Once we know more about New we'll get other leads.'

Tom nodded at the window. 'This looks like the first guy coming. You know, I can't see a squaddie using a hypo as a weapon. Too sophisticated and chancy. Unless he's a medical orderly.'

'Your money's on the Galloping Major, is it?'

'Until we discover where he's galloped off to, yes.' He went to the door. 'Shall I wheel him straight in?'

'Yes. You can kick off. I'll break in if I have specifics. We'll keep quiet about the cause of death.'

Sergeant Putter gave wary replies, his gaze flicking to the silent Max every so often. He claimed not to have been a close friend of Brian New, but they had shared an interest in ice hockey and went to games together. He knew little of the dead man's personal life.

'Brian only talked generally when we went to the stadium. He was good enough company but, after the game, he was never keen to make a real night of it.'

'You mean a pub crawl and a session with a local tart?'

Putter scowled at Tom. 'Brian was the quiet sort.'

34

'How about mess dances? Did he have a regular partner for them?'

'No. He was on the Entertainments Committee. Spent most of the evening as MC, more often than not.'

'Not what you'd call a ladies man, then?'

'Oh, the girls had their talons out, but they never hooked him.' His eyes narrowed. 'Why're you asking all this? It was a road accident, wasn't it?'

Max answered smoothly. 'There were no witnesses, so we're just trying to establish what happened. Thank you, you can go.'

When Putter left, Tom said Brian New sounded an unlikely candidate for murder. 'A decent type, moderate drinker with a restrained sexual appetite. No regular woman in his life.'

'Not one he was prepared to woo openly.'

Tom grinned. '*Woo*! Do men still do that? I heard they simply buy a stranger a drink then take her to bed when she finishes it.'

Max laughed. 'Our victim sounds more the wooing type to me.'

'The nurse in his car?'

'Possibly.'

'Maybe he was just giving her a lift. It was a filthy night.'

Max felt the familiar lurch of his heartbeat. It was frequently happening. How long would it be before references to cars and stormy weather no longer touched a raw nerve?

'Someone'll soon give us the truth about their relationship,' he said. 'Where the hell is the next man on Steele's list? We'll be here all night at this rate.'

One aspect of Sergeant Putter's evidence was borne out by the two women who had known the victim well. Sergeant Diana Fogg was upset, and euphoric in her description of the dead man. Corporal Karen Smythe had worked with New and had clearly fancied him in a big way. Curious. A man women really went for who didn't respond to them.

'Think he was gay?' Max asked as the pretty NCO departed.

'Could be. You never know. If so, why was the nurse in his car that night?'

'Like you said; it was a filthy night and he offered her a lift. It happens,' said Max tonelessly.

The next man reiterated what had been said. The victim had been well liked. A social drinker rarely unable to handle his intake; a nice-looking man girls propositioned without much success. Although the two women had not questioned the interest taken by SIB, this man did.

'Brian was one of the straightest guys around, sir. A very responsible driver. Can't understand him just losing control of his car.' He frowned at them. 'Is there something suspicious about this? Is that why you're here?'

Max said smoothly, 'We're trying to get to the bottom of why the car left the road. The *Polizei* asked for our co-operation. They're always reluctant to tangle with the British

36

Army, and we'll almost certainly need a favour from them one day.'

When the door closed behind the man, Max stretched and yawned. 'God, it's stuffy in here! How many more to go?'

'Four. Not getting far, are we? Seems New had no enemies. Not one who'd want to put an end to him, anyway.' Tom crossed to open the door to allow more air in. 'I don't like this one. It's too specialized, and the chance of finding a motive among his immediate colleagues is looking slim. That leaves the Galloping Major.'

'*Someone* wanted New dead, and planned it carefully. No violent quarrel ending with impetuous shots being fired, or a knife flashing. A swift, silent toxic jab with a needle in an unsuspecting victim. Unless New was leading a double life, nothing in this case adds up.'

'Apart from an officer vanishing the following day. There has to be a link.'

'The link could be that we'll find the Major's body pumped full of an as yet unidentified poison,' Max said thoughtfully. 'If police forensic experts are baffled by it the toxin might be peculiar to the armed forces. One of their secret weapons. If that's so, and our killer has stolen some, he's probably taken more than a single fatal dose.'

Tom blew out his cheeks. 'You think we're after a serial nutter?'

'I hope to God not. My guts are beginning to tell me New wasn't killed because of something he'd done, but because of something he

37

knew. Could even be unaware of knowing.'

'How about the Major?'

'If he's dead, too, bang goes your prime suspect. As soon as we've seen the rest of these people who're taking their time in reporting – so much for Steele's "steady stream" – we'll tackle the 2IC about last night's vanishing act.'

The next three men more or less confirmed what the rest had said, and each questioned SIB involvement over a road accident. Max gave the same bland reply, then raised a fresh issue by asking if New had friends in the medical world. He apparently had not.

Max elaborated on this angle with Tom before the last man came. 'We should check whether New was involved in or connected with tests at Porton Down.'

'Tests that went wrong?'

Max shrugged. 'Or New could have kicked up a stink about how volunteers were treated; threatened to leak details to the Press.'

'And he was silenced? With a poison no one recognizes?'

This deep scepticism was met with a grin. 'Thriller writers would give their eye teeth for that plot. I've often thought we'd make a mint if we adapted some of our cases for the silver screen.'

Tom wagged his head. 'Couldn't stand working with those luvvies.'

'Wouldn't have to. We'd just write the stuff and hand it over to them. Could be a profitable way to fill time waiting around like this for witnesses to show.'

Sergeant Sam Dawkins was worth waiting for. He had been the victim's close friend. His sense of loss was immediately apparent. Even more so was his hostility.

'I can't get my mind round this. A car smash on a filthy night I have to accept, even though Brian was a first-rate driver. But SIB asking everyone about his private life suggests something I'm not at all happy with.'

'What d'you imagine it suggests?' asked Tom.

'That Brian was *involved* in something.'

'We're simply trying to piece together what happened, as there were no witnesses,' Max explained.

'Why SIB and not traffic cops? Is there more to Brian's death than we're being told, sir?'

'We're the ones asking questions,' said Tom crisply. 'Do you know Sergeant New's plans that evening; where he was returning from?'

Face set, eyes cold, Dawkins said, 'He'd booked a table at the Golden Key out on the Kesselhof Road.'

'For himself and Vera Maitland?'

'That's right.'

'Were they in a relationship?'

'I guess so. Brian injured his foot. He met Vera at the hospital just a few weeks ago. They began dating right off.' He passed his large hand over his face in distress. 'Jesus, what a mess! He was serious about her. Wanted to settle down, have kids. That evening at the

39

Golden Key was going to be crunch time.'

'He was going to propose to her?' probed Tom.

Dawkins nodded. 'Depending on how she took the news about Hong Kong.'

'Hong Kong?'

'He married a Chinese girl when he was out there in 95. It didn't work out. She refused to leave her family. He came home without her and they divorced at long distance a year later. It made Brian very bitter. Then he met Vera and was certain they were meant for each other, but he worried that she wouldn't like the idea of being his second wife. Women can be funny over something like that. Jacki was educated at a convent school and a real corker to look at, but she wouldn't come to England with him.'

Max beefed up the questioning. 'Did New tell you much about this woman he hoped to marry? What about her background and education?'

Dawkins looked mulish. 'What has that to do with a road accident.'

'Just answer the questions,' ruled Tom.

No pushover this sergeant. 'Sir, I know you have the right to interrogate anyone you like, but SIB investigates serious crimes. Before I say anything more I'd like to understand what's behind all this. My best pal was killed in a car smash two days ago. You can find out all about Jacki on his service record, but I don't feel comfortable betraying things he told me in confidence about Vera, when I'm

40

ignorant of why you want to know. They're both dead. Strangers raking up details of their personal lives is rather tacky, in my opinion. Let them rest in peace.'

Max saw his point and gave a little ground. 'Your friend's death touches on a case we're investigating. We need to know why Sergeant New's car should run off what was apparently an empty road.'

Still resistant, Dawkins said, 'I can't help you with that, sir. I wasn't there.'

'If you had been, you'd probably be dead, too.' Seeing they would get nothing more from the man he told him he could go.

Perversely, Dawkins showed reluctance to leave. Still seated, he said, 'Brian and I go back a long way. We were squaddies together. He was a loyal friend, a fair man and a bloody good soldier, sir. There's no way he'd be involved in anything criminal you're investigating.'

'We didn't suggest he was,' said Tom, getting to his feet. 'You're dismissed, Sergeant.'

As the door shut behind Dawkins, Tom said, 'He's too close to the tragedy.'

'I agree. At least he told us why New was uninterested in women in general.'

'Wonder if he got a yes or no from the nurse at the Golden Key.'

Max stood and stretched. 'We'll never know. Let's quit this sauna and find someone to give us a cup of tea.'

It was not a relaxed relationship at the best of

times. Right now it was decidedly frosty. Major Roger Kennedy was ill-tempered from hosting the small group of Frenchmen who had made no secret of their opinion of the British Army's present standard weaponry. Ben Steele, with no option but to own up, struggled to make his case for revealing details of Simon Kington's disappearance.

'When you said I was the best person to liaise with SIB I naturally assumed it was because I was Duty Officer last night.'

The Second in Command was livid. 'I specifically stated that two Redcaps were coming to ask questions about Sergeant New. Why would you *naturally assume* something else?'

Ben fought his corner. 'I don't recall that you actually mentioned Sergeant New, sir.' He hastily added, 'Not in *that* context. You did, of course, speak to me yesterday about his fatal crash. We were told then that it was a road accident.' Not liking the look on his superior's face, he poured more oil. 'I had no reason to think SIB would be involved there, so I assumed they had been called in on Major Kington's disappearance.'

Roger Kennedy blew his top. 'You spend too much time *assuming* and not enough on using your brains. You must have some or you'd never have been accepted as an officer in this regiment. You've been with us long enough to know when you should keep your mouth shut; when not to blab to the bloody constabulary because one of our number doesn't go home one evening.'

Ben went down fighting. 'My duty report gives full details of Mrs Kington's call for assistance, and the measures I took to promote a search for her husband. Sir, he *did* go home. And vanished! Surely the police should be alerted. He's no ordinary regimental officer; he's privy to top secret EU stuff. His disappearance is very suspicious.'

Kennedy's eyes narrowed. 'You read too many downmarket thrillers. Major Kington has simply forgotten to inform his wife of an overnight appointment. He follows a demanding schedule. Understandable that things sometimes slip his mind.'

Ben opened his mouth, then shut it again. It suddenly occurred to him that this man must be in on the truth, because no one of intelligence could truly believe what he had just said. Kennedy clearly knew where Simon Kington was; had organized a further search this morning merely as a smokescreen. There must be something big underway. A top security op in the planning stages. Something so big it was vital for Kington to go underground until it came off. So big even his *wife* was kept in ignorance?

Developing that thought, the heat of humiliation rushed through him. Had she put on a performance last night to maintain the secrecy; made him drive around in a bloody downpour half the night looking for the handsome husband she knew was safely elsewhere? What a gullible fool she must have

43

thought him. Rightly so. Only an idiot could believe a man would drive up to his carport, then walk off in to the night without a word to his wife and vanish from a guarded military base.

Now anxious to do a disappearing act himself, Ben made his apology. 'Sorry. I misread the situation, sir. It won't happen again.'

'Be sure of that,' came the cold response. 'Any future instructions I have for you I'll write down in words of one syllable you can't possibly misread.'

About to repeat his apology, Ben decided silent retreat would be wiser. His escape was foiled by the two large SIB men waiting in the outer office. Captain Rydal smiled, transforming his otherwise stern features into the brand of aloof attraction women often found irresistible.

'We've finished our questioning. Sergeant New appears to have been a man of considerable worth and loyalty. You've lost an excellent NCO.'

'The regiment has.' Ben made the distinction, still sensitive to the accusation of disloyalty by speaking out of turn about a fellow officer. The honour of the regiment must be protected. If the rank and file did not always appreciate that, its officers were expected to. 'Were they helpful? Give you any leads?'

'None, I'm afraid, sir,' said the Sergeant Major. 'But we'll get there.'

'You didn't actually tell me why you're

treating the car accident as suspicious, did you.'

'No, we didn't,' Rydal agreed equably. 'We'd like a word with Major Kennedy. Would you make the introductions?'

The last thing Ben wanted was to face the 2IC again. 'I do have a very hectic schedule. Well ... yes, of course.'

The thundercloud expression deepened at his reappearance in company with the 'bloody constabulary'. But Roger Kennedy was never less than courteous to visitors and he made a real effort as Ben introduced men who were mostly unwelcome when on official business. No regiment wanted criminal activity in its ranks. When there was, commanders preferred to deal with it internally.

Kennedy shook hands, apologized for being occupied when they arrived, and waved his hand at two chairs. As Ben made to leave, he was told to stay.

'Sergeant New was one of yours, which is why I brought you in on this in the first place.'

Swallowing a sigh, Ben perched on the edge of the computer bench. Rydal was certain to bring up the subject of the missing Major. The 2IC knew that. The bastard was adding salt to the wound.

'I was surprised, to say the least, when one of your bods rang with the news that there was an element of suspicion attached to the death of Sergeant New,' Kennedy began. 'Only yesterday I was informed that he had

45

died in a car crash. Are you suggesting someone deliberately ran him off the road?'

Rydal shook his head. 'Forensic examination revealed a lethal dose of poison in the victim's system. He would have died at the wheel, leaving the vehicle uncontrolled.'

Even Kennedy's urbanity was shaken. 'Poison! You mean something like salmonella, food poisoning?'

'No.'

'Then what the hell are you saying?'

'Sergeant New was murdered, sir,' said the Warrant Officer.

Words burst from Ben. 'There must be some mistake. No one would poison Brian New. He was a quiet, good-living man. Not the sort to make enemies.'

'So we were repeatedly told this afternoon,' Rydal said drily. 'But someone deliberately put an end to his life, and to that of a young nurse who was a passenger in the car. She died of injuries sustained in the crash, so we're regarding her as an accidental victim until we learn more.'

'Surely this is a matter for the *Polizei*,' Kennedy protested. 'The act was committed off-base.'

'There's no proof that a German was the perpetrator. Until there is the ball stays in our court. Nothing we heard this afternoon pointed to the victim having close ties with any locals.'

Kennedy looked intensely annoyed. 'But the bloody killing took place out on the

46

streets, man. Someone had a grudge. You know how it is. *Get the Brits out of our country.* Or a local Lothario's girl is commandeered by one of our riflemen. There are even nutters, grandsons of Storm-troopers, who are still fighting the Second World War. They have their grandfather's loaded pistol primed and ready to fire at the first opportunity.'

Ben's tongue ran away with him. 'He wasn't shot, sir. He was poisoned.'

Max Rydal deflected the certain snub from Kennedy by making the situation even worse. 'We understand one of your officers went missing last night. Would you give us the details?'

After a lightning scathing glance at Ben, the 2IC said, 'I'm afraid Lieutenant Steele has a somewhat runaway imagination. No one has *gone missing.*'

Sergeant Major Black quoted from memory. 'Major Kington drove home, parked his car, and vanished. His wife called the Duty Officer who organized search parties. You, sir, augmented them this morning. Has the Major now turned up?'

Ben wished he could sink through the floor. Roger Kennedy clearly wished he had put him there, flat out and unconscious. 'Major Kington is our Defence Liaison Officer. As such, Mr Black, he is forever on the move. Lieutenant Steele was not entirely *au fait* with his schedule, that's all.'

'So where is Major Kington, sir?'

The brow darkened. 'You're here to enquire

47

into the death of one of our sergeants. If we can be of further help with that we shall, of course, cooperate fully.' He got to his feet. 'I have a meeting in thirty minutes, before which I must compile a report on the visit of a French armaments deputation.'

It was a dismissal, and Ben intended to depart with them. The lamb marked for slaughter hiding within the flock. Max Rydal did not budge.

'If you have no objections, we'd like to talk to Mrs Kington before we head back.'

Kennedy stiffened. 'The lady can cast no light on Sergeant New's character or private life. I suggest your time would be better spent tracing whoever he had fallen foul of in the local community.'

Rydal smiled. 'We shall certainly check that out if evidence points us in that direction. For now, I'd like to ask Mrs Kington where her husband is, as you seem reluctant to give us the facts.'

While Ben silently enjoyed this battle of wills, he had no doubts that hiding in the flock would be to no avail. Kennedy was surely preparing the sacrificial altar.

'Captain Rydal, there are times when officers of military forces engage in activities of a secret nature. Activities to which a security tag is attached.'

'I engage in them myself sometimes,' Rydal replied coolly. 'At the moment I'm investigating the murder of a member of *this* military force, and the fact that an officer mysteriously

48

vanished the night after the killing could be significant.'

'That's an outrageous suggestion!'

'I'm suggesting that Major Kington might be another victim.' His tone grew crisper. 'Shall we stop all this fencing? Lieutenant Steele's imagination might be colourful but, unless Mrs Kington's is the same, something very strange occurred last night. Defence Liaison Officers don't attract attention to their secret activities by fading into the night and instigating widescale searches. They depart in the normal way saying they have to attend a routine meeting. "Another boring get-together with EU old farts", they tell their wives. Then off they go to make world-shaping decisions.' He paused and fixed Kennedy with a cold eye. 'Will you ring Mrs Kington and tell her we're on our way?'

The other man's hostility increased. 'This is a purely regimental matter, Rydal.'

'And it's a very serious matter, sir. A sergeant of your regiment has been murdered in a most curious manner: an officer of your regiment has *vanished* in a most curious manner. Both within two days. Why Brian New should have been killed we don't yet know, but Major Kington's disappearance has disturbing possibilities.' He cast Ben a glance. 'His laptop has also gone, you said?'

Ben jumped in at the deep end. 'Sergeant Major Busby swears he was carrying it when he left the office, but Mrs Kington told me it wasn't in the vehicle when she went out to see where her husband had got to.'

Rydal turned back to Kennedy. 'You see the worrying implications? On that laptop there might be info that should never fall into the wrong hands.'

'I know that, man,' Kennedy snapped. 'That's why I need to keep this in the family.'

'We are members of that family, Major Kennedy,' Rydal snapped back. 'In or out of uniform, our loyalties are the same as yours. Right now, we need to speak to Major Kington's wife, if you please.'

They all drove to the large quarter on the far side of the base, despite Rydal's smooth reminder to Roger Kennedy that he had a report to write before a meeting in half an hour. Ben hid a smile as the 2IC bluffed his way out of his earlier plea of heavy commitments. His own self-assurance had returned now he was certain Tara Kington had not made a fool of him last night. He was intrigued by SIB thought processes. Not for a moment did he support Kennedy's theory of a nutter still fighting a world war, but it seemed likely that the murder of Brian New and Kington's disappearance *could* be linked in some obscure way.

Tara Kington greeted the four men quietly and invited them through to the sitting-room. In tailored cream trousers and jade silk shirt she looked as immaculately striking as usual. She had either swiftly changed and applied make-up after Roger Kennedy's call, or she was one of those women who never let their standards drop. Ben thought it was probably the latter. His eyes were so busy appreciating her silk-moulded breasts he missed the wariness in hers as she faced them all.

Max Rydal added to Kennedy's more effusive apology for descending on her *en masse*, then got down to business.

'Mrs Kington, we'd like to hear from you what occurred last night to make you call up the Duty Officer. So far, we've been given an account that suggests your husband vanished into thin air after driving up to the house. We know that's impossible, so we have to consider the alternatives.'

She appeared unflustered by this direct approach. 'By all means, but let's have tea while we talk. I've put the tray ready in the kitchen.'

'Ben can see to that,' said Kennedy swiftly. 'He might as well make himself useful.'

Ben's rising anger subsided as Tara turned a wan smile on him. 'Would you be a dear, Ben? You've just to push down the switch on the kettle. I've prepared the rest.'

He went like a lamb to the kitchen which was large and immaculate. Gleaming copper pots and pans hung along one wall. Surely they had never been used! Appliances adorned the worktops: mixer, electric can-opener, toaster, assorted cafetières, coffee grinder, toasted-sandwich maker, water purifier, pasta cutter. Spices and condiments in matching labelled pots stood there like a rank of soldiers on parade. Brown eggs filled a basket lined with padded green and white checked cotton. Onions were in another. A large dark-green bowl held a selection of fruit.

As he poured water in the china pot Ben reflected that the Kington family must eat well. Yet he somehow couldn't imagine the elegant, enticing Tara out here in an apron whipping up delicious meals for her talented husband. They must employ a cook.

When he carried the tray through to the sitting-room, Rydal was attempting to make sense of the facts. 'Why telephone the Ferrari Club despite hearing your husband drive up to the house? If he had planned to go there without mentioning his intention to you, surely he would have gone in the Ferrari direct from his office.'

Tara met that calmly. 'You can't have been listening to me. I've said several times I knew Simon couldn't have vanished as he appeared to have done, but I was bewildered and not a little frightened. In such situations one pursues even the most unlikely explanations.' She frowned. 'When children are late arriving home, parents phone everyone they can think of in the hope they will be there, no matter how impossible it would be. It's known as clutching at straws.' When this was met with silence, she asked, 'Have you any children?'

There was a curious pause before Rydal said thickly, 'No. None.'

'Then it's useless for me to try to make you understand my actions.' Glancing up at Ben,

52

she thanked him. 'If I pour, perhaps you'd be good enough to hand the cups around.'

Sergeant Major Black was immediately on his feet. 'I'll do that, ma'am.'

Recognizing this deferment to rank by the only non-commissioned man present, she smiled warmly. More warmly than at me, Ben reflected with disappointment. Of course, Tom Black was a good-looking man whose years of experience had added an aura of tough dependability women would be drawn to in times of stress. A gawky young subaltern just a year out of Sandhurst would not inspire such trust.

The questioning continued. 'Mrs Kington, how would you describe your relationship with your husband?'

Roger Kennedy reacted angrily. 'For God's sake, Rydal! We're only here because you have a wild theory that Simon Kington's unexplained absence could have some bearing on your case. Keep your questioning pertinent, or I shall ask you to leave.'

Rydal answered in clipped tones. 'He left his office to drive home but never entered it. That decision was either made by him or for him. Two explanations. One, he had strong reasons for leaving Mrs Kington open to distress and speculation through his actions. Two, he was taken against his will by persons unknown. In view of his specialist work the latter is more likely, but before we set in motion a high-profile international search we have to satisfy ourselves that his is not a voluntary absence due to domestic or marital incompatibility. Mrs Kington has said she is bewildered and frightened, which suggests she wants a speedy resolution to this affair. If she objects to anything I ask, I'm sure she's capable of telling me herself.'

Ben's admiration increased. Tara might be distressed but she was keeping her head admirably. 'Simon and I have a close, immensely contented marriage. We love our boys and spend as much time as possible as a family when they come over for the school holidays. I didn't have a row with my husband yesterday. We rarely disagree. I can't even recall when we last had a spat. Unusual, I know, but we're both intelligent enough to respect each other's individual needs and wishes.'

Rydal pursued his point. 'So you're unaware of any reason why your husband would behave in such a curious manner?'

'I think I've already made that abundantly clear.' She held his uncompromising gaze for some moments, then asked, 'What did Roger mean about linking this to a case you're investigating?'

'A sergeant of this regiment was murdered two nights ago. An officer of this regiment went absent the following day. We have to follow any possible leads in cases of homicide.'

Tara's teacup landed heavily on the low table as she cried, *No!* Simon hasn't ... It's out of the question. You don't know him.

You're quite, quite wrong!'

'We're simply following routine procedure, ma'am,' put in Sergeant Major Black.

Kennedy got to his feet. 'Tara, I've already ruled the notion preposterous. I apologize again for submitting you to this nonsense. Rest assured the regiment will do all in its power to trace Simon. With far less heavy-handedness, I promise,' he added, glowering at the SIB duo.

Muted trilling sent Black through to the hallway with his mobile phone, while the three officers prepared to take their leave. They were halted when the Sergeant Major returned to request a private word with his boss. Ben's heartbeat quickened in anticipation of what might have developed. A swift glance at Tara showed how tense she had grown. He wished he could comfort her, but she was a major's wife and he was a lowly subaltern. Any comforting should be done by Kennedy, but he was studying his wristwatch with impatience. A martinet on timekeeping, that man!

Rydal reappeared and addressed Tara with more gentleness than before. 'Mrs Kington, we've been informed that a body was discovered this morning by a dog-walker on heathland three kilometres from the main gate of this base. There are no means of identification – the man was only partially clothed – but the *Polizei* had reason to think he might be a member of the British forces and contacted my section headquarters an hour ago to ask if we had been advised of anyone going AWOL. Two of my sergeants investigated. They've given us a rough description. Five eleven, well-muscled, close-cropped dark hair, brown eyes. Age probably mid-thirties.'

'Dear God!' breathed Kennedy. 'What's going on here?'

Ben edged instinctively closer to the woman being told she was possibly a widow, and swiftly volunteered to drive to the mortuary for preliminary identification. He guessed foxes would have been busy with the corpse overnight. Better for him to view what remained than subject the woman who loved Simon Kington to such an ordeal.

Three

Tom Black went with the young subaltern to the local German hospital. He well knew why his boss opted to return to their headquarters to garner evidence from Sergeants Bush and Johnson, who had questioned nursing staff about Brian New's girlfriend. Also to set in motion an investigation into Simon Kington's duties as Defence Liaison Officer for all units quartered at that base. Any man who had been called to identify his pregnant wife's badly crushed body would never dissociate that memory from any hospital he later entered. Viewing bodies in mortuaries was a regular aspect of their job, but thankfully none had yet been linked to Tom's personal life.

As he drove his five-year-old Ford to the main gate Ben Steele was quiet, whether from thoughtfulness or shock Tom was unsure. The lad was very young; had probably not yet encountered violence aside from the gung-ho brand revelled in during mock battles. There was a hint of chivalry in the way he had instantly volunteered for this unhappy duty, to shield Tara Kington from possible distress. Life in today's world would soon knock that

57

out of him, Tom thought with regret. His own life with Nora and their three loving girls followed traditional lines and was highly successful. So far! He felt a touch of chivalry now and again could ease some of society's present problems.

Once on the road that would take them past the oaks in to which Brian New's car had smashed, Tom asked if his companion had known Major Kington well.

'Only in the Mess, really. He was frequently away at meetings, unlike the regimental officers one deals with on a daily basis. I liked him. Everyone did.' He glanced swiftly at Tom. 'This is completely beyond my under-standing. Anyone bent on grabbing his laptop could've waylaid him along this road en route to a meeting. Quick and easy. Flag him down dressed as traffic cops, drag him among the trees to finish him off, then drive away in his car *avec* laptop. No one's wise to the op until the meeting's well underway and someone reasons he wouldn't be so late arriving. But *this* way! Presuming they laid in wait for him at his quarter, how the hell did they smuggle him out? Guards at the gates *swore* everyone they checked was spot on, and I personally examined the perimeter wire for breaks or signs of tampering. None.'

His speed had increased with his enthusi-asm, so they flashed past the tree with a splintered and gouged trunk, where a young nurse who might just have accepted a pro-posal of marriage had been fatally injured

58

alongside a man already dead.

Ben Steele's thoughts remained on the other fatality. 'I suppose it's your job to find out how he was spirited from a secure establishment so easily. Wait a bit, though. How did the abductors get in in the first place? Unless ... no, I can't believe it was an inside job.' He cast another glance at Tom; dangerous at that speed. 'Did your men say how he was killed?'

'There's no evidence that he was, sir. Word I got was that the cadaver appeared to show that he suffered a heart attack,' Tom said, keeping his suspicions to himself.

The car swerved wildly as the driver stopped watching the road. 'Simon was superbly fit. Men in his condition don't have heart attacks, and they certainly don't remove all means of identification and half their clothes first. Come on, Mr Black, you surely don't accept that.'

'I'll accept what the post mortem reveals. We're nearing the hospital entrance, sir, and you've just passed a speed restriction sign at double the figure displayed on it.'

The mortuary was at the rear of the hospital, reached by a short offshoot corridor at the end of a long one giving access to a number of wards. The two men found themselves unconsciously marching in step over polished flooring that squeaked beneath their boots. Tom pushed open the last set of doors to allow the subaltern to walk ahead of him, and the familiar smell of these storehouses of

59

the dead washed over him. Two sergeants in red headgear, with RMP armbands, rose from their seats and saluted. It was Tom one addressed, however.

'They know you're coming, sir. Body's in that small room to the left of the office.'

The sound of their voices brought a white-coated attendant to greet them. 'Thank you for coming so swiftly, sir,' he said to Ben Steele. 'You're here to check if the body is that of one of your officers?'

'That's right.'

They were led to a small room much in the style of a funeral parlour. More dignified for grieving relatives than pulling out a long drawer bearing their loved one. The body lay on a raised table skirted with dark cloth; the atmosphere was curiously muted suggesting soundproofing. The attendant drew the sheet back as the young officer stepped forward and stood respectfully gazing at a strong face topped by dark curly hair.

He stood for so long, Tom thought he must actually be saying a prayer over the dead man. Eventually, he asked, 'Well, sir?'

Steele turned looking very shaken. 'It's Colin White, Commander of Four Company. He went off yesterday morning for ten days' mountain trekking in Bavaria.'

They all worked late in to the night. Apart from Staff Sergeant Pete Melly, who had gone down with the vicious stomach bug presently circulating, the whole team sat in

60

on Tom's briefing.

'After a few weeks of relative quiet we're faced with what looks on the surface to be some kind of vendetta against the Cumberland Rifles. The murder of an officer and a sergeant; the possible abduction of another officer. With a view to a third killing?'

He pointed to the information on the board. 'Initial conclusion: Captain Colin White suffered a coronary spasm instigating cardiac arrest. The pathologist will check for the presence of a toxin in his bloodstream, at our request. Result tomorrow, if we're lucky! I want to set up three separate investigations with a regular interchange of info. Piercey and Beeny have already begun questioning staff and diners at the Golden Key, so they'll stay with that. Bush and Johnson, you'll switch to tracing the whereabouts of Major Kington. The CO and I will concentrate on the curious death of Colin White. I've no doubt all three investigations will soon overlap, and that needs to happen as soon as possible.

'Let's take Brian New first. His colleagues claim he was an all round good guy. Divorced but no womanizer; drank sensibly, had no debts, was a loyal friend. Company commander gave him top marks. A man respected by officers and men alike.'

'About time he joined his fellow angels,' muttered Phil Piercey.

Tom fixed him with a fierce gaze. 'Tell that to the poor bugger's parents.'

61

The ripple of amusement swiftly died as Tom's gaze embraced them all. 'Our pre-liminary inquiries failed to turn up any obvious motive for his murder.'

'Which will be a double homicide if we prove whoever injected the victim knew he was about to drive off with a passenger in his car,' interjected Max from his seat beside Tom.

'We went to the Golden Key in company with a local cop, sir,' said Derek Beeny, the more laid back of the two sergeants. 'The victims ate dinner at a table for two in a rear corner of the restaurant. It was very busy, but the staff were unaware of anyone approaching the pair aside from the table waiter and the wine waiter. They had drinks at the start of their meal, but didn't order more. Piercey and I reckon both waiters are in the clear because of the time element.'

'We know the substance hasn't yet been identified,' added Piercey, 'but a slow-acting poison would have produced some effects – palpitations, sweating, blurred vision, lack of concentration – before New left the Golden Key. He might even have found walking difficult. Someone would surely have noticed. We've details of those diners who reserved tables, and those who paid with plastic. We'll only trace the others by asking them to come forward. We've already interviewed three couples living within easy distance of the restaurant. Nothing to report. Two others weren't at home when we called.'

'We plan to tackle the rest first thing tomorrow,' said Beeny. 'but we reckon the attack must have taken place in the car park.'

The irrepressible Piercey cast a glance round the room to ensure everyone was attending. 'Not easy to approach someone in a crowded restaurant with a syringe full of poison, jab him in the arm, then walk away without anyone knowing. Especially the victim. Much easier in the car park. It's dark, it's pissing down. Heads bowed, shoulders hunched, not looking where you're going. A contrived collision, a swift puncture ... and the victim's certain dead.'

'Which would mean the killer did know he had a passenger,' declared Heather Johnson. 'It also means we have eff-all hope of identifying him. Could've been anyone from anywhere.'

Connie Bush presented their findings. 'We spoke to six people who knew Vera Maitland well. She had a serious relationship with a dentist in the UK. He walked out on her a year ago. She speaks good German, so she applied for an exchange post in a hospital out here to get away from bad memories. According to her friends there's been no man until Brian New turned up. Then it was wham bam, here I am!'

'Can I have that in adult language?'

She grinned at Tom. 'Love at first sight, sir.'

'Motives? Friend who had her eyes on New; jealous male nurse or doctor with hopes in Maitland's direction?'

'Nothing obvious, but I suppose we should not discount some psycho in the lower hospital echelons who has a seedy bedsit papered with photos of her.'

Tom pursed his lips. 'That sort are more usually stalkers or voyeurs. What we have here is a killer who possesses an unknown quantity of a unique toxin and who knows how to inject it. I agree there could be a medical link. The facts suggest the murder was committed by someone who knew the pair would be at the Golden Key that night. In to that category fall hospital staff and personnel of the Cumberland Rifles. If we presuppose Colin White's death is a copycat murder, I'd say the scales come down on the side of the RCR, the Royal Cumberland Rifles. We then have to conclude that the nurse was simply a tragic innocent victim.'

He glanced round the room. 'As always, we'll keep an open mind and chase up all possible leads. For instance, both men could have been secret members of some political organization. We all know nothing is unlikely in this game. Simpson and Jakes, I want you checking local clubs and societies for membership lists. New liked ice hockey. Did Colin White? Could they have met a common contact at the rink, maybe someone from a minor crime syndicate that's exacting revenge on those two by killing them?' At that point Tom turned to their CO. 'Sir.'

Max got to his feet. 'After an easy spell we've been landed with a real humdinger. Mr

Black has laid out the possibles; I'm going to let my guts add to those.' He gave a faint smile. 'You're all familiar with them by now. I believe the answer to this lies with the Cumberlands. The nurse unfortunately got in the way. We have two deaths and an unexplained disappearance from this regiment, all within three days.

'Colin White drove from his house at oh eight hundred hours yesterday morning heading for Bavaria, his car loaded with mountain walking gear. He was killed just three kilometres from his base later that night. His body was clad only in a tee shirt and underpants. It had been attacked by animals overnight, but they don't remove outer clothes. He would have been wearing civvies, so no way would a stranger know he was in the RCR. Which leaves us to conclude the killer either knew that fact in advance, or it was a random killing for kicks. There's no evidence of pre-death torture, beatings or sexual assault, although the scene of crime had been heavily trampled suggesting a struggle. We'll get more as the SOCOs make progress.

'Questions swiftly needing answers: have the victims a common link with a local organization that could employ professional hitmen, or with someone working at an MOD experimental establishment? Also, why wasn't Captain White killed at around eight twenty when he would have been driving past the heath, and where is his car? Lastly, how

65

could a man privy to defence intelligence be abducted from outside his home and spirited from a secure base?'

'In the boot of a car,' suggested Piercey.

'Since that case of stolen ammunition, vehicle checks have been absolutely meticulous,' said Tom. 'The Corporal of the Guard that night swears the Major couldn't have been smuggled out through those gates.'

'Then he's still on-base, buried in a shallow grave.'

Heather Johnson, who did not get on with Piercey, said acidly, 'Someone jumped him in his own car port, jabbed a needle in his arm – I take it we're considering the same killer? – then took the body through a base alive with people at that hour, dug a grave totally unnoticed, covered the body up again still unnoticed before swanning out through the gates with his laptop? Let's get real.'

'Let's get back on track,' Tom demanded quellingly.

'A massive search was conducted by the Cumberlands. Major Kington is nowhere on-base. Even in a shallow grave,' Max added. 'The German police are searching the heath and the woods beyond for a second body. Sergeants Bush and Johnson will liaise with them and follow up on any reported sightings of the Major. There'll be hoax calls, mistaken identity, and so on, but the missing man is a security risk. He doesn't deal with top secret stuff, but what he knows is restricted information.'

66

Connie Bush asked, 'Are we considering him as the possible killer?'

'We're keeping an open mind until you and Sergeant Johnson come up with more evidence. My guts tell me we need look no further than the RCR for a motive, despite the murders being committed on civilian territory.' He wound up. 'That leads me to conclude that Major Kington will also be traced off-base. Either dead, or alive and guilty of anything from multiple murder to breaking the Official Secrets Act.'

Max walked to his nearby lodgings leaving his car in the vehicle compound as he had no need of it that night. He usually enjoyed the brief stroll from Section Headquarters to *Frau* Hahn's large house at the far end of the street. More than a village, yet hardly a town, Frühberg was conveniently situated for the several military establishments served by 26 Section, Special Investigation Branch. The younger members complained that Frühberg was just a haven for 'the grey brigade', but Max liked it. He wasn't a city person and this peaceful, pretty hamlet was surrounded by long, green vistas that soothed a body and brain laden with evidence of humanity's downside.

For his first weeks in Germany Max had occupied an apartment in a trendy new block in the nearest town, but he had been driven from it by young, party-mad neighbours. The sounds of loud pop music, nocturnal comings and goings, to say nothing of squeals and grunts to the accompaniment of groaning bedsprings on the other side of his bedroom wall were more than he could stand at the end of the day. He had been working on a complex murder case then, too.

As he walked along the near-silent street, gazing at the stars, Max reflected that he had found with this elderly German widow the nearest to a family home he had ever known. His mother had died after a long illness when he was six. Being an 'Army brat' he had gone from prep school to boarding school, spending holidays with his father whenever service postings made it possible. Max had found little in common with the sport-loving womanizer his parent had become and was usually glad to rejoin his schoolfriends.

Frau Hahn had six children, thirteen grand-children and twin great-grandsons aside from brothers, nieces and nephews. A bachelor brother lived with her, and there were frequent visits from family. Although Max ate with them when he was able, his rooms over-hung the large rear garden and were virtually soundproof.

As he let himself in an hour before midnight he heard the murmur of voices from the front parlour. A game of cards was underway. A pram piled high with packets of disposable nappies and tinned baby food told him Ulrika and Johann were here with their twins. Walking through to the huge old-fashioned kitchen, Max picked up the tray left out for him whenever he missed dinner. Just as a mother would!

His spacious high-ceilinged bedroom had a covered-in balcony that made an ideal eating area, where he kept a kettle and toaster to make his own breakfast. Taking off his jacket and tie he settled to eat the selection of cold meat and sausage with tomatoes and potato salad, first pouring thick, aromatic soup from the flask into a Dresden bowl. Aah, two babies in the house and not a sound!

After his meal Max poured a small whisky and left it beside the bed while he took a shower in the adjacent bathroom. No sleek, modern en suite this, but he delighted in the early postwar equipment that unfailingly sent down a deluge of hot water.

Sitting in bed with his whisky he tried to make sense of the attacks on Royal Cumberland Riflemen. Why take the life of a young nurse who was surely unconnected with the vendetta – for a vendetta must be what they were dealing with here? What had the killers done with Colin White between grabbing him early morning and killing him late in the evening? Why wait so long? Was there a need for that delay, and had Simon Kington somehow influenced it? Was the Major one of the perpetrators or a third victim of the unknown poison? Max's gut feeling said the latter. Dear God, it was essential to get to the bottom of this before a regiment was decimated.

It was another bright spring morning when

the alarm woke Max. If there had been overnight developments he would have been
called. So, no sightings of the missing major,
and no more bodies pumped full of a toxin
that had experts baffled. Which didn't mean
there wouldn't be more!

He swiftly showered and dressed in lightweight trousers and a shirt beautifully laun-
dered by *Frau* Hahn's maid of all work. While
he buttered soft rolls to fill with slices of
cheese and ham, he listened to one of his
CDs of lush mandolin arrangements of
Neapolitan love songs – his favourite relaxing
breakfast time listening. With a large cup of
black coffee beside his plate, and his ears
filled with Mediterranean witchery, he
watched the antics of red squirrels as they
chased each other in the row of trees at the
far end of the garden. They were one of the
delights of taking lodgings in this rambling
old house.

The cycle of changing seasons and the
variety of flora and fauna in this village gave
Max some respite from the frequent grimness
of his job. He loved to walk the many paths
around Frühberg, whatever the weather, and
listen to the birdsong, the breeze rattling
through bare branches, the refreshing rush of
clear water in the brook. On one Sunday
before the snow melted, he had walked beside
a stand of conifers and, in the silence, had
heard the cones cracking open as the sun un-
froze them. The simplicity, the unthreatening
staccato sounds in a hushed white world had

70

been balm to his troubled mind following the winding up of a bizarre murder case. Now he was facing another. Thank God for fir cones and gambolling squirrels to offset the madness of man!

When Tom arrived to pick him up, Max greeted him lightheartedly and told him about the squirrels. He grinned in response.

'All I've seen this morning is Nora in her bathrobe, and three chattering girls in various stages of dress keeping up a continuous parade from bedroom, to bathroom, to kitchen. Life in a house with four females is a fair challenge. A man is best out of it when it's time to get ready for school.'

As Tom drove from the village out to the autobahn, Max outlined the thoughts he had had before sleeping last night. 'The Cumberlands have to be at the root of this business, Tom. The killings are carried out away from their base through a curious regimental loyalty. Don't sully your own doorstep! It's even a quiet, clean method. No blood, no wounds, no dismemberment. Little suffering for the victims, I imagine. A sudden excruciating pain in the chest, then everlasting night. Ties in with my theory that the RCR is our man's god, so he does the job with quiet efficiency.'

'It's a sound enough theory,' Tom said, 'but surely it rules out Major Kington. He's unlikely to take out two men then scarper, throwing suspicion on his god.'

Max shook his head. 'If he was our killer,

71

he'd stay put not run. He's too intelligent for that. He's most probably another victim.'

'In a shallow grave on-base, as Piercey thinks?'

'Ah, there you have me. How he was lured or taken from a secure establishment I don't yet know, but we can be sure he was.'

They drove for a while in silence. The roads were growing busier as Germans set off for work or ferried their children to schools. No one took much notice of the British Army vehicle. They had grown used to the presence of these soldiers on their roads.

'It's as if someone seeks to rid the regiment of those he sees as bad apples,' Max said thoughtfully, pursuing his theme. 'Rather like James Harkness murdering Major Bekov in the manner of death by firing squad, because his great-grandfather had been executed that way in 1917. He believed Bekov deserved the punishment his ancestor had not.'

'But Harkness was wrong about the crime of his victim. He acted through a fanatical obsession with family and regimental honour.' Tom glanced at Max. 'You think we have a similar set-up here?'

Max frowned. 'I just think we should look carefully at anyone who has no next of kin, no friends back home, no hobbies. A person who regards the regiment as his family and home. Such people are often obsessive, very protective of what they value. Could be male or female. A woman could have carried out these murders. No great strength required.'

'But I can't see a woman making a regiment her god. One member of it, maybe, but it's not usually an aspect of the female psyche to feel inordinately passionate about an organization of warriors. That's a man's thing.'

'Agreed. So let's discount that possibility.'

After some thought, Tom said, 'Bad apples? Brian New was anything but, apparently. Liked and respected all round. Good living. A credit to the regiment. According to Lieutenant Steele, Major Kington was the same.'

'Also according to Mrs Kington.' He glanced across the cab and gave a light laugh. 'OK, duff idea ... but if we discover Colin White was whiter than his name, I'll start to think the British Army is fostering a regiment of paragons and get *really* worried about this case.'

Tom grinned. 'The Stepford Wives aka the Cumberland Rifles?'

'Something along those lines.'

'God help us!'

The Medical Officer was with Christine White when they arrived. She looked to be in a state of collapse, sobbing wildly while fending off the man attempting to give her an injection. He looked up as Mrs White's friend led them in to the room and announced who they were.

'Wrong time,' he said sharply. 'She's not up to talking to you.'

The widow struggled up from the sofa and lurched towards them. 'I am. *I am.* You can

73

tell me who did it.' She thumped Max's chest with her fists. 'Who bloody took him from me? *Who?*'

Max seized her wrists and held her steady, moved by her grief. He too had suffered such grief just a few years ago. 'We're here to ask your help to find the answer to that. Let the doctor give you something to ease the pain, then we'll talk.'

'I'll make tea,' said the friend, walking to the kitchen as Max and the MO coaxed the distressed woman back to the sofa. She continued to sob while the sedative was administered.

Max glanced around the room. Vastly different from the Kington home. The furniture looked well-used; there were toys everywhere. A few dirty patches on the walls suggested scribbling had had to be erased. The Whites' children were clearly not in school in England and, judging by the toys, were all young. Maybe even pre-school age. Fatherless now.

The MO packed away the syringe and empty ampoule, snapped shut his case, then approached the SIB men. 'My name's Clarkson. I don't think you should bank on getting much out of her today. She was really stressed out before this happened. Last straw. She gave birth to a second set of twins two months ago. The other pair are barely three and a half, but they attend a nursery on weekdays. They had a German girl helping with feed and bathtimes, but when Christine heard the terrible news she damn near strangled the girl, apparently. The neighbour who's making tea called me to her quarter where Heidi had run for sanctuary. Christine's been calling down curses on the entire German race since I got here.'

'There's no proof Captain White was killed by a German,' said Tom.

Clarkson frowned. 'He was found out on the heath.'

Max had no wish to pursue that line. 'You said Mrs White was very stressed trying to deal with four small children, yet her husband set off yesterday for a mountain trek leaving her to cope on her own.'

'He went on my advice. Christine's parents and sister are due to arrive later today. They did their utmost to prevent Christine marrying into the Army, and they snipe at Colin at every opportunity. A ghastly, overbearing family. When they last visited, Colin booked himself a room in the Mess and totally avoided them. They've now invited themselves over, ostensibly to see the new babies, and Christine's the type who can't seem to make a stand against them.'

'Yet she defied them over the marriage,' Max pointed out.

'Ah, she discovered she was pregnant. And she was crazy about Colin. They went off, tied the knot, then told her people.'

'Adding fuel to the fire,' Tom observed.

'I guess there must have been a huge bust-up that set the future pattern. It seemed to me to be a good thing for Colin to take a break right away from them. He's also been stressed: not sleeping, working all day and going home to four noisy, messy kids when he's dog-tired. I felt it unfair that he should live in the Mess while Christine's people took over his wife and home. So I advised him to go off and recharge his batteries.' He sighed. 'Christ knows what's behind this demise of a good-natured guy like Colin.'

The neighbour entered with a tray, causing them to turn back in to the room. Christine White was deep in a sedated sleep.

Max regarded Clarkson speculatively. 'That was strong stuff you gave her. Perhaps *you'd* answer some questions about your patient.'

'That's confidential medical data.'

'Nothing like that,' Tom assured him, taking a cup of tea from the neighbour. 'Maybe you could add some info, ma'am.'

'I'll be glad to, if it'll help. I'm Joanne Maybury. My husband's commander of Three Company.' She glanced at the comatose woman. 'Poor thing! However will she cope now Colin's not here to buoy her up? Her family were told of his death last night. When they get here they'll take over, of course. It's my guess they'll never let go. Chris will be swallowed up and the kids'll be raised by Gran and Grandad along their own narrow, prejudiced lines. What a tragedy!'

They all sat to drink their tea. Max asked the MO if Colin White had been planning to team up with anyone. 'Bad policy to walk mountain tracks alone, especially with the snow starting to melt now.'

'He usually went out with three others. In the summer they also climbed. Easy to slightly difficult ascents only.'

'These three were Brits?'

'Yes. Mark Lang's a tank commander; Sanders and Benson are with a Signals Squadron. I believe they'd climbed as a team back home and knew each other well. Important when indulging in that tricky sport. Good to know you can trust the guy on the other end of the rope.'

Tom asked if Colin White was intending to meet these friends yesterday.

The MO shook his head. 'No idea. But you can check. I'll give you details of where they're all stationed.' With a faint smile he added, 'Colin used to go on somewhat about his passion in the Mess. No one could help knowing all the facts.'

'He was the same with us,' said Joanne Maybury. 'Luke – that's my husband – has no interest in climbing. He even told Colin they were reckless fools who put in danger the lives of men who have to rescue them when they get stuck. But Colin continued to bend his ear when he got back from his jaunts.' Her voice thickened. 'How could this have happened? Colin was a simple, genuine guy who doted on Chris and the kids. Who'd have been so cruel as to kill him and dump his body out on the heath?'

Max turned his attention back to Clarkson.

'Captain White was rather a bore in the Mess?'

'No, no! He was a very lively member. Well liked. That's why he had his leg pulled so often about his craze for climbing. The lads played all manner of tricks on him, but he always took it in good part. Joanne's right. Joining the armed forces means you put your life on the line, but not this way!'

'Did he have German friends, maybe in the climbing fraternity?'

'Mark Lang would be better able to answer that.'

'Colin and Chris knew a family in Bergdorf,' said Joanne Maybury. 'It was through them that the girl came to help with the new twins. You don't think *they're* responsible, do you?'

Max avoided that. 'As far as you're aware, Doctor, the victim had no enemies ... apart from his in-laws?'

Clarkson set down his cup and saucer, and got to his feet. 'I wasn't one of Colin's intimates but, from my knowledge of him in the Mess and my surgery, I'd say he wasn't the type to provoke animosity deep enough to lead to murder. Now I must deal with Sick Parade. I'm already running late.'

'One last question, sir,' said Tom, also rising. 'Were Captain White, Sergeant Brian New and Major Kington generally fit men?'

The MO's eyes narrowed speculatively. 'You're expecting Simon to be a third victim?'

78

'We have to consider the possibility,' agreed Max.

'Colin and Brian New were, yes. I sincerely hope Simon still is.'

'As we do, sir,' said Tom calmly.

It was a warm spring evening. Ornate gates stood open at the foot of a long drive bordered by shaved lawns, which led to a large grey stone house. An impressive private residence a multimillionaire with a passion for Ferraris had turned in to an exclusive club for others like himself.

Ben Steele drove his standard Ford through the entrance gates and was daunted by the array of four-wheeled magnificence parked there. He knew it was possible to bluff one's way in to such places with the right amount of assumed swagger, but he wished his car was at least a BMW. He was sure no fault could be found with his appearance. Regimental blazer, pale trousers, open-necked shirt, silk scarf. A gold Rolex would have added the final touch. One day, perhaps!

He parked in a space half hidden by trees, then made his way to the shallow steps forcing himself to saunter rather than march. Oh, for a glamorous girl hanging on his arm. Tara Kington, for instance. Yet he had heard she did not share her husband's fervour for these cars, so never accompanied him to rallies or club activities. Maybe it was a men only club.

That thought was immediately banished on entering. He spotted several vivid young women talking in the foyer with silver-haired men in more expensive versions of Ben's smart-casual clothes. His heart sank. The suspicion he was loath to face rose up. Had Simon Kington lost his head and run off with a rich bimbo almost half his age? In this set-up temptation would be very strong.

He was drawn from his flight of fancy by a firm but discreet voice asking his business. Crunch time! In fluent German he told the porter he was there to meet Major Kington on an urgent matter.

'I'm flying to Japan tonight. My schedule is tight, so he asked me to call in here.' He glanced at the clock in the small cubicle. 'I'm a little early, I see. When he arrives be good enough to tell him Lieutenant Steele is waiting in the bar.'

He headed purposefully for the room in to which the silver-haired sugar daddies had taken the girls, half-expecting a protest. But his imposture had worked. Time for action plan two.

The club's icon was celebrated in oils, watercolours, silver and bronze. In addition, the walls of the high-ceilinged bar were adorned with photographs of worldwide rallies, and of designers and eminent owners from launch day to the present.

As he wandered the room looking at it all, Ben sensed a touch of eccentricity in such worship. It filled him with unease. Could someone *kill* for a car? Would a man who coveted a model owned by someone else commit murder to get it? Fabulous diamonds had often left a trail of blood through their history. As had *objets d'art* and beautiful women. The annals of crime were full of instances. If the desire to possess was powerful enough, removing whatever stood in the way took extreme forms. Rare stamps, exotic birds' eggs, ancient coins. Why not cars?

Sane thought returned with a rush. Simon's Ferrari was still at his house. Besides, a maniac collector would have set about the business along a dark lane where a body could lie hidden even for years. Ben sighed. Back to the theory of a bimbo who had inspired temporary madness.

'Are you a new member?'

Ben turned swiftly to find one of the girls he had seen in the foyer. He felt his colour rise. She was astonishingly beautiful. Red-gold hair fell past her shoulders, pale green eyes were remarkably clear against her tanned skin, her body would induce temporary madness in any man. Her smile was full of invitation.

Gathering his senses, Ben said, 'I'm here to meet up with a friend. Simon Kington.'

'How nice!' She immediately switched to English and offered her pink-tipped hand. 'I am Sonja Meikel.'

Ben completed the introduction while studying her slender shape in the rich blue dress ending at mid-thigh. 'Do you know Simon?'

'Of course. Everyone knows him. He has a

so famous father in medicines. Gerhardt Wolf is his sworn enemy.' She waved a hand to indicate one of the silver-haired men, then gave a delightful laugh. 'Do not take that seriously, Ben. Gerhardt's company is the German equivalent of Grant Bonner Kington, that is all. Would you like an introduction?'

'I'd rather talk to you.'

She laughed again. 'Are you flirting with me?'

'You must be used to men doing that.'

'Ah, but not your military friend.'

It was said in a teasing tone, but Ben took her up on it. 'I find that hard to believe.'

'Then you do not know him. The only ladies Simon finds attractive have four wheels, an exciting chassis and turbo engine.'

'Isn't that true of all the members; why the club exists?'

She linked her arm through his and led him towards the bar. 'There is "in love" and there is "crazy passion". I am in love with Ferraris. Simon regards them with passion.'

Curious, he asked, 'Do you own one?'

'Of course I do. I could not otherwise be a member.' Her eyes grew large with speculation. 'You thought I was what you British call a *rambo*?'

Ben's laughter was spontaneous despite the fresh colour in his cheeks. 'The word is *bimbo*. I did think you must be a member's daughter,' he lied.

'And so I am. My father is there talking to

82

Gerhardt.' She indicated the group of men he had taken for sugar daddies. 'They are all great rivals for winning at rallies. But they are not happy last year. I came top with Simon just behind me. Third was Hilde Wengen. That is she by the window showing much of her legs.'

Gorgeous legs they were, but Ben now knew better than to imagine all they did was wave in the air. When he managed to draw his gaze from them he discovered Sonja was holding two drinks.

'It is time for cocktails, yes?'

'Yes ... but please allow me to buy them,' he muttered, unused to super-rich girl rally winners.

Her inviting smile washed over him. 'You are very quaint, Ben. Rolf will charge them to *Vatti*'s account, as usual. Now drink and relax.'

It was some cocktail! He was beginning to believe this girl could knock back quite a few without visible effects, but he meant to keep his head clear for why he was here. To do a little private investigation.

'So you beat Simon last year. How did he take being sandwiched between two competitive women?'

She eyed him provocatively over the rim of her glass. 'That is not very polite. I and Hilde are the bread; your friend the tasty filling.'

'I didn't mean...'

'Simon was happy to make high speeds on the track he cannot make on the autobahn. It does not matter to him to win, just to drive fast. Me, I like to be the best.'

I'll bet you do, he thought, finding her sexual challenge getting to him. To ward it off, he asked, 'Are any of Simon's particular friends here this evening?'

Light from the windows burnished the shining fall of hair as she shook her head. 'He comes, he speaks with the committee, he enters his name for rallies, then he leaves. Once or twice he will eat here. Mostly, he does not linger like others.' She twisted to the bar and replaced her empty glass with a full one already lined up by Rolf. 'You are too slow, Ben. The cocktail hour is so short one must be quick to enjoy it fully. Here is one already waiting for you.'

'I actually have to go,' he said hastily. 'It looks as if Simon's been detained. He wasn't here earlier, I suppose?'

'I have not seen him all this week. He travels away a lot. And he has other passions, you know. If he should concentrate on driving he would be unbeatable. But he rides his horses and flies his aeroplane. Now he has the new craziness for the tiny one.'

Ben frowned. 'The tiny one?'

'It is so curious.' She tossed back the remainder of her second drink and reached for the one Ben had declined. 'How can a man race a superb Ferrari then switch to one of those ridiculous machines? I have seen pictures. One or two large men sitting on a small toboggan that has a motor. It is like a children's story. The magic flying carpet. So silly!'

Ben suddenly felt as heady as if he had drunk half a dozen of her cocktails. A microlight! The answer to how a man could be spirited from a secure base. Hop over the perimeter fence, grab the victim as he gets out of his car, then hop back over the fence ... and vanish!

Four

Max was deeply frustrated after a restless night. Thoughts had bombarded him like neutrons raining down on a barren planet. Intuition, experience – what he referred to as his guts – told him the Royal Cumberland Rifles *must* be at the root of this case, despite both murders being committed outside their regimental base.

Klaus Krenkel was conducting his own investigation, liaising with SIB, but the *Polizei* were getting no further than the military detectives. Neither Brian New nor Colin White had had close affiliations with German civilians that could have led to violence, and Krenkel was losing interest in what he felt was a purely British affair. Max did not argue with that, but he was glad of his German colleague's transcripts of interviews. It left his own team to concentrate on the internal investigation.

After a tussle with Christine White's aggressive parents, Sergeants Bush and Johnson had managed to talk to the widow. She had painted a picture of a supportive husband and father whose only fault, so far as she was concerned, had been a compulsion to risk his life climbing mountains. Connie Bush added her opinion that had White fallen to his death from a high peak his wife could probably have handled it. She had broken apart completely over this; likely to remain that way while her family took over her four children lock, stock and barrel.

Max had questioned all the RCR officers about Colin White, while Tom had done the same in the Sergeants' Mess in respect of Brian New. Both sessions had proved unproductive, prompting Max to reiterate his comparison with the Stepford Wives.

'These men were so perfect they could have been robots, Tom. D'you think the Cumberland Rifles are fantasy soldiers created by some machiavellian budding world dictator?'

Tom had replied drily, 'If they are, it'll be the first time we've been on the right side.'

If there were squirrels in the trees that morning, or any other wildlife activity of interest, Max failed to notice it. He made toast, but it remained in the toaster while he drank several cups of strong black coffee and brooded over the tragic death of Vera Maitland. She had surely just been in the wrong place at the wrong time. If she had just accepted New's proposal of marriage, she would have climbed in that car full of happy plans for her future, unaware that she had no future.

Max gazed unseeing from the windows, caught up in painful memories of Susan. Whatever future she had hoped for had been denied her on a morning of her twenty-sixth year. Although time was working the healing process and he was able again to find pleasure in pastimes he had always enjoyed, car crashes in adverse weather invariably revived the sense of loss.

Next minute his attention was caught by *Frau* Hahn's twin great-grandsons, who emerged in to the garden to totter uncertainly after Franzi, the great woolly hound standing as tall as they. Despite the dog's size and friskiness, he never seemed to bowl the toddlers over and they had no fear of him.

Watching them induced warmth to drive away the chill that had threatened, and Max smiled with pleasure as the tiny boys collided and plonked down heavily on their padded rumps. The years of innocence. Thank God for them!

On arrival at Section Headquarters, Max had a swift consultation with Tom before a more general briefing. There was still no news of Colin White's car, and no real clues to where he had been between leaving the base and being found dead just three kilometres from it. The forensic report added to the puzzle. He had eaten a light meal of white fish, buttered potatoes and asparagus before death occurred, washed down by pure water. Slight traces of semen on the underpants suggested willing sexual activity. There were no signs of bondage or manhandling, apart from bruising and lacerations inflicted post-mortem and conducive with the body being dragged across heathland.

The victim had died between nine and midnight. There was nothing to show where the actual killing had taken place, but the body had been in contact with a rough blanket at some time. Possibly to transport it from the scene of the crime to where it was found.

Max invited discussion on this. 'Two murders have been committed by someone who has a supply of a toxin experts can't yet pinpoint. He may have more available.'

'He's a serial killer?' asked Connie Bush.

'We need to catch him before he gives us the answer to that,' Max declared. 'I want your thoughts; input we can discuss, analyze, attach some sense to.'

Sergeant Beeny said, 'There have to be two men in on this. One couldn't hold him down and inject at the same time.'

'No sign of manhandling,' his partner Piercey reminded him. 'He did this one the same way as the first. Bumped into his victim and stuck in the needle in passing. Easy enough to do in the narrow spacing between parked vehicles, especially when it's dark.'

'But Captain White didn't drive away and crash like Sergeant New,' Heather Johnson pointed out.

'Because he'd arrived somewhere and was getting *out* of his car,' Piercey said smugly.

'Arrived where?' mused Connie Bush. 'This would have occurred around nine p.m. He'd had supper and sex before he died. So, he spent the day with a woman, then drove to a *Gasthof* intending to book in and leave for his mountaineering trip next morning.'

'But who would have known of his plans?' asked Beeny.

'The woman he'd been with,' Connie concluded.

'You mean she had sex with him, gave him supper, then followed and finished him off?' challenged Beeny. 'After that, she rolled him in a blanket in the car park, drove the body to the heath and carried it from the car without help?'

'What if she's the wife of a Cumberland Rifleman,' suggested Sergeant Olly Simpson. 'Husband came home early, saw them at it, followed White and got rid of him.'

'You're all wandering in the realms of fiction,' said Tom with evident disgust. 'Two murders by a highly unusual method on consecutive nights. Apart from the regimental link there *has* to be another. Start living up to your training and experience and come up with something real. Which of you checked with his regular climbing partners?' Seeing blank expressions, he exploded. 'Christ, what've you all been doing since this case opened ... apart from reading the bullshit detective fiction you quote instead of using the brains you're supposed to possess? Get on it *now*, Beeny!'

Max, who rarely saw Tom in a high passion, said with some acidity, 'I assumed that had been followed up yesterday.'

Tom turned to him quickly, 'My fault, sir. I put it out as one of the tasks to be tackled. Didn't allocate specifically.'

'You shouldn't have to spell it out in words of one syllable.'

'But I should've checked someone had got on to it.'

Max agreed. He should have. 'So we have no corroboration of the Medical Officer's statement that Captain White set off on a walking trip two days ago?'

'Not yet, sir.' The twitching muscle in his jaw and the frequent acknowledgement of rank told Max the Sergeant Major was furious with himself. A martinet for efficiency, he could not bear to face his own lack of it on the few occasions he lapsed.

Watching Beeny conversing on the phone by his desk, dark flop of hair moving as he nodded, fingers drumming on the computer, Max considered a hypothesis. What if Colin White had *not* been waylaid by the heath early in the morning? What if he had driven off in the opposite direction to meet someone and had later been killed there? His body could have been driven back in the dead of night to the heath, where the killer would have been reasonably certain dog walkers or joggers would come across it.

Beeny returned to his seat in the rough circle. 'I spoke to Lieutenant Lang himself, sir. There were no plans to meet up; said the other two in the usual team are on UK leave. He sounded upset by the news. They'd been

91

friends a long time.'

'He's had no contact with Captain White regarding leave this week?' probed Tom.

'No, sir. Last contacted him to give congrats on the birth of more twins. Almost two months ago, that was. Said he guessed there'd be no climbing for a while with four small kids on the go.'

Max then aired his hypothesis. 'It could account for those missing hours,' he pointed out. 'Pathologist can't prove time of death, nor estimate how long the body had lain where it was found. Most of the night, because of fox damage, but where was he killed? We need to delve deeper into the victim's life. He must be more complex than the man everyone describes. Sergeant Beeny, go with Piercey to interview Lieutenant Lang in depth. Men who climb together have implicit trust in each other and are likely to confide things kept secret from others. Sergeants Bush and Johnson, take the assumption that Captain White drove from the base in the *opposite* direction. Question shopkeepers, garage attendants etcetera along that route. Intensify the search for the missing car. It should yield evidence of what he was doing prior to his death, who he was with, even *why* he was killed. Get the answer to this death and we'll have a head start on the other ... and maybe the chance to prevent a third.'

Tom was still angry. 'Pull your fingers out and put in some real work! Both murders were cleverly planned. Forget random killing; forget mistaken identity. Those two men had to be taken out. Somewhere beneath their apparently blameless lives lies the reason why they posed too much of a threat to go on living. I don't want to see any of you again until you've got some real leads.'

Certain his guts were giving him the right signals, Max turned his back on trays filled with paperwork and set out for the present home of the Royal Cumberland Rifles, with Tom at the wheel.

'I think we should have another word with Major Clarkson,' he said to the silent man beside him. 'Was that a load of bull about recommending a trekking holiday, or did he really believe Colin White had taken the advice? I'm no medic, but to send a stressed man getting little sleep and facing the prospect of hostile in-laws invading his home on a break that demands knowledge of the terrain, clear judgement and peak physical condition sounds irresponsible to me.' After a moment or two, he added, 'Cast off the hair shirt, Tom. You can't chase after them every minute, and you shouldn't have to.'

'No, I shouldn't have to, but we've wasted a whole day because no one checked out the obvious man to confirm where the victim was heading.'

'We still don't know. There's so little to go on with both these crimes. Nobody saw or heard or knows anything, yet those two were killed for a reason hidden deep beneath lies

93

that are disguising an obsessive murderer. The m.o. is indicating something we're too slow picking up on. I've looked at it from all directions, but the solution is hovering one flash of inspiration away.'

'Then you're doing far better than I am, sir.'

'The best I've come up with is a man taking revenge for a brother, a pal – a girlfriend, even – who is suffering from Gulf War Syndrome. Death by injection. Highlights his point!'

Tom pulled up at a red light; glanced across with pursed lips. 'We've come across wilder motives, but wouldn't this guy be bumping off people in the MOD who authorized that cocktail of drugs? Or the medics who administered them? Why kill off men who probably were given those same drugs? The RCR served in the Gulf back in 92.'

'Another duff idea,' Max conceded, as the Land Rover moved off again. 'If the scientific boys could only ID that toxin it would surely throw some light for us to follow. The very fact that it's unidentifiable by those in the know makes its use in a case like this so puzzling. Are we looking for a mad scientist, Tom?'

'Running amok in the Cumberland Rifles? Why?'

Max looked from the window at the guarded gates they were approaching and sighed. 'Because he's deranged. Because he hates khaki. Because he needs to check that the new poison he's developed does its job. God

94

knows why! Maybe White and New *were* just in the wrong place at the wrong time. My guts aren't infallible. This regiment could have no connection with what's going on here. The victims could merely have been two handy guinea pigs.'

Tom showed his ID to the guard, who saluted then raised the barrier. As he drove on to the perimeter road, Tom said quietly, 'You don't really mistrust those guts of yours, do you?'

'I wish like hell I did,' he confessed. 'Then we could offload this case on the *Polizei*.'

'You think Klaus would buy the idea of a mad scientist on the loose?'

Max smiled. 'We could try him with Major Kennedy's theory of a German still fighting the last war with his grandad's gun.'

Tom finally relaxed and smiled back. 'Let's stick with your guts, for now. I think they're right. Human guinea-pigs conveniently appearing, both members of a British Army regiment, is too far-fetched. Besides, there's the missing Defence Liaison Officer, also RCR, which swings the pointer back here.'

The disappearance of Simon Kington had been followed up in the usual manner. Checks at airports, rail stations and ferry ports; questioning of friends, colleagues, those who looked after his Ferrari, his horses and the Learjet he part owned. Nothing.

Max knew a man could not self-destruct or be abducted by aliens, yet Kington had some-how left a secure establishment without being seen. Due to his Defence links his absence was potentially worrying, but with nothing to work on SIB were concentrating their efforts on the known crime of double murder. There was always the possibility that Kington had behaved stupidly over a woman and would soon return with his tail between his legs. If so, he would deeply regret his moment of madness. Both his career and his marriage would suffer badly.

Max gave Tom a long thoughtful look. 'Are you expecting a third body to be found before long?'

'If it is, bang will go the prime suspect. My money's still on the Galloping Major as our killer.'

'Really?'

'His father is a pharmaceuticals baron. Easy for him to lay hands on a new toxin being developed in their laboratory.'

'Motive?'

Tom swung the vehicle round to pull up outside the Medical Centre. 'Getting rid of bad apples?'

Max shook his head. 'My theory, I admit, but I can't see it applying to a man who spends so much time racing horses or his car. To say nothing of flying his quarter-owned jet. Speed is Kington's god, not his regiment.'

As they entered the red brick building, Max said, 'This man also has access to drugs and chemicals; knows how to use a hypo with expertise. We need to talk seriously to him.'

Major Charles Clarkson was dealing with

the tail-end of the morning sick parade. He did not look pleased to see them, but asked an orderly to rustle up coffee and biscuits for the visitors while he attended to the ills of a sergeant with a large dressing on the back of his right hand, and a woman corporal who looked to be in the early stages of pregnancy. The SIB men recognized the sergeant. Sam Dawkins, close friend of Brian New.

'I'll nab him when he comes out,' said Tom quietly. 'He told us about his pal's saintly persona. Now he can give us the flip side. New must have had one and, somewhere along the line, he upset someone enough to die because of it.'

Max frowned. 'Ditto Captain White. But what links the two? We know they had little to do with each other; not even in the same company. No interests in common. White was very married; New was divorced years ago. So there wasn't even a wives' friendship to work on.'

'The link is the Cumberland Rifles. Must be.'

They took mugs of coffee from the orderly and prepared to wait. When Dawkins came from the treatment room with a fresh dressing on his hand, Tom put aside his drink and tackled him.

'We want to talk to you again when we've finished here. Where will you be in the next hour or so?'

Dawkins had a question of his own. 'Why didn't you say Brian had been murdered?

There's word going around some nutter's got it in for the Cumberlands. What's going on?' he demanded red-faced.

'We'll discuss that later. Where will you be?' Tom persisted.

'In Number Two Store, stocktaking. I'm on light duties because of the hand.'

Max asked what he had done to it, and hostile eyes turned to him. 'Tore it on wire, sir. It's got infected.'

'The perimeter wire?'

'The dog runs. There's no break in the perimeter wire. No one took Major Kington out through *that*. Sir.' He added the respect of rank without conviction.

Watching the man stomp his way down the path, Max's frustration grew. 'We have to make headway on this before morale is undermined by the threat of mass murder of Cumberland Riflemen.'

Tom plainly took the comment as further blame for the slip-up over the mountaineering Lieutenant Lang. 'We're working in the dark. Even the best of us can't make headway when everything's a blank, sir.'

The military mother-to-be then came from the consulting room, followed by the Medical Officer who asked his unwelcome guests to enter.

'I don't have a lot of time to spare,' he announced, making no attempt to sit. 'As I indicated yesterday, I can't divulge confidential medical information.'

'If it was in practitioners' jargon we would

not understand it, anyway,' Max replied calmly. 'You're busier than most regimental doctors I've met. You had to rush away from our last meeting, and you have urgent business now. Is this a particularly unhealthy regiment?'

Clarkson's dark eyes hardened. 'I specialized in venereal diseases at Med School. I hold a clinic locally every Thursday from thirteen hundred to fifteen hundred hours. What can I do for you?'

'We've discovered Captain White made no plan to follow your recommendation. Were you aware that he had ignored your advice, sir?' asked Tom.

'I gave you details of the men you should check that with.'

Max asked, 'Is it usual to suggest that a man who's stressed and badly in need of sleep should indulge in the hazardous sport of trekking over mountain peaks during the spring thaw?'

Clarkson was a tall, swarthy man, the kind who soon looked intimidating. 'Have you had medical training, Captain Rydal?'

'It merely seemed counter-productive to me.'

'As your investigation does to me. Yet I wouldn't think of questioning your methods, because I know nothing of detective procedures.'

'They're very simple. Check everything and everyone. Then go through it all again taking out those factors that don't add up. Like a doctor who gives such a heavy sedative to a witness she goes out like a light before she can be questioned. And who advises an exhausted patient to scale a few high peaks,' said Max, irritated by this man's attitude.

Tom went right to the point. 'Would you tell us where you were on Sunday and Monday nights, sir?'

Storm signals lit up the eyes. 'On Sunday my wife and I gave a dinner party that went on rather late. On Monday our children had friends to sleep over. I played games with them until bedtime. Plenty of witnesses on both occasions.' He reached for his cap and medical bag. 'Am I to understand you regard me as a murder suspect?'

'Two of your colleagues were killed by lethal injection. A medical weapon, wouldn't you agree?' asked Max staying in the doorway.

'The injections I give more often than not *save* lives. If, for some obscure reason, I'd wanted to kill those two I'd have put a bullet through them. Dig a little deeper and you'll discover I'm the crack shot of the Army Rifle Club.' He gave a tight smile. 'It's what *I* do when stressed and badly in need of sleep. Get rid of built-up tension by blasting at targets that can't run away. You should try it. Now, if you'll move aside, I'll be on my way.'

They let him go. Back in the Land Rover going to interview Sam Dawkins, Max said thoughtfully, 'A man of considerable passion, apparently. A far darker mood than yesterday.

I wonder what caused the change.'

Tom swung the vehicle around a mini roundabout with unusual recklessness. 'Professional tug of war. Spends his days sorting out troops with a dose of clap and girl corporals having babies. It's what he chose to be trained for, but he now has ambitions to be a real shooting soldier. The star of the Rifle Club comes down to earth amongst the bedpans.'

Max regarded him with surprise. 'That's very deep and psychoanalytical.'

Tom gave a caustic laugh. 'It's a load of crap. His wife probably boiled his breakfast eggs too hard.'

'How were yours?'

'Cereal and toast.' Silence hung heavily between them until Tom said, 'We've never had a blind alley case like this one. A fatal jab with a needle. No kitchen knife, no blunt instrument. No cartridge cases, no powder burns. No scenes of crime, even. We assume Brian New was attacked in the restaurant car park, but have no witnesses or proof. We have no idea where Colin White was given his lethal injection, and his car has vanished. We can't find a link between the victims, or an obvious motive, because they were both bloody paragons. And where the hell is Major Kington?' he finished explosively.

They sat outside Number Two Store making no move to leave the vehicle. Professional impotence weighed on them. After a while, Max said, 'There was an old black and white classic on TV last week. Ended with a man-hunt through the sewers of Vienna under quadruple occupation. Dated, but terrific acting.'

Tom looked askance at him. *'The Third Man?'*

'Exactly! Our victims had no common link that we can find, so they must both have had one with a third person. Maybe even without each other's knowledge.'

'The Galloping Major? Apart from the obvious regimental connection, neither victim was rich, talented, ultra-intelligent or interested in horse and motor racing. Nor did they have shares in a private jet.' Tom's brow furrowed. 'But, as you once said, Brian New might have been killed because of something he knew rather than what he'd done. That was before Colin White's body was found. What if they both had evidence against Kington that was so damaging they had to be put out of the way?'

'Would he have killed, then run and put suspicion on himself? I still believe he'll prove to be a third casualty. All the same, we've probed the lives of the known victims but neglected his. I suggest we pay Mrs Kington another visit this afternoon and dig a little deeper this time.'

The interview with Sam Dawkins yielded little that was new. He made no secret of his hostility or of his opinion that SIB were laying down on the job. He even went so far as to suggest all they had to do was round up

102

everyone who had been at the Golden Key on the night of the murder and use Gestapo tactics until the guilty man cracked.

'They invented the technique. Why not use it on them for a change? Pull out a few finger or toenails, stick their heads in buckets of water, crush their balls with pliers.' Dawkins was angry and full of grief for an old friend.

Some light was grudgingly shed on Brian New's personality, but it did nothing to further the investigation. He had been as lively as the average young soldier – drinking, chasing girls, betting on horses, kicking up larks on-base and around town in Hong Kong, until he fell for the girl he married. He had sobered practically overnight and, surprisingly, stayed that way after the divorce. Tom commented that the circumstances surrounding the divorce would have made most men break out and hit the bottle.

'Not Brian. He put all his energy into his career. Said he wanted eventually to apply for a commission, be the man giving orders.'

'As a sergeant he gave orders,' Tom pointed out.

'He wanted more power than that.'

'Is that what he actually said? More power?'

'His very words, sir. He was deeply humiliated by Jacki refusing to stay with him. Made him look a wimp in front of the lads. He was determined to show what he was really made of. It became almost an obsession. Which was why I was surprised that he fell so quickly for Vera. I never thought he'd risk a second marriage.' Dawkins cleared the thickness in his throat. 'Wonder if he got around to asking her before...' He glared at Tom defiantly. 'If I knew who'd done that to them, I'd sort him out personally.'

'Leave that to us,' Tom warned. 'We won't crush balls with pliers – we're civilized – but the killer will pay heavily for his crime.'

They left Dawkins unconvinced, their own doubts in no way eased by the encounter. Max suggested they had some lunch before tackling Tara Kington, so they went their separate ways to eat and glean any snippets of gossip that might prove useful.

Unsurprisingly, Max found himself isolated at the long table. The diners were mostly young single men, or visitors with a regimental host. He was happy enough quietly to mull over the two interviews that morning, in a large room hung with gold-embossed boards filled with the names of illustrious former members of the regiment, and paintings of long-ago battles in which it had distinguished itself. He was taken abruptly out of the realms of history when someone came to sit opposite him at the polished table.

Ben Steele smiled, hoped he was not intruding on serious deliberations. Max demurred with a return smile. He felt well disposed to this subaltern whose eyes many girls would envy for their size and depth of colour. Perhaps because he was still full of post-Sandhurst enthusiasm.

'Have you made your peace with Major Kennedy?'

'An uneasy peace. I always seem to be putting my boot in.'

Max grinned. 'Comes of being new to the game. The boot tends to behave itself as time passes.'

'It's a bit of luck running into you,' Ben confided. 'I've been wondering what to do about it.'

Max set his knife and fork down on a plate that had held a large slice of chicken pie with vegetables, and sat back replete. 'Do about what? The errant boot?'

The young officer leaned forward conspiratorially after glancing at a laughing group at the far end of the table. 'I've done some investigating and come up with an exciting result.'

Oh dear, thought Max, it *was* the errant boot! 'Investigating into what?'

'Major Kington's abduction.'

'We don't know that he was abducted. He could well have gone under his own steam.'

The youthful face was pink with eagerness. 'That's what I thought. At least, it's what I didn't want to think. Couldn't believe he'd put Tara through distress knowingly. So I did some asking around and hit the bull's-eye.' Another swift glance to check that those at the far end weren't eavesdropping, then his story came out in a rush. 'So it's evident Simon wasn't interested in the girls at the club, although any man with a wife like his wouldn't have a roving eye. So that led me back to the abduction theory, and how he could have been taken without using the gates or cutting the wire.'

After waiting for Max's reaction and getting a satisfying prompt, more words tumbled out. 'By two-man microlight! Hop over the perimeter wire, snatch him, then hop back again. The entire op is over in a matter of minutes and no one's any wiser. Here's the punchline,' Ben added triumphantly. 'Sonja Meikel told me Simon's latest craze is *flying microlights*!'

Max grew interested. His team had checked out the Learjet, but no one had taken the aircraft up for two weeks. A microlight was altogether different. Kington could have flown anywhere with no means of tracing him. No flight plan to be logged, no contact with ground control for permission to land. It could also be hidden very effectively.

'So what d'you think?'

Max was drawn from his thoughts. 'It's an interesting theory, but it has flaws.'

'So has the fact that someone vanished the way he did. But this surely solves the biggest question, doesn't it?'

'And poses a number of others. How did the abductor know exactly when Major Kington would arrive home, and how was he forced to go with him? I'd say two were needed to manhandle an unwilling hostage.'

Ben sighed with impatience. 'That applies to any theory on his disappearance. But he *has* gone. So the microlight clue is worth following up, isn't it?'

'Of course. We do that with any promising piece of info. The most unlikely facts often spawn valuable leads,' Max said. 'Have you an idea who the abductor might be?'

'Someone after defence intelligence Simon would have. There are any number of organizations who'd want it.' When Max made no comment, he asked aggressively, 'Who else would snatch him?'

'You'd know that better than I. Did he have enemies? There must be a few who're envious, resentful of his affluent, fast-track lifestyle. Has he been promoted over someone's head? Did he beat another man to the job of Defence Liaison Officer? Has someone's bored wife ever made a play for him?'

It was clear Max had put his own boot in now. The confidential manner was replaced by indignation. 'Simon's one of our most popular officers. He's never flaunted his wealth or talents, and he's the last person to play around with another man's wife.'

Ramming his boot well and truly home, Max asked, 'Is it possible that he committed the murders, then ran for it?'

Ben rose, face set. 'You're clutching at straws instead of listening to what people tell you about Simon. The *Polizei* would make a better job of getting to the bottom of this than you are.'

Max watched the young officer's swift retreat wryly. A touch of hero-worship? Or was it his undeniable infatuation with Tara Kington that made him believe the man she had chosen to marry must be perfect? Life's rough edges would bring cynicism to temper such judgements, but Max admired his loyalty. Within a year or two, the Cumberlands would have a fine officer in their ranks.

He drank coffee well away from the group of hearty young men Ben had joined. Microlights! Why had no one in the team come up with that idea, himself included? Unless Kington turned up soon – dead or alive – he knew MI5 would take over the case. The EU Defence connection would demand their intervention. He always disliked that. Working with Klaus Krenkel and the *Polizei* was normally reasonably harmonious, but on the few occasions MI5 had arrived on the scene every aspect of the case had grown more complicated.

Priority would have to be given to the missing officer. He had been gone three days without any reported sightings or contact with his wife, so they must now seriously consider the possibility of his being a third murder victim. All the more essential to discover what clues his background might hold to shed light on the darkness enveloping this multifaceted case.

Ben Steele had given a glowing description of Kington. This further account of character perfection worried Max. What was this facade of virtue hiding? Two, possibly three, men could surely not have been killed because of their utter goodness.

Tom's hour in the Sergeants' Mess, eating a meal that would have Nora muttering darkly about cholesterol, gleaned a few facts. Nothing to get too excited about, but he related them to Max en route to the Kingtons' house.

'Sar'nt Major Busby is definite the Major had his laptop with him when he left the office that evening. Seemed his usual friendly self. Busby heard the car start up and drive off, but he didn't see who was in it. Several witnesses who've already testified that they saw him heading for home, today admitted they recognized his car and *assumed* he was driving it. None would swear to who was at the wheel.'

'So there's no proof Major Kington left that car outside his house. His wife only heard and assumed, like the rest. He could have been grabbed, or have sneaked away, outside his office.'

Tom nodded agreement. 'My money's on the latter. Abduction would be too risky – lights from office windows and too much human activity at that time. Suppose he went out to his car, drove it a couple of blocks to where an accomplice was waiting to take over? Kington then slipped into the cavity beneath one of the huts and lay low until his partner came along much later, driving a truck carrying a legit cargo. The Major hung to the underbelly of the vehicle as it passed through the gate, then dropped off when it halted at the junction leading on to the autobahn. They only check the underside of traffic entering, not leaving.'

They were now parked in the road outside the missing man's home, and both sat staring at the 4x4 someone had put there three nights ago.

'It's possible,' said Max eventually. 'It sounds more like one of the fictional plots you accused the team of hatching, but we all know from experience that villains get away with the most audacious plans. It would explain how he left the base, but it raises a hell of a lot of question marks. Did he leave because he had committed two murders, in which case the accomplice was an accessory to the crime, or has he defected with a computer memory filled with not terribly secret data? The accomplice is then guilty of contravening the Official Secrets Act.'

Tom sighed heavily. 'Facts: he has gone and so has the laptop; two murders have been committed. His absence has to be linked with the killings, or with the specialist work he does. The laptop might be misleading. It's what he holds in his head that's the key.'

'There's the other angle. He could be the third victim. A swift jab in the thigh as he leaves his vehicle.' He nodded at the car port. 'The body could then have been taken out with a legit cargo, as you suggest, stuffed into a box marked as part of the consignment.'

'That leaves our killer on-base.'

'I've always believed that.'

'But why top the Major here, when it's so chancy, yet attack the others outside? Don't sully your own doorstep, you said.'

Max gave a faint smile. 'I say too much, Tom. Why the hell does none of this add up? Why isn't there a pattern? Why are these reputedly perfect soldiers being targeted this way?'

Spotting movement, Tom spoke sharply. 'Uh-oh, the lady's about to leave.'

Tara Kington had emerged from a side-door, dressed in jodphurs, boots and tailored black jacket, and was unlocking the door of the Ferrari.

The two detectives left their vehicle and approached her. 'Mrs Kington, we'd like a word with you,' said Max. 'It won't take long, but perhaps we could go inside.'

She paled, studied them fearfully. 'Have you found him?'

'I'm afraid not.' Tom spoke quietly, and put out an arm to indicate the door through which she had just left. 'Just a few questions about his contacts and interests.'

The interior was as immaculate as when she had known they were coming. Whatever her present fears she was keeping up appearances. Model home, and faultless personal grooming. It suddenly struck Tom that this woman was yet another paragon. She even had her emotions tightly under control. How different from what they had encountered at the Whites' quarter. Tara Kington would

111

never need a tranquillizer from Major Clarkson.

Max went straight to the point. 'In spite of intensive enquiries, I'm afraid we have no clues on your husband's whereabouts. There've been no sightings, no evidence that he has left Germany by any regular means.' He gave her a penetrating look. 'Has he made any contact with you, Mrs Kington?'

'I would have told you immediately,' she replied coolly.

'You've not been contacted by anyone else?' asked Tom.

'Whoever is holding him, you mean? Again, I would have told you.'

'Such people always threaten reprisals if the police are alerted, ma'am, but there are ways of getting around that,' he said gently.

Her right hand played with the hard hat she held, the only sign of her nervousness. 'I *would* have told you.'

'Who do you think might be holding Major Kington?' asked Max.

She turned to him with a graceful movement. 'Someone who's well aware of the work he does. Simon deals with important, influential people. Influential in Defence, that is. It's not only what's discussed at meetings, but what's confided outside the conference room. He's a brilliant linguist, so he often overhears private conversations between men who have no idea he understands what they're saying. I'm afraid someone has now realized this and taken him out of circulation until the vital

112

time has passed.'

'The vital time?' queried Max.

She shrugged. 'When a controversial vote will be taken. When a far-reaching decision will be made. Some ground-breaking directive affecting Europe on which there has been undercover coercion, bribery, threats. All to guarantee the result desired by one powerful member nation. Simon's eavesdropping could expose and ruin the endgame.'

'And you think once their object has been achieved these people will release your husband?' As Tara stared at Max, he added, 'If your theory is correct, Mrs Kington, he knows too much ever to allow him to reveal what he overheard. You have to face that fact.'

Tom approached a new angle. 'Do you know what the Major's views are on European military cooperation?'

Her head shot round. There was an angry sparkle in her eyes. 'If you're suggesting he'd be in cahoots with vote-rigging or coercion you don't know Simon very well.'

'We don't know him at all,' Max pointed out. 'That's why we need your help with this situation. As a brilliant linguist he'd be able to talk to men of most nationalities during conferences, get to know them socially between sessions. People who speak other languages are generally keen to learn about the country and customs also. Did your husband form any particular friendships among the delegates?'

Her mouth twisted. 'Quite a few, I imagine.

He has great charm. He's also a true patriot and values his regiment second only to his family. He would never do what you're hinting at.'

'We don't hint, we deal with facts,' Max told her. 'We've found nothing to support the theory that he was abducted from your car port, so we're looking into the premise that he went off voluntarily. I'll ask again; did he form any special friendships with foreign nationals?'

'Almost certainly,' she replied icily. 'I can't say more than that. My husband never speaks about his work. Not only is most of it confidential, he values his off-duty time. He has a great many hobbies and interests.'

'The latest being microlights?'

Tom glanced at his boss in surprise. Where did that come from?

'You certainly do your homework! It's his latest enthusiasm.'

'Does he own one?'

'Bought last week.'

'For you both to fly?'

'I prefer horses. They stay on the ground.' She glanced pointedly at the clock. 'I have to go. The groom will have my mare saddled for me.'

Following her along the hallway to the front door, Max said, 'I'm afraid the Range Rover will have to be searched again. We believe someone else drove it here from your husband's office.'

She swung round to face him. 'My God, of

course! I didn't *see* Simon, only heard what I thought was his arrival. So they took him as he left his office?'

'Or he made his getaway from there,' Tom said.

'No, you're wrong, quite wrong on that score. Ask anyone who knows him.'

Out in the early afternoon sunshine Tom studied the tough vehicle. It certainly didn't drive itself to where it was neatly parked. A scene-of-crime duo had already dusted the bodywork for prints – too many to be of use – and examined the ground in the vicinity for evidence of a struggle or the presence of others in the car port. Now the inside of the vehicle must be gone over with a fine-tooth comb. If an accomplice brought it here he would have left signs of his presence, however tiny. The problem would be trying to pinpoint whoever had left them. It was frequently impossible without a stroke of luck.

Tara Kington spoke through the open window of the dark green Ferrari. 'I'll let you know immediately if I hear anything.'

'Have you told your children what's going on?' asked Max.

'No, they'd be deeply unsettled.'

'Where are they?'

'Winchester. Simon's old school. They come here for the long vacs. In between, they see my in-laws.'

Tom said, 'You should tell them. Get the grandparents to explain what's happened. We've managed to keep this from the media so far, but it won't stay that way for long. You won't want your boys to learn about it from the gutter press and become the butt of pupil persecution.'

She suddenly appeared to droop. 'They shouldn't have to suffer this terrible waiting and uncertainty. Jumping at every knock on the door, every telephone call. I long to go to them, but I must stay for Simon's sake. I've arranged to go riding because I can't stand another afternoon alone. Find him! Find him soon, and punish whoever has taken him from us.'

Starting the powerful engine, she shot out from the car port with dangerous speed, turned on squealing tyres, and raced away with an expensive roar.

'So the lady does have emotions,' Tom murmured, watching the car disappear.

'But not strong enough to respect her missing man's precious toy. I'd say she's completely unused to driving it, wouldn't you?'

'If I'd gone missing Nora wouldn't dream of playing around with my scale models of famous steam engines. She'd more likely cosset them. Women are funny that way. Kissing something their man has held; taking to bed a pair of his underpants when he's away.' Seeing Max's expression, he hastened to add, 'Not Nora, but she told me some do. Maybe the Major's no longer so passionate about his Ferrari. Puts all his enthusiasm into his new toy. Where'd you get the info on the microlight?'

'From the regimental Miss Marple; Lieutenant Steele. He's been doing some private investigating at the Ferrari Club. I contacted Sergeant Simpson right away. Told him to check with the Flying Club if one of the machines is missing. If Kington *did* go from the base by clinging to the underside of a truck, he could have used a microlight to reach his final objective. Land in a field somewhere, push it beneath an open barn. No reported sightings! I'll persuade Klaus Krenkel to get his men on that search. Find Kington and we'll probably make progress on the rest.'

Tom's mobile trilled. He took the call as they walked down from the house to their Land Rover, saying little but nodding frequently. Disconnecting, he said with a smile, 'We *have* some progress. Bush and Johnson have located Colin White's vehicle. It's in the rear car park of a private clinic specializing in vasectomy ops.'

Five

He lay staring at two squares of lighter darkness wondering what they could be. Concentration was elusive so he soon abandoned the effort. Images once more paraded behind his closed lids; fragmented images that passed too swiftly to identify fully. Faces he might once have known, long-legged creatures racing off to the endless distance, a huge hornet buzzing above him. The phantoms slowly melted away into welcome oblivion.

The squares of light were recognizable when consciousness returned. Windows. He could glimpse a great splash of stars in a night sky; a full moon. He raised his throbbing head, pushed himself into a semi-sitting position. Movement was painful but those windows beckoned.

Fighting giddiness, he slowly crawled towards them then hauled himself to his feet by gripping a sill to steady himself. Outside, water stretched to the horizon. It shimmered darkly under the gloss of moonlight. To his right and left was blackness. No lights from shipping or houses. Yet he was not at sea. The undulating sensation had ceased, and moonlight revealed a jutting tiled roof directly below him. He was in a room high in a brick building beside a large stretch of water.

A warehouse on a dock? No, there would be gantries, stacked containers, noise. He could hear nothing save his own laboured breathing. Holding panic at bay, he turned his back on the mystery outside. On the floor he could just make out a mattress with heaped blankets. Just that and a portable lavatory in the corner. He suddenly needed to use it and sensed that he had done so before. It was only a hazy recollection, like that of being fed with a spoon by a dark, silent figure. Fear now gripped him. Why did he feel so ill? Where was he? *Who* was he? There was no doubt he was being held prisoner in this room, but he lurched over to the door to confirm it. Locked!

He began shivering violently, so he shuffled back to reach for the rough blankets to wrap around his near-nakedness. He instantly lost his balance and collapsed on the mattress with a sharp cry.

The sound of footsteps; a key turning in the lock. A bulky figure in black trousers and top stood for a moment assessing the situation. Then it went. It was soon back, crossing to where he sprawled helplessly, half-covered by the blankets. The person bent to put a cup to his mouth. He sipped cautiously. Cool water. Desperately thirsty, he drank all the cup held. The shadowy figure immediately vanished before he could even begin to form questions.

Still shivering, frighteningly exhausted, he

curled up in a ball beneath the cheap blankets and tried to make some sense of what was happening to him. Within minutes cohesive thought grew impossible. He felt himself falling back into the blackness where the elusive images returned to torment him.

By the time Tom drove in to the large walled area at the rear of the Reinhardt Klinik the sun was low in the sky and the temperature was dropping fast. Several kilometres from a small riverside village, the clinic was a converted manor house of mid-Thirties vintage set among trees that shielded it from the road. Very discreet and very expensive, thought Tom. The perfect cover for murder. But why take the body back to the heath when there were acres of anonymous countryside here, where it could have lain undiscovered much longer?

A German forensic team was examining Colin White's car. Sergeants Bush and Johnson were nearby in conversation with a young *Polizei* officer. All three were smiling and nodding. When they caught sight of Tom the two women sobered and broke away, leaving the good-looking German to turn his attention back to the job in hand.

Connie Bush waved her hand in the direction of the car. 'The boot's loaded with a backpack, survival kit, heavy boots, thick sweaters, wet weather gear, a tent, and everything necessary for several days and nights in the mountains. Camouflage to disguise how he really planned to spend his leave. Even fooled his wife. When we interviewed her she said nothing about his planning to get himself neutured.'

Irritated by her phraseology, Tom snapped, 'It's a decision people prefer to keep to themselves. Mrs White is being bullied by her family and is shattered by the murder. She's unlikely to reveal intimate facts about her dead husband to two women who appear to find the subject amusing.'

Looking suitably serious, Heather Johnson said, 'Captain White *was* booked in, sir. We checked. He arrived just before ten hundred hours and had the op early afternoon. The nurse we interviewed also told us all patients were served with a light supper which matched the contents of the victim's stomach. During the course of the morning he gave a sample for a sperm count. Hence the trace of semen on his underwear?'

'So we know the victim was alive to eat the supper. What time was it served?'

'Eighteen hundred hours. Patients are expected to settle early for the night,' said Connie Bush.

'Captain White was dead four to five hours later. When was he last seen by anyone here?'

'Presumably when the orderly collected the empty supper plates. He's off-duty today, so we've been unable to question him. If he hadn't actually seen our man he wouldn't have thought it odd. All the rooms have en suite bathrooms. The patient could have been in there.'

With half an eye on the activity around the car, Tom said, 'What about bedtime drink, pills, etcetera?'

Connie shook her head. 'Nothing after supper except water. A full jug is delivered with the meal.'

'So when *did* they bloody realize he'd gone?' he demanded angrily.

Heather shivered in the growing chill. 'The nurse said it was the next morning. They thought he was regretting his decision and wanted to be shot of the place. It happens, she said.'

'You mean men walk out in the early hours without saying anything?'

'She admitted this case was unusual.'

'Yeah, he was grabbed and murdered. I hope to God that *is* unusual.' He waved his arm at the vehicle being searched. 'Why the hell did they imagine he left his car?'

After exchanging what's-up-with-him glances with her friend, Connie said, 'The clinic staff don't concern themselves with how their patients arrive and leave. They never study what's in the car park.'

'Would they have noticed a rusting heap after it had been there five or six years?' Tom fumed. 'What about his wallet, keys, mobile?'

'All gone. The room was empty.'

They all began walking towards a small wrought iron gate in the wall surrounding the car park. Tom was glad of movement in the deepening chill. They passed through to an extensive lawned area bordered by flower-beds, then up steps to a stone terrace. This rear wall of the manor was broken by four sets of French doors on the ground floor. Four more above them opened on to small balconies. The two women halted outside the place where white-overalled investigators were conducting a thorough search.

'This was the room Captain White occupied,' said Connie. 'Ground floor access made the killer's job a doddle. No evidence of forceful bruising or of rough handling on the body suggests the victim was killed in that room. Easy enough in a clinic for someone to don a white coat and enter a room with a hypo. The victim would believe a plausible medical explanation and submit to being injected. Colin White was probably still unaware of being murdered as he breathed his last.'

'He'd die very quickly,' Heather continued. 'His body would then be taken out through these French windows, across the grass and out by that gate to a waiting vehicle. It's dark, blinds have been lowered in the rooms, staff have departed aside from the nurse on call.'

'Just one nurse to deal with any emergency?'

'No, sir. The Reinhardts live in an apartment on the second floor. Both are medically qualified to perform vasectomies, but neither would speak to us.'

'And you accepted that?' questioned Tom fiercely.

Connie assured him they had tried. 'Refused to consult with female soldiers. Their very words, sir. Boris Mann – the police guy we were with when you arrived – told them their patient had been found murdered the morning after he booked in here, and they immediately clammed up.'

'They quoted professional confidentiality,' Heather added. 'Mann got very little out of them, he said.'

Tom grunted. 'I'll have a word with Mann. After that, I'll cross-examine the Reinhardts. A British officer vanishes from their clinic and is murdered by a means that links up with common medical practice. I'd say the staff of this place are all suspect, including the two surgeons.'

Leaving his two sergeants to interview other patients in company with a nurse, Tom crossed to Boris Mann and introduced himself. He had a working knowledge of German, but the tall, blond *Polizei* officer answered in impeccable English.

'You will wish to speak with the Reinhardts. They are very aloof and say they cannot discuss details of their patients.'

'Huh, this one was murdered on their premises. They'll either talk to us here or at your headquarters. From where I'm standing they and their staff are serious suspects.'

Blue eyes gazed back frankly. 'There is nothing to prove the killing took place in the clinic.'

'The victim was last seen alive in that room.

He didn't drive off in his car, and he wouldn't have walked forty-eight Ks in darkness to the heath. He was *taken* there. His body showed no signs of a struggle against human restraint, so we have to accept that he was dead before he left the clinic.'

'Perhaps he went willingly after being told of some misfortune to his wife or family.'

'No, no. In that event, whoever staged it would have had to approach him through the staff to make it appear genuine. Captain White was a trained soldier. He'd never have fallen for an alarmist yarn offered by some stranger knocking on his French door.'

'And if that person held a gun?'

Tom smiled, and if it was slightly patronizing he was unaware of it. 'In these days of high security our troops are schooled in how to deal with threat of any kind. Believe me, the victim would never have been spirited away like that unless he was already dead.'

Mann nodded and put out a hand to indicate the side entrance to the building. 'I also believe that. So let us find some proof, if we can.'

The Reinhardts protested that they were about to eat dinner. Mann courteously apologized before emphasizing the importance of his questions. Then he introduced Tom. Oskar and Trude Reinhardt were a handsome couple; he silver-haired, casually but expensively dressed, she at least fifteen years younger with the blonde, fine-featured elegance of upper class Teutonic women.

125

They were both haughtily hostile and, although they would almost certainly be fluent in English, they spoke in their own language to the young policeman and ignored the 'British soldier'. Tom found their pure dialect difficult to follow, so Mann had to translate. The Reinhardts pretended not to understand Tom's basic German, which led to a three-sided interrogation. Added to the dislike he'd felt at first sight, this disdain raised Tom's temper. But this was *Polizei* territory and he had to respect the boundaries.

The room they were in reflected the affluence of its owners and, presumably, the quality of their medical skill. Antique furniture, rich rugs scattered on polished wood, original masters hanging around the walls all spoke of professional success. Tom had time to size this up during the long-winded questioning and he was curious about the financial gain of such a selective enterprise. Unless they had a private source of income, this pair must be raking it in from men driven to make themselves sterile. Colin White could have believed the outlay well balanced by the confidence of having no more children to raise and educate. Well, that was a certainty now.

The young German first confirmed the details given earlier by the nurse. 'The doctors prefer that their patients relax for twenty-four hours after treatment. They say it is advisable.'

'I don't know much about this procedure, Boris, but it surely isn't a spur-of-the-moment arrangement. Wouldn't the Reinhardts have prior consultations with the prospective patient, his wife and his own doctor before consenting to perform the operation? Captain White's medical officer gave us no indication of knowing about his decision, and I'm fairly certain his wife was also ignorant of it. If the decision had been reached after discussion with them, Captain White could have had the treatment in the local hospital. Why would he come here and pay over the odds? Ask them how many meetings they had with him prior to his arrival.'

The air of superiority vanished with Oskar Reinhardt's swift reply. Mann translated. 'The patient made all the arrangements by telephone. His military duties did not allow him to drive here during regular consulting hours. He faxed the documentation requiring vital details, and these were checked on arrival. The clinic is very strict on these matters.'

Tom looked hard at the two doctors. 'Perhaps you'd produce the faxes and all documentation you have in Captain White's file.'

The Reinhardts tried every argument from patient confidentiality to the excuse that their secretary kept the keys to the filing cabinets and she had gone away for a long weekend.

The interrogation lapsed into English as questions were flung at the clinic's owners by both policemen. Thoroughly rattled and too obviously trying to cover something up, Trude conceded that they would, of course, erase any charges incurred by the unfortunate captain's brief stay at the clinic. She now seemed eager to discuss what might have befallen their patient.

'After their supper the men are left to rest until morning. It is then that there are sometimes regrets. It is a big step to take,' she added, glancing significantly at Tom's flies. 'So, particularly if he is a young man like your captain, they creep away like a wounded animal.'

Disgusted by her crude simile, Tom said harshly, 'Without saying anything to the staff? And leaving their car here?'

'We do not concern ourselves with...'

'Then you should,' he countered. 'For a man to have such strong regrets means he was emotionally unsure of his decision at the outset. Surely it's your professional responsibility to discuss his fears or doubts with every patient before going ahead.'

'But yes, of course,' she said breathily.

'So why weren't you concerned when Captain White "crept away like a wounded animal" three days ago?'

Looking nervously at her husband, she said, 'We tried to speak with him ... but he was not answering his mobile number.'

'So you simply shrugged and told yourselves he'd made the decision and must learn to live with it?'

'What more could we do?' put in Oskar. 'We

are only responsible for patients who are in our care. If they choose to leave the clinic that is entirely their own business.'

Knowing he was basically right, yet suspecting this set-up was somewhat dubious, Tom left that side of things to the *Polizei* and concentrated on his murder investigation.

'How easy is it for anyone to walk in to the clinic without arousing suspicion?'

Patently relieved at the change of direction, Trude replied more warmly. 'We try to be very relaxed here. Visitors may come and go at all times until half an hour before supper is served. We believe our patients should be restful before sleeping.'

'So the doors are locked at half past five each night?'

The Reinhardts exchanged looks. 'The side entrance is open for our guests. Our children and friends frequently visit us.'

Boris Mann threw in a question. 'So an intruder could use that door after dark?'

They remained uneasily silent.

'You have drugs here; medical appliances. Stuff worth stealing.'

'They are in locked areas,' Oskar snapped. 'I check that these doors are secure when I leave the operating theatre each day. There is no chance of theft.'

'But there is opportunity to commit murder,' Tom countered. 'Easy for someone to enter by your side-door in a white coat posing as a member of staff, give Captain White a lethal injection then take him out through the French door to a waiting vehicle.'

'That is preposterous!'

Trude put a warning hand on her husband's arm and spoke with a return of the former hauteur. 'This is not a military camp with secrets or dangerous weapons to protect with wire and guns. We are responsible only for the medical treatment of men who elect to attend our clinic. You should not expect us to have alarms and guards patrolling with savage dogs. We have never before had evil occur here. We have never before treated a British soldier. I think we shall be more discriminating in future.'

The Medical Officer's eyes narrowed when he spotted Max at the door of his office. He leaned back with a sigh. 'What now?'

Max went in and sat uninvited. 'Can I suggest a session at the Rifle Club when you finish here? You seem stressed enough to need it.' At the lack of response, he added, 'I'm trying to get to the bottom of two murders and a possible abduction. I need all the help I can get.'

Charles Clarkson relaxed, nodded. 'Yes. Sorry. Lot on my mind. What's the problem?'

Max explained where they had found Colin White's car. 'He'd booked in for a vasectomy. Were you aware of that?'

'Of course I wasn't bloody well aware,' came the vehement reply. 'I'd have counselled against it. Four kids isn't excessive. I've four myself, more widely spaced than Colin's,

130

admittedly. But he wasn't in the right frame of mind to make a decision like that.'

'Had he mentioned the possibility, even lightheartedly?'

'No. Good God, he's ... he was thirty-three, crazy about Christine and superbly fit. Two pregnancies are par for the course. Just happened that each produced two babes. I fully intended to have a serious chat about contraception when he returned from leave.' Clarkson frowned. 'Why the hell didn't he confide in me before ... had he actually gone through with it?'

'It appears so. What can you tell me about the Reinhardt Klinik?'

'Zero. Never heard of the place.'

'Mmm. My people think it's a bit shady and the *Polizei* officer there with them plans to investigate. The Reinhardts clammed up when asked to produce Colin White's file. Tell me, in such cases shouldn't the man's wife and GP be consulted?'

'Ideally, yes. His wife should be in agreement, for obvious reasons. His doctor should discuss the whys and wherefores, taking into account the man's physical and mental state when opting to take that step.'

'As I imagined. According to Sergeant Major Black the Reinhardts appear to accept bookings willy-nilly. They're both eminently qualified to do the op, but the human emotional side doesn't seem to concern them. The fees very definitely do.'

Clarkson sat forward intently. 'There's

another puzzle. The Whites could ill afford private medical costs. If both Colin and Christine had been unshakeable about doing this I could have fixed it for him locally. None of it makes any sense to me.'

'Nor me. But my concern is to discover who entered that clinic, gave him a lethal injection, then drove his body back to the heath to dump it.'

'And *why*,' added Clarkson heavily.

'If I knew more about the victim I might get some clue. It has to be someone who knew where he was going to be that night.'

The doctor's eyes glittered with sudden comprehension. 'Hence why you're questioning me? If you don't believe I wasn't in on his decision, I can prove I wasn't anywhere near that clinic.'

Max smiled and shook his head. 'Not necessary. Unless you're a crack liar as well as a crack shot your reaction to the news dispelled any suspicions I might have had.' He got to his feet. 'Who were his particular regimental friends?'

Clarkson gave a slow shake of his head. 'Can't help you much there. I only use the Mess on dining-in nights, or when I need an informal chat about items on my monthly account. My wife likes to entertain, and there are four kids to chauffeur to ballet lessons, Scouts, the cinema, swimming club and so on. Family takes my life over when I leave this surgery.'

'No wonder you need to let off steam at the

Rifle Club,' said the man who had no experience of fatherhood.

'I'm actually going there now.' He stood and began locking desk drawers. 'I'd say the men Colin climbed with are your best bet.' He summoned up a smile. 'I know I loosen up after a session at the targets. The guys there probably know more about me than I do myself.'

From his car Max called Mark Lang and made arrangements to meet at 21:00 in a hotel near the base housing Lang's regiment. It was sixty kilometres distant, but Max first wanted to visit Christine White. Knowing it would be difficult he prepared for either a slow and patient interview, or a speedy exit hastened by White's in-laws.

The general view seemed to be pity for Christine at the mercy of her domineering family, but there was another aspect to it. Now a widow with four children under five, in a foreign country, obliged to vacate the married quarter within a specified time, and with no other home to return to, maybe having bulldozing parents to sort everything out would be a godsend. At least during this traumatic period. Two pairs of twins would surely benefit from firm handling.

He drove through the base lost in thought. The MO claimed his four children took over his off-duty life. Tom had much the same experience with his three girls. If Susan hadn't been in that car during the fatal storm, would they still be together? A threesome

133

with baby Alexander. Would they have more children? How would it feel to return home and find it full of small offshoots of himself, demanding games, bedtime stories, or chauffeuring to various eager activities?

With the sun starting to sink below the line of trees, turning the sky red-gold and enriching the green of the lush grass, Max felt a sharp shaft of grief for what might have been. As he drove past the rows of married quarters, where lights now glowed in downstairs windows, he suffered the familiar pain of emotional isolation.

The balding, middle-aged man who opened the door was unexpectedly small. Visually not the bruiser Max had imagined. There was nothing small about his voice or attitude, however.

'If you're another God-wallah you're wasting your time. My girl's had that "the Lord will provide" crap up to her ears. Neither He nor the effing Army are able to provide. It's me and the wife who'll do it. We told her all along not to get tangled with a soldier, but he did the dirty on her and she had no choice. We've stood by her, all the same. When it comes to the bottom line it's *family* who rally round, not some khaki dog-collar.'

With the door fast closing in his face, Max said calmly, 'I'm a khaki policeman. I have some information about Captain White I think your daughter should know. I'd like to see her.'

The door was pulled open again. 'What

kind of information? I'm not having her upset.' Dark gimlet eyes bored into Max's. 'Have you found out who did it?'

'We'll only do that by talking to everyone who knew him and discovering who might have reason to kill your son-in-law. Can we please continue this indoors?'

The interior was overheated and even more cluttered than before. The sound of raised female voices and infants' laughter floated from the upper floor suggesting bathtime for the older twins. The eight-week-old pair must be already tucked up for the night.

The lounge-diner showed evidence of the present chaos. Max felt momentary sadness for the man who had driven away three days ago unaware that he was abandoning forever all he held dear. It was essential to stay aloof from the tragic aspect of his work, but Max was still in the grip of 'what if' in relation to his own life.

He offered his hand to the belligerent little man. 'Max Rydal. I'm with Special Investigation Branch.'

After reluctance from the other man, the handshake was accompanied by identification. 'Jim Slater. You'd best tell me what you have to say and I'll pass it on to our Chrissie. She can't take any more.'

'I really need to talk to your daughter. There are some questions I must...'

'Haven't any of you lot got feelings?' cried Slater. 'That bastard's dead, and he's left her with four nippers. *Four.* None of them old enough for school. She doesn't want questions, she wants answers. Who's going to pay for their food, their clothes? Who's going to pay for hers? Who's going to help her pack this lot up and take it back home? Where's she going to live when she gets there? Tell me that.'

'Army Welfare will...'

'Pah! Do-gooders! Got no time for them. Had a woman here yesterday trying to barge in with a handful of pamphlets. Sent her on her way sharpish. I told her, it's *family* that knows what's needed at times like this.'

Max fought rising anger. No wonder Colin White found it impossible to deal with this bigot. 'Mr Slater, you say the Army is doing nothing, yet you're apparently turning away everyone offering help.'

The hard mouth tightened further. 'We don't need their charity. The sooner our girl gets shot of this place the better. Now, say what you've come for and go.'

Short of storming the upper floor in search of the widow Max was powerless. He tried one last shot. 'You may not be aware that a sergeant of this regiment was murdered by the same method the night before your son-in-law. It's my job to bring to justice whoever killed these men. I won't do that meeting with prejudiced attitudes like yours. Please allow me to see Mrs White.'

Slater moved towards the front door. 'Chrissie has nothing to do with your investigation. She's the *victim*.' He opened the door and stood waiting. 'Take a tip from me. Soldiers are no more than trained killing machines. If there's no war on, they start knocking each other off.'

Out in a dusk growing chill, Max found he had time on his hands. He drove to the incident room provided by Ben Steele and made coffee before calling Tom's mobile number.

'Got nowhere with Colin White's father-in-law. Makes Jack Connor seem like a pussy-cat,' he said in reference to one of the Army's fiercest RSMs. 'The only way we'll get to speak to Christine is when he leaves the house. Might have to put a twenty-four hour watch on it.'

'What I heard from Connie Bush is the mother-in-law's as bad. Might have to lure the widow away instead.'

'We'll let it ride for now. I've fixed a meeting with Lieutenant Lang later on tonight. The MO thinks he might be useful. Clarkson didn't know about the vasectomy. Upset him slightly. Felt he should have been consulted. I've crossed him off our list, by the way. How's it going with you?'

'Boris Mann is continuing the investigation of the Reinhardts' business methods. He's trying to break them over the keys to their filing cabinets they claim the secretary has. She's gone for a long weekend someplace they don't know, according to them, but Boris has two of his guys searching for dupli-cates they must hold on the premises.'

'Sure they do.'

'Questioning the patients was pointless. None of them were here on Monday night. The members of staff we interviewed saw nothing, heard nothing. Familiar?'

'Too right. Have you finished there for now?'

'More or less. The *Polizei* are sending a flat-loader to take White's car to their headquarters for further examination. Mann has assured me we'll get all their results.'

'I've checked the section update. The toxin has been confirmed as vegetable based, but it's still a mystery. Something rare.'

'It would be.'

'No luck checking microlights, either.'

'Who's surprised?' said Tom in disgust. 'We have saintly victims, a rare toxin, a dodgy vasectomy clinic, no apparent motive, no obvious suspects and a vanishing defence expert complete with laptop. Why should we have any luck with microlights? I'm off home.'

'As Scarlett O'Hara said, "Tomorrow is another day", Tom.'

'Yeah, right at the end of the film. We never got to see what tomorrow brought her! Goodnight, sir.'

The Head Office of Grant Bonner Kington just outside Cheltenham was ablaze with lights in the murky dusk. In the highly competitive international pharmaceuticals market round the clock business hours were essential. Deals with the Americas and the Far East went down during late evening or the early hours. There was also the expanding market in China to capture.

Sir Chetwin Kington had just phoned his wife to tell her he would have to miss their friends' dinner party – the third time in ten days he had done so. Her caustic response lingered in his ear. They were spending less and less time together. He rarely saw his twin grandsons when they were staying at the house. Molly knew them well, and they loved her because she devised interesting things to do during their short school breaks. But Grandpa was little more than a name on birthday and Christmas cards.

Regret touched him momentarily. Success bore a heavy price. He had spent no more time with his own son than with *his* sons. Simon appeared not to have suffered as a result. He was doing well in the Army after achieving academic laurels at Cambridge, and had made an excellent marriage. No cause to feel he had failed his only child, surely. In any case, Molly provided a family anchor. Always had, always would. Good woman, Molly. Must try to spend more time with her.

The telephone rang to interrupt his thoughts. It was Migeles in Rio. Sir Chetwin had been waiting two days for the sly bastard to agree terms. During the subsequent hard bargaining, his PA entered to put a long white envelope on his desk. Fifteen minutes later, another deal just a signed contract away, Sir Chetwin set down the receiver with a satisfied sigh. Deserved a celebratory drink for carrying that off.

Crossing to the concealed bar he poured a generous shot of brandy and drank it looking from the window at the illuminated snails that represented the homeward rush-hour traffic on the dual carriageway. Yes, success bore a heavy price, but would he want to be one of those snails heading for a mortgaged semi to spend another evening staring at the TV with a careworn wife and demanding, malcontented teenagers? No, sir! Earlier regret was kicked aside by the buzz he now felt. He'd chanced his arm with Migeles, and it had paid off richly.

Back at his desk he picked up the envelope Estelle had brought in, unopened because it was marked Private and Confidential. He slit it with his paper-knife, pulled out a single sheet and a four by six inch colour photograph.

We have your son. We'll sell him back for £1,000,000 in large denomination notes *unmarked in any way*. You will be contacted within the next four days with further instructions. This photograph shows Simon has not so far been harmed. If you do anything stupid or inform the authorities, your son will start to suffer. We're sure you fully understand our terms.

In a daze, Sir Chetwin studied the head and shoulders shot of Simon in uniform, hair tousled, slightly frowning. Behind him a pair of hands held a copy of *The Daily Telegraph* showing the date and headline he had read over breakfast that morning.

Heart pounding, he pressed the intercom button. 'Estelle, who delivered the letter you just brought in?'

'A courier, sir. Is there a problem?'

'Hold all calls, no matter who. I don't want to be disturbed.'

Snapping off the intercom he picked up the receiver of his private line and punched out Simon's home number in Germany.

'Mrs Kington speaking,' said the familiar cultured voice.

'Tara, it's Pa. I need to speak urgently with Simon.'

She was immediately concerned. 'Is something wrong? The boys? Molly?'

'They're all fine. Put Simon on, please.'

'He's not here. There *is* something wrong. You sound—'

'I'll get him on his mobile.' Preparing to cut the connection, he was halted by her next words.

'He can't be contacted at the moment.'

His hand stilled. He took a deep breath. 'Where is he, Tara? *Tara!*' he prompted, alarm growing by the second.

'I ... I don't know. No one does.' His normally controlled daughter-in-law suddenly

broke down, confessing tearfully, 'He vanished four days ago. I've been going nearly crazy
waiting for news. I'm so afraid he's been—'

'What do you mean, he vanished?' Sir
Chetwin demanded tersely. He listened with
incredulity to her account of his son's
inexplicable disappearance from outside his
own home, but he then knew the letter he
held was genuine. People who could spirit a
man away from a military base must be
members of a highly professional organization that didn't play games. They would do to
Simon what they threatened if the money was
not handed over.

'I was sure SIB would soon trace him,' Tara
continued jerkily. 'I said nothing to you
because I didn't want to worry Molly or the
boys unnecessarily.'

High on adrenalin, Sir Chetwin snapped,
'Tell the Redcaps to leave well alone, for
God's sake! I've just received a ransom demand. I can't have soldier detectives trampl-
ing this sensitive business with their hefty
boots. These people aren't averse to violence
if they're crossed. I'll deal with them on my
own.'

'A ransom demand? Then he's still alive,'
Tara breathed. 'Thank God. Oh, thank God!'

'I'll need proof that he is before I pay,' he
told her, 'and any outside interference could
jeopardize my negotiations.'

'But you don't know the full story, Pa. An
officer and a sergeant of the regiment were
murdered at the same time as Simon

142

disappeared. SIB think he's either a third victim, or...' She faltered. 'Or that Simon killed them then ran.'

'That's *indefensible*!'

'I know. So I *must* tell Captain Rydal about the letter you've had. It's proof of Simon's innocence.' Her voice thickened again. 'I've had the cold shoulder from those ignorant enough to think he was involved in the murders, and I've suffered the stares and whispers of others who believe he's run off with another woman. You've no idea what these last days have been like for me.'

Filled with barely controlled rage, he said, 'What the hell's going on out there? My son is snatched; two men are murdered! I thought top security was in place due to the terrorist threat. Anyone who could believe Simon capable of ... I understood he was held in great esteem by the regiment.'

'He is. You *are* going to pay the ransom? You *will* get him back for me?'

'Of course. Of course. Tara, listen to me. I don't want this development made public. Instruct that SIB captain to call me. I'll deal with him direct.'

'Yes, I'll tell him, but please do whatever they say. Get Simon free before those bastards do anything to him.'

'There's no fear of that, my dear,' he assured her falsely. 'I know how to handle complex situations. Trust me, Tara. I'll stay in constant touch. Goodbye, my dear.'

After cutting the connection Sir Chetwin

sat for a few moments facing the fact that his son's fate lay in his hands. Men at the top were perpetually vulnerable to extortion. During his upward climb he had resolutely steered clear of those carnal or venal temptations to which many high-flying men succumbed. Denied the opportunity to blackmail him, these devils had resorted to kidnap.

A million pounds – the value of a life to these evil creatures. The twins would inherit less, but better for them to have a father than money to squander as Simon admittedly did. Horses, a Ferrari, shares in an aircraft; none of them cheap. Simon was spending his grandmother's legacy very freely. But why not? He was in the prime of life. The perfect time to live to the full before age and infirmity put a damper on such things.

He gave a long sigh of anguish, telling himself he might not have given his son much of his time over the years, but he would do whatever he must to save him now. He picked up the phone and got through to the private residence of his banker.

Half an hour later he asked Estelle to tell his driver to bring the car to the side entrance. Then he put on his coat and scarf, the triumphant deal with Migeles forgotten. He would have Barnes drive him to Winchester before heading home. A private word with the twins' headmaster would ensure an unobtrusive watch over the boys until the crisis was over. He would protect Molly by working from home for a spell.

In the car he opened the minibar and poured a much-needed hefty brandy. As the Daimler purred along the bypass, the out-raged father and prominent citizen vowed to raise one hell of a stink in the national press about lax military security. But not until Simon was safely back with his family.

Six

Lieutenant Mark Lang was an outgoing man of substantial build with brown curly hair. Already ensconced in a corner alcove with a tall glass of lager, he identified himself with a raised hand.

'Military haircut and English clothes. Knew who you must be as soon as you came in,' he said as they shook hands. 'What'll you have?'

Max smiled and indicated the glass. 'What you've got there looks about right, thanks.'

As they settled on the padded bench seat, Mark frowned. 'You've made a lengthy journey, but I don't think I can tell you any more than I already have. I haven't seen Colin since our last climb. Must have been four, five months ago. He e-mailed the news of the latest twins. I e-mailed congrats and my expectation that there'd be a considerable gap before we tried another ascent.'

He drank from the beaded glass and wiped froth from his mouth. 'We didn't tackle the very difficult climbs. You need to put in a hell of a lot of practice before taking them on, and we weren't able to do that. We simply liked scrambling up a rock-face for the satisfaction of getting to the top. Don't get me wrong. We

146

are experienced mountaineers, but we climb for the pure enjoyment of the sport.' He gave a faint smile. 'None of us in the team labours under the illusion that peaks have personalities we have to dominate to prove ourselves. None of that crap about man against nature. Believe me, we aren't prepared to risk death just to stand on a summit and have a photograph taken.'

Any hint of levity vanished. 'Having said that, poor old Colin would rest more easily in his grave if he'd been killed in a fall. But *this*!' Brown eyes gazed unhappily at Max. 'Who'd want to kill a harmless guy like Colin? I find it hard to accept.'

Having let him get all that off his chest, Max said, 'We're trying to discover who would have known his movements on his last day. We've traced his car. Forty-eight kilometres from where his body was found, parked behind a vasectomy clinic.'

Mark's hand stilled halfway to his glass. '*Vasectomy* clinic?'

'Had Colin ever mentioned such a decision to you?'

'God, no.'

'We believe his killer masqueraded as a member of staff to give him a lethal injection once the patients had settled for the night.'

'Jeez!'

'So the killer knew of his intention. The MO at his base didn't, which is unusual. I thought Colin might have confided in you, sought your opinion. In that situation I'd want to talk

147

it through with someone. You're a friend, a trusted climbing partner, living at a different base among men who didn't know him. The ideal confidant.'

Mark shook his head. 'I'd no idea he was contemplating ... what about Christine?'

'Her father is refusing to let us speak to her, but I suspect the decision was made without her knowledge.' Max paused momentarily. 'We have to assume he believed his sperm would fertilize two eggs every time. A prospect so daunting he made that decision while deeply stressed.'

The other man sighed. 'I wish I'd telephoned my congrats. We'd have chatted. He might then have mentioned his fear, and I would have advised him to give it time before doing anything so drastic.'

They sat quietly, letting the chatter of German drinkers fill the silence. The well-dressed socializers were smiling and gossiping lightheartedly, unaware of the tragedy being discussed by the army men in the far corner of the elegant lounge.

Eventually, Max said, 'Don't think you might have saved his life if you'd known what he intended to do and talked him out of it. I'm convinced he'd already been marked down by the killer, who'd been obliged to follow him to the clinic to do the job. There'd been another killing by the same method. And there's a possible third. We're trying to find a common link between these victims. Mrs White is in no state to tell us about her husband, even if we could see her, so I'd like you to give us as full a background sketch of Colin White as you can manage.' He stood. 'While you give it some thought, I'll get us both another lager.'

He walked to the bar and ordered, then indicated where they were sitting. Studying Mark Lang as he strolled back, Max decided the young officer was genuinely shocked and upset. No suspect, this man.

Mark looked up as Max returned. 'A background sketch? We were at Sandhurst together for a while. Colin was on the senior course when I joined, so we didn't share class or field work. We sometimes came across each other socially, but I had my own cronies and spent most of the time with them. After Sandhurst I didn't bump into Colin again until I joined a local climbing club near Catterick. Colin was also a member. We discovered we had interests in common and became friends. At RMA he'd been a prankster whose tricks had a spiteful kick in them. He'd also been rather acid-tongued, inclined to drone on about people's weaknesses which further undermined their confidence. I believe he was even once officially warned about it.'

Their lagers arrived and they both drank lengthily. Max then prompted Mark to continue. 'Colin had changed when you met up again?'

'Absolutely! Quieter, more easygoing. Seemed to have adapted to military routine completely.'

'How long since you'd known him at Sandhurst?'

Mark thought for a moment. 'Three, three
and a half years. Long enough for the rebel in
him to settle down, I guess.'

'What d'you know of his background?'

'Won an army scholarship at grammar
school. Father's manager of a glass factory.
His mother ran a small hairdressing salon
until she was diagnosed with MS. Colin's
sister lives nearby and looks after her. He felt
somewhat guilty about that.'

'Surely no one expected him to resign his
commission and nurse his mother.'

'No, no. But he's served longer overseas
than at home, which meant he saw little of his
parents. He was here in Germany for the first
six months after commissioning, then his
battalion was sent to Hong Kong in the run
up to the handover. He met and married
Christine within two months of his return
home.' Mark grimaced. 'Seems Colin was
very quick off the mark and made Christine
pregnant. He once hinted to me that he
suspected it was deliberate on her part. She
fancied him like mad and wanted to break
free of her family.'

'Now she's firmly back in their grip.'

'What a bloody shame!'

'Fortunate that Colin offered to marry her.'

'Oh no, he was crazy about her. The pregnancy merely advanced the event. Her family
gave them hell, of course. Colin was relieved

when this posting came up. Christine's sweet, but she's also very malleable; totally unable to stand up against her domineering parents. If they'd stayed in England he was afraid the marriage would have foundered. The Slaters were forever calling on Christine when Colin was on duty. Then there'd be rows because she seemed unable to send them packing.' Lang's brow furrowed. 'I think Colin eased his growing frustration by climbing. He loved it. Said the clean air, the silence and the ability to achieve what he set out to do gave him a great sense of freedom.'

'From the marriage? Did he regret it?'

'He regretted her bloody family. The last time they came on a visit he lived in-Mess until they left. Told me it was easier on everyone, particularly the kids, not to have aggro from morning till night. I advised him to put his foot down and deny them entry to their house. Know his reply?'

'I can guess,' said Max. 'I met the father-in-law this afternoon. Only a raised drawbridge and a wide moat around the place could stop him ... and then he'd probably swim over and dynamite the drawbridge.'

'He's that bad?'

Max gave a rueful smile. 'We've just established a reason for Colin White to commit murder, but none for why he would be the victim of it. Are you aware of any strong political or racial beliefs he held? Was he a member of any local radical clubs? Or any back in the UK? You said he used to be acid-tongued, tended to undermine others' weaknesses.'

Mark shook his head. 'He'd outgrown that. I'd say it was a sign of insecurity at Sandhurst. Putting others down raised his own confidence. No, Colin was a truly nice guy. It's unbelievable that anyone would want him dead.'

'I suspect it's more a case of *needing* him dead,' offered Max. 'The sergeant killed by the same method only the day before was also a truly nice guy, according to his colleagues. That leads me to conclude that their deaths were necessary due to something they knew rather than something they'd done.'

'Something they *both* knew?'

'Yes. Can you throw any light on that at all?'

'Christ, I wish I could. We only ever talked about the usual things. I don't recall anything that suggested Colin possessed vital info, or had knowledge that would put the finger on anyone. He was just an infantry officer, plain and simple.'

'Not as simple as he appeared, because someone believed he was too dangerous to leave alive. I hoped you might have...' He broke off as his mobile rang. A glance at the wall clock showed it was just before midnight. He asked Mark to excuse him while he answered a call from his sergeant major, and walked out to the foyer.

'Yes, Tom?' He half expected to be told of another death.

'Mrs Kington has contacted us to report

152

that Sir Chetwin has received a written ransom demand for the return of his son.'

'*Sir Chetwin?*' echoed Max, taken aback by the development.

'They want money, and he's the man who's got it.'

Max frowned. 'No mention of release of prisoners, or the withdrawal of our troops from some benighted zone?'

'No. Nor cranks demanding cessation of work on experimental drugs.'

'Simply our average extortionist with an eye to the main chance? That doesn't add up, Tom.' He moved to a quiet corner away from a chattering group who had come from the restaurant and were saying their farewells. 'Can this kidnap actually be purely coincidental; nothing to do with the murders?'

'Beginning to look that way. Sir Chetwin wants to handle it solo, but Tara Kington insisted on telling us as proof her husband isn't the killer.'

'We can't allow him to operate alone. His son is a serving British officer. People behind this type of high profile operation aren't playing games. There'll be a time limit on payment. When it runs out they'll start carving their hostage up, piece by piece.'

'I've already informed the Home Office, sir, so it's basically out of our hands now.'

'I wonder! I'll talk to Sir Chetwin first thing tomorrow. He has to be made aware of the possible bloody outcome.'

★ ★ ★

Tom Black was making himself a cheese and pickle sandwich by the glow from the open fridge when the overhead light clicked on. Nora stood there smelling of talcum and bedtime warmth.

'You still awake, love?' he asked unnecessarily.

'I wasn't, until you "crept" in in your usual flat-footed fashion and began crashing around.'

'Crashing around? Tiptoed like a cat after a mouse.'

'Yeah. Tom and Jerry style!' She shut the fridge door. 'You yell at the girls for leaving that open.'

Tom grinned, took a huge bite out of his sandwich and mumbled, 'Anything more you want to tell me?'

'Plenty.' She switched on the kettle.

'Such as?'

'Such as you're a great big handsome mutt, who manages to get away with anything after midnight when I'm in a nightie and you're hungry.'

Tom sat on one of the cushioned chairs and munched contentedly. He was so lucky to have found his soul mate first time around. He thought briefly of Max returning to an empty bed where he'd lie awake with his troubled thoughts.

Tara Kington's news certainly put a different slant on the investigation. It also cleared his own prime suspect of the two murders. All the same, something didn't add up in the

Kington affair. The average extortionist Max had referred to was simply after money. Sir Chetwin Kington was a multimillionaire and ripe for plucking. That was straightforward enough. What Tom found puzzling was the choice of hostage. There were twin grandsons at school in England. Surely a double abduction would multiply the emotional pressure to guarantee swift payment. And so much easier to grab a pair of unsuspecting boys. So why decide to pluck their father from the midst of a secure military establishment? Not so secure, apparently. But if Simon Kington was somehow considered a greater prize he could have been snatched at the stables, *en route* to the Ferrari Club, or at the airfield where he kept the microlight. Why do it the most chancy possible way?

Nora put two mugs of tea on the table and sat facing him. 'Plot thickened?'

'Couldn't get much thicker. One aspect has branched off in a new direction. What little sense I was making of the two murders has now been shot to pieces.'

'Want to talk it through?'

'We've all been doing that for four days and got nowhere. We've nothing to work on. *Nothing*. Scaremongers are putting it around the ranks they're going to be knocked off one each day. The 2IC is getting het up over our lack of progress, and tonight's development will have him really jumping up and down.'

Nora sat quietly drinking her tea. Tom knew he could trust her with confidential information and it helped to voice his thoughts. 'There *has* to be a connection between the killings and the abduction. I find it too much of a coincidence that extortionists should pick the most difficult of kidnap victims, and even more coincidental that they should strike at exactly the time two men of the same regiment at the same base are murdered.'

Nora's eyes gleamed. 'You've proof that Simon Kington *has* been abducted, not killed?'

'His father's received a ransom demand.'

'There's your link!'

'What?' he demanded.

'Drugs. Sir Chetwin's company produces all kinds of potent substances. Those men were killed with one. What if there's a group of fanatics protesting against the manufacture of toxic drugs, or drugs in general? An odd-ball religious sect who believe doctors play God and should let nature run its course. Like most zealots who contradict their own dogmas when it suits their purpose, these people are fixing their activities on the military to highlight the controversial subject of permanent damage to health by multiple injections given to troops to counteract biological or chemical weapons.'

Tom pursed his lips. 'Max already came up with that. We decided the murder victims would more usefully be the medical staff who gave the injections. The Cumberland Rifles were on the receiving end. Bright idea, though.'

'I still think it's the link you're looking for.'

'Mmm. If the kidnappers were demanding closure of the pharmaceuticals company, it'd be a valid point. But they want cash. Stacks of it, you bet. That's the spanner in the works for me. There are any number of millionaires out there to milk under duress. Why pick a difficult target like Major Kington?'

'But he wasn't, was he? Snatched in seconds beneath the nose of his regiment. Easy peasey!'

As Tom watched his wife rinsing the mugs at the sink, some light shone in the darkness of incomprehension. Of course it had been easy, because Kington had never left that base. A lethal injection as he climbed in his 4x4, and the dying victim is carried to another vehicle standing by. The hit is over in seconds. In the four hours that pass before the Duty Officer begins making inquiries, Kington's corpse is secreted within the establishment until the ransom is paid. Then it can be dumped where it will be found. Whether or not Sir Chetwin paid up, he was not going to get his son back alive.

Frau Hahn had left out a plate of cold meats with a flask of soup. Max had eaten a light meal before driving back, so he put the large platter in the fridge and took just the flask to his room. A mug of soup would go down well while he prepared for bed.

In his pyjamas, he sat mulling over the unsettling development. It knocked all his earlier theories into a cocked hat. Kington had not been killed by lethal injection, nor had he deserted to work for new masters. At no time had Max seriously believed in an abduction. Now this complication to a case obscure enough already! He no longer trusted his guts; no longer had confidence in his detecting skills. He was up a blind alley. As of now he had no idea what to do next, how to instruct his team at tomorrow's briefing. The last thing he had considered was a straightforward kidnap to screw money from a millionaire businessman.

As he sipped the warming soup it occurred to him that the ransom demand provided a jarring note. If it had concerned military or political demands it would have conformed to the pattern. Of course, the money could be used to buy arms or hitmen to wipe out a despot. Clearly, MI5 were thinking that way by taking command of the affair. Max pursued the jarring note idea, and it struck him that there was another slant on this development. What if Kington *was* another murder victim, left where his body had not yet been discovered? The delay could prompt someone – anyone who knew Kington was missing – to chance his arm at wringing money from a rich, influential parent before the corpse was found. Afraid he could be right, Max determined to alert Sir Chetwin to the possibility in the morning.

Heavy in spirits he eventually settled for sleep and turned off the light, but his brain was a treadmill revolving facts, ideas and fancies continuously. He recalled the entire conversation with Mark Lang several times, sure there was something significant hidden there that he had failed to recognize. The very 'goodness' of Colin White and Brian New was a constant irritation. Then, through the clutter of stored information, came two statements that focussed his thinking anew.

Sergeant Sam Dawkins had said Brian New had indulged in drinking, chasing girls, betting on horses, kicking up larks as much as the average young man until he married and sobered almost overnight. He had stayed that way even after his divorce, so it was not necessarily the Chinese girl who had wrought the change in him. But change he had, from being a normal headstrong lad to a near paragon.

Mark Lang reckoned Colin White had been a sly prankster with an acid tongue – had been reprimanded over it – then turned in to another universally popular, upright member of the regiment.

In Max's experience a man's personality stayed much the same through the years unless he suffered trauma of some kind. Battle horrors could do it; life changing injuries, also. In spite of the time-honoured adage, he had never come across a wayward man who had been tamed by 'a good woman'. Temporarily, maybe, if he was obsessed with her, but the devils invariably re-emerged as passion cooled.

One battalion of the Cumberland Rifles had participated in the first Gulf War; possibly in Kosovo or Afghanistan, where atrocities could have triggered a dramatic personality change. Tomorrow he would question Tara Kington about her husband as a person rather than as a Defence Liaison Officer who had mysteriously vanished. Had he also undergone a sobering experience? Although Max's section was now off that case, there was no reason why he couldn't ask for information that might elucidate the other two they still had to solve.

He fell asleep still unsure why the fact of soldiers suddenly becoming models of correctness should throw any light on why they had been murdered now. Yet he felt it was important.

First thing on arrival in his office Max called the contact number Tara Kington had given for her father-in-law. Not surprisingly, it was busy. It remained busy for the following half hour, but Max felt he must speak urgently to Sir Chetwin before the morning briefing, and persevered.

A smooth, cultured female voice finally answered, saying neutrally, 'Grant Bonner Kington. Good morning.'

The PA, without a doubt. 'Please tell Sir Chetwin that Captain Max Rydal, Special Investigation Branch is on the line, as requested.'

'Ah yes, Captain Rydal. I'll put you

through, but please be brief. Sir Chetwin is conducting an extremely sensitive negotiation.'

She made it sound like a tricky business deal, Max thought. Then, on reflection, he supposed it was, except that he was buying his son's life not a foreign franchise.

A voice suddenly bombarded his ear. 'I asked you to call so there would be perfect understanding between us on this affair, but you jumped the gun without the courtesy of speaking to me first. The bloody Spooks were on my doorstep before I reached it last night. My wife is deeply distressed by their invasion of our home, the tapping of our telephones, armed men in the grounds and, most particularly, a detective keeping an unobtrusive eye on our grandsons. *So* unobtrusive, dammit, the entire bloody school is aware of his presence and speculating on the reason for it.'

'Sir, your son is—'

Max was cut off by further furious words. 'I'm regularly dealing with greedy, grasping men attempting to manoeuvre me in to a corner with my back to the wall. I know how to handle crises and emerge unscathed, Rydal. My son's life is at stake here. When he is free and back with his family, *then*, and only then, should there be police involvement. But not the ham-fisted military kind! If harm comes to Simon due to your interference I'll see to it your career takes an immediate downturn.'

The line went dead.

Giving Tom a resumé of the hardline attitude as they walked to the briefing, Max aired his nocturnal suspicions, only to learn Tom had had the same thoughts.

'We might be considered ham-fisted, but this supposed abduction has too many holes in it to be on the level, Tom.'

'Mmm, but we're off the case now.'

Max smiled reflectively. 'So we are. Must remember that.'

The members of their team were all as surprised as they by news of the ransom demand. Tom said to them, 'As it's a case of simple extortion it's no longer considered to be a military matter.'

'But he was taken hostage on military premises,' Connie Bush pointed out.

Tom glanced swiftly at Max and received a slight nod. 'It's possible the ransom note was sent by someone trying to profit from Simon Kington's disappearance. Although there's been no mention of it in the UK papers, our investigation has been relatively widespread – ports, border controls, the Major's clubs. And his regiment, of course. A large number of people know of his absence and one of them could be trying to cash in on it.'

'So we're still regarding him as a possible third murder victim?' asked Heather Johnson.

Max said neutrally, 'The only aspect of Major Kington's disappearance that officially concerns us is that it's unlikely he killed New and White. We concentrate on their murders. If we uncover anything else along the way...'

'Like a body in a shallow grave on-base?' put in the irrepressible Piercey.

Tom glared at him. 'I want total effort on this. Question everyone again. Chase any lead, however slight. The killer had to know the movements of both victims. New told Dawkins about his date with Vera Maitland. Maybe he also asked around for the name of a place suitable for a special occasion meal. The nurse could have done the same at her hospital, but that wouldn't tie in with the second murder.'

'It could, sir,' put in Connie Bush, always right on the ball. 'What if someone there is friendly with a member of staff at the Reinhardt Klinik and knew Captain White was booked in?'

Annoyed that it hadn't occurred to him, Tom nodded. 'Good point. Check it out. The rest of us will go with the most probable surmise that the killer is a Cumberland Rifleman.'

'Rifleperson. Could be a woman,' murmured Piercey.

'There'll be another body in a shallow grave if you don't sober up,' snapped Tom. 'Pity your wit isn't sharp on valuable input.'

'Sorry, sir.'

'We've so far failed to find anyone Colin White confided his plans to. The MO wasn't in on his decision, nor was his close friend and climbing partner. Staff, team up with Sergeant Johnson to question those officers he worked most closely with, or any who were particular friends. *Discreetly*, for God's sake. We don't want the whole flaming regiment knowing the victim's very personal decision. But *someone* knew, and we have to discover who that was.' Tom swung round on Piercey. 'You and Beeny check out every twenty-four and forty-eight hour pass issued for the relevant nights. Then interview all personnel who were off-base, and follow up where they claim to have been.'

Max fixed his attention on Sergeant Jakes. 'Anything yet on that toxin?'

'No, sir. I've checked with all the experimental establishments again. Nothing missing from any of them: none are working on anything new. Yesterday, I talked to a couple of guys at Wolf Oberfeld. The company's big in Germany. On a par with Grant Bonner Kington. Only experimental stuff they're doing right now concerns hepatitis. Nothing on toxins.'

'Mm, if it was an industrial secret they'd deny it, anyway. We can't push any further there. It's *Polizei* territory. I'll have a chat with Klaus Krenkel. Find out if they have anything on that company.'

Jakes said, 'Simpson and I plan to tour the farm and pesticide suppliers in the area with a couple of his German guys today. Thought we should check their toxic products and sales. Someone might be mixing their own poisonous brew in the garden shed.'

'Good thinking. Keep at it,' said Max.

'There's one thing, sir,' said Olly Simpson,

the most studious member of the team. 'A girl at Wolf Oberfeld happened to mention that Gerhardt Wolf, the managing director, owns several Ferraris. He'd possibly know Simon Kington.'

'And his father, who's also in pharmaceuticals. Are you making a point, Sergeant?'

He shook his head. 'Just feeding in info.'

'Always useful,' Max agreed.

Tom cast a look around the room where they clustered attentively. 'We need a breakthrough on these murders. *Urgently.* So get to it! There's no guarantee the killer won't strike again. We need to get to him before he does.'

'Or *she* does,' murmured Piercey true to form, as they dispersed.

As Tom drove through the main gate, Max said, 'We should rightly make a courtesy call on the 2IC, but I think we'll do it *after* speaking to Mrs Kington.'

'We pass the senior officers' quarters first, so it's logical,' agreed Tom with a grin. 'He'll see it's pointless shutting the stable after the horse has bolted.'

'I wouldn't count on it,' Max said drily.

Tara Kington invited them in with every sign of assurance. 'I have coffee infusing in the belief that policemen would arrive exactly when they said they would.'

They followed her through to the familiar room, which was as immaculate as before. So was she, in violet velvet trousers and cream silk shirt. Max did not warm to her any more than he had before. She was too cool, too

165

controlled. Christine White's hysteria he had understood. This he did not.

'It must be an extremely anxious time for you,' he said as they settled around the low table bearing three cups and saucers.

She glanced up from depressing the filter of the cafetière. 'No, it's such tremendous relief to know Simon's *alive*.'

'Has your father-in-law been given proof of that?' Max asked sharply.

'A photograph with yesterday's *Telegraph* held behind Simon.'

Was she really so naive as to believe that guaranteed her husband's survival? Max decided against elaborating on the suspicion they had and merely answered her query on how he preferred his coffee.

'And you must now withdraw those terrible accusations you made.'

'I don't believe we made any accusations,' he countered.

Her gaze met his frankly. 'But it was perfectly obvious you believed Simon had either run off with another woman, or with a laptop holding high security information. Worse, you suspected him of killing two men and fleeing from justice,' she added, handing him a cup of coffee.

'We have to consider every possibility in the course of an investigation, Mrs Kington.'

'None of them was the *least* possibility,' she argued, giving Tom coffee. 'I told you my husband would never do any of those things. However old-fashioned it might sound, he's an honourable man. I defied his father's ruling on police intervention because I could not allow defamatory rumours concerning Simon's disappearance to continue circulating the regiment.'

'The rumours were certainly not instigated by SIB. We kept our inquiries strictly impersonal, ma'am,' put in Tom.

'Because we know nothing of your husband's personal life,' added Max, setting down the bone china cup and saucer. 'Perhaps you'd enlighten us.'

A slight frown marred her smooth forehead. 'To what purpose? Sir Chetwin is arranging to pay the ransom. Simon will be back with me by the start of next week, latest. He's of no further interest to you. Surely you should be concentrating on those two murders to the exclusion of all else.'

Irritated by her supercilious tone, Max decided to put some cards on the table. 'Our years of experience tell us that two killings and a highly professional abduction within the same regiment on the same military establishment within the space of three days have to be connected. Why your husband was treated differently we'll discover in time, but his disappearance is almost certainly allied to the murders. At present, we have no leads apart from the m.o. used in the murders. It's possible your husband was injected with a milder dose of the same substance – enough to render him incapable of resistance – then given an antidote once he was safely away.'

'We need to find a rational link between the three cases,' said Tom. 'We already have general profiles of Captain White and Sergeant New. We'd like you to fill us in on your husband's personality and social habits for comparison.'

'How extraordinary!' she exclaimed. 'Colin was a run of the mill officer with a silly wife who was detrimental to his career. Not that he had much military ambition. He was interested in little else than scrambling up mountains. Bored on about it at mess cocktail parties.' She gave a faint smile. 'Christine's only conversation was Pampers and baby foods. A couple to be avoided at those obligatory affairs, believe me.'

'And?' prompted Max.

Her large eyes regarded him candidly. 'I can't think why you'd imagine there could be a common link between Colin and my husband. And there would certainly be none between Simon and one of our sergeants.'

It was so dismissive, Max dug in his heels and asked for another cup of coffee, adding pointedly, 'I'm sure Mr Black would also like more.'

'Yes, please,' said Tom, understanding the way things were going.

She handled the unexpected move well, demonstrating a social grace that would be an asset to *her* husband's career. But she was an intelligent woman, not easily fooled. As she refilled their cups, she said, 'When Simon returns you'll doubtless want to hear his story. Then you'll find out all you need to know about him.'

'How long have you been married?' Max asked conversationally.

'Fourteen years. Our boys are approaching their teens. I've been warned all hell may then break loose.'

'My oldest girl will be at that stage in six months,' Tom told her. 'It seems she'll grow moody and rebellious, wanting to dye her hair scarlet and paint her lips black.' He smiled as one parent to another. 'Boys apparently yearn to drive a motor bike or a souped-up car, and experiment with alcohol and drugs.'

Tara Kington returned his smile. 'When they're not chasing the girls with scarlet hair and black lips.'

Max speculated on the sudden softening of her manner. Could this sophisticated, assured woman be a doting mother? Of sons, perhaps, especially if they resembled their father. The silver-framed wedding photograph on the sideboard showed Simon Kington as impressively good-looking.

'Your father-in-law seems to command respect from others. He'll surely keep teenage grandsons on the straight and narrow,' he commented.

'Yes. Pa's very good with them.'

'How about your husband? Is he strict?'

She shook her head. 'He doesn't need to be. Dom and Toby are in awe of him.'

'They're afraid of their father?'

'Of course not! It's a type of adolescent hero worship. Simon's so multitalented, you see.'

A case of having to live up to a parental example? Max wondered. 'They're fortunate to have two such accomplished parents,' he said pleasantly. 'I imagine you met at Cambridge.'

'Yes. During Rag Week.' Her expression grew softer. 'We were all crazy in those days. Went to extremes, like most undergrads. Simon was the ringleader of every mad caper. It's amazing he had time to study enough to gain firsts in both subjects.'

Max's interest was dramatically heightened by what she had said without realizing she was actually giving them the information they had come here for. As a student, the very correct, 'honourable' Defence Liaison Officer had been a student tearaway. Colin White had been a troublemaker at Sandhurst before settling down, and Brian New had indulged in all the excesses of the average young soldier before marrying and growing quietly responsible. Was this the link they were looking for? What had happened to affect these three?

Light began to dawn at the end of the dark tunnel. Had these men suffered a shared trauma that had changed them irrevocably? Some deeply shocking experience in company with another person on whom it had had the *reverse* effect. A quiet, moral soldier who became evil because of it. Someone who then felt impelled to destroy those who had emerged from the appalling event as *better* men. Had Kington, White and New witnessed something during that time that the fourth man was driven to protect at all cost?

If the hypothesis were true it would make sense of what had so far failed to add up. It would also support the belief that Simon Kington was lying dead somewhere not far away.

Seven

Ben Steele had had a hell of a day. He'd led his platoon over a gruelling cross-country endurance course. Men had dropped out through exhaustion towards the end, but he had been obliged to grit his teeth and push on to where trucks waited to drive them back to base. One of the 'privileges' of being an officer was that he must never expect his men to do what he could not.

Standing under a hot shower Ben considered skipping dinner and falling in to bed, but that would be viewed as weakness by Roger Kennedy. The 2IC was certain to be in the mess bar to check on the stamina of the subordinate who had dropped him in it with SIB over the Kington affair. Ben had not yet been forgiven.

As he towelled down, he considered the news given to him by Alec Nixon on his return thirty minutes ago. Ready to drop, covered in mud, sweaty and seriously wondering why he had chosen such a demanding career, Ben had merely mumbled an acknowledgement as he plodded past to his own room. Now he felt more human he was able to give thought to what Alec had said. He found it difficult to believe. Sir Chetwin Kington was being told to fork out some of his fortune to buy the release of his son.

Lost in conjecture, Ben stopped rubbing his chest dry. Within the space of four days 'they' had somehow entered a secure establishment, taken by force from outside his home a very fit man, and smuggled him out unnoticed. They had then approached Simon's influential father in the UK with their financial demands. Even without knowing the finer details, Ben wondered at the extent of the risk purely for the sake of cash.

He fixed the towel around his waist, padded along the corridor to his room and began to dress, still mulling over what he had heard.

He had never believed Simon to have absconded, but that the kidnap must surely have a military or political motive. This development was at odds with what he knew of the affair. Why take the laptop if money was all they wanted?

In shirt and underpants he ran his electric razor over his face. Being very dark his stubble was heavily visible fourteen hours after his early morning shave. The girls in his platoon still looked fresh-cheeked at the end of a long day. Lucky devils, girls! Didn't have this twice-daily chore.

The telephone rang, startling him enough to nick his chin and draw blood. Swearing, he dabbed at it with his face flannel while crossing to take up the receiver.

'Lieutenant Steele,' he said, keeping the

damp cloth pressed against the cut.

'Corporal Fox, sir. Main gate.'

'I'm not Duty Officer. You want Captain Hicks.'

'No, sir, there's a young lady here asking for you.'

'What?' He was still dabbing his chin. 'There's some mistake.'

'No mistake. She's asked for you by name, sir.'

Baffled, Ben stared at the tiny circle of blood on the wet flannel, unable to get to grips with this curious conversation. His brain was as weary as his body right now. 'Who is she, Corporal?' he asked irritably.

'Says her name's Sonyer Michael. She's a *Fraülein*, sir.'

Blood rushed through Ben's veins. Sonja Meikel, that gorgeous girl at the Ferrari Club? How could she be at the main gate? How did she know where he was based? How could she possibly be asking for him after such a brief meeting?

'Are you still there, sir?'

'Yes ... yes,' he stammered. 'What does she want? I mean, are you sure...?' Oh Christ, he was behaving like a kid on the verge of puberty.

'The lady claims you'll vouch for her if I let her through. Was you expecting her, sir?'

'No. I mean, I hardly know...'

'Want me to say you're not on-base?' There was now a definite 'knowing' tone in his voice. He clearly believed Sonja had been a one-night stand about to make things awkward for him.

'No! Look, Corporal Fox, I'm only just back from that cross-country,' he explained, trying to accept that this beautiful, wealthy, racetrack champion was seeking him out. 'Please take your time entering her details, then impress on her there's a strict speed limit within the base.'

There was a chuckle on the line. 'Do my best, sir, but I can't see her observing it in what she's driving. Reckon she'll be outside the Officers' Mess in less than five.' He was still chuckling as he cut the connection.

The reserve of energy trained servicemen manage to call on was summoned as Ben frantically changed his casual shirt for a plain cream one, knotted a somewhat jazzy tie under the collar, and stepped into a pair of dark trousers, all the while intermittently pressing a tissue to the nick that refused to stop bleeding. His heart was pounding. Sonja was a total knock-out, and he hadn't put on a very sophisticated act in that swanky club. So what was this all about? If he wasn't downstairs before she drove up in her Ferrari, half a dozen of his lusty colleagues would be flocking around her.

In a desperate attempt to cauterize the tiny cut he liberally splashed aftershave over his chin, then gave a soft cry as it stung his flesh. But as he hastily ran a comb through his thick hair his heart sank. He smelled like a ponce. A swift facial scrub with a soapy flannel weakened the tangy fragrance.

Further attentions had to be abandoned when he heard an expensive roar from the area below his window. Sonja had arrived! On the point of leaving his room he swiftly turned back to scoop up his wallet, small change and his watch. Half running along the corridor he fastened it around his wrist, yet again wishing it was a gold Rolex.

Bursting through the front entrance, still adjusting the collar of his soft leather jacket, Ben was furious to find the 2IC standing beside the silver Ferrari, bending to speak to the girl behind the wheel. Just his luck.

'Good evening, sir,' he said breathlessly, then added, 'Guten Abend, Sonja. *Wie geht es Ihnen?*'

Roger Kennedy scowled at him. 'I was just asking the young lady who she had come to see. You should have been here to greet her, Ben. Bad manners!'

'Sorry about that,' he said stiffly.

'Yes ... well! Show her where to park this splendid machine. You can introduce us properly when you bring her in for a drink.'

With a smile for Sonja he walked away before anything more could be said. A good thing, because Ben was out of ideas on the subject. No way would he let this fabulous red-head anywhere near his red-blooded fellow officers. He'd dreamed of her for the past two nights. He wanted her to himself, whatever the reason for this unexpected meeting.

'Are we to go in for a drink, Ben?' she asked softly through the lowered window.

She looked even lovelier than he remembered in a jacket of dark fur and dangling diamond earrings – both the real thing, he was sure.

He lied swiftly. 'Guests have to be booked in in advance. Let's go in to town.'

She smiled, quickening his pulse further. 'That is what I wish. Jump in!'

His hesitation was only fleeting. He'd be a fool to suggest they go in his Ford. He walked round the gleaming car and slid on to the soft leather, longing to be the one at the wheel and she his passenger. He felt further humbled when she said mockingly, 'Now I show you how expert is the bread of the sandwich.'

Ben's thoughtless simile had not been forgotten.

Nought to a hundred in sixty seconds was nothing to this girl. They raced to the main gate overtaking other traffic along the perimeter road, drawing the attention of pedestrians, until Sonja decelerated to perfection several feet from the barrier. Corporal Fox wore an expression that was part smirk and part envy as he noted the occupants and went to raise the red and white bar.

'Have a nice time, sir,' he said, the smirk broadening. 'Hope you're not too fagged out after the cross-country!'

Ben knew there would be lewd yarns circulating the ranks after this. Squaddies enjoyed taking the piss out of subalterns when the chance arose. This stunning girl in this superb silver car offered them the perfect ammunition.

For the first five minutes Ben practically held his breath as they overtook other vehicles, and negotiated bends in the narrow road with centimetres to spare. Then they were on the autobahn with miles of straight road ahead. He relaxed, acknowledging her expertise. Resented it, too, if he were honest. A natural masculine reaction to a desirable woman demonstrating outstanding prowess at a skill men liked to regard as unique to their sex.

Knowing better than to offer a compliment, which she would very likely consider patronizing, Ben decided it was time he took control of the evening.

'I know a decent place for a drink. I'll give you directions,' he said, confident enough to stop watching the road and feast his eyes on her.

'We shall go to my club. *Der Kaninchenstall.* I have already planned it.'

Despite its name The Rabbit Hutch was a very trendy, upmarket club with membership fees only high-flyers could afford. The evening would cost him an arm and a leg for drinks alone, and he was ravenous enough to eat all they had on offer. Still, what the hell? Sonja had come chasing after him, and army officers were trained to handle any eventuality. He'd damn well earn that smirk on Fox's face.

The Ferrari swept off the autobahn and raced along a country road to where the club lay in extensive grounds. The car didn't stand out among those neatly parked outside the discreet entrance. Ben estimated there must be several million poundsworth of engineering sitting on the tarmac as Sonja drew to a halt beside a BMW sports model.

'So, Ben, we are here. Shall we go in?'

'After you've answered a few questions,' he said firmly. 'How did you know where I was based?'

'Phoo, that was easy.' She smiled seductively. 'You have very sexy eyes, *mein Soldat*.'

Ben tried to ignore her perfume, the gloss on her kissable mouth. 'I want to know why you came to the base unannounced, asking for me. What's behind this, Sonja?'

'I came because I wish to know you better. And because of those sexy eyes,' she teased, leaning towards him.

As he was trained to handle every eventuality, the kiss she began he completed with military command and expertise, set to continue until the objective was gained. But she had other ideas.

The interior of *Der Kaninchenstall* was plush and subtly lit, with wall paintings of rabbits smoking cigars, posturing beside smart cars, dining *á la carte*, or watching the races through binoculars. Sonja had to sign Ben in as her guest, and he then discovered only members could buy drinks or pay for meals. He protested, but she waved his words aside.

'It is nothing. I always sign chits and my father settles the account each month.' She tugged on both his hands. 'Come, I want to show you to my friends.'

After several heady cocktails on an empty stomach Ben shrugged off his early suspicions about this crazy date, and took pleasure in being one of this alluring girl's group of friends. Sonja had shed her fur jacket to reveal a jet-beaded top with a very short black chiffon skirt that gave Ben the delight of studying a generous expanse of shapely leg.

The drink kept flowing – Sonja had an amazing capacity for alcohol – and Ben began wondering how soon they would eat. He was growing light-headed, if not a little drunk. He urgently needed to counteract the liquid with food, yet he couldn't make the move to the restaurant as he would if he was allowed to pay for their meal.

An hour later, despite drinking very slowly, Ben was growing bemused. Sonja's friends were speaking in a mixture of German and English in deference to him, but his knowledge of their language wasn't good enough to let him follow all their bright, rapid comments. Until his weary senses caught a name he knew. Simon Kington.

Sonja turned to him with a smile. 'That is how I knew how to find you tonight. You said he was a friend, so you must work at the same place, yes?'

'Yes.' He leaned towards her somewhat groggily. 'What was that guy saying about

Simon? I didn't catch it.'

She let her hand rest on his thigh, rather higher than was advisable, he thought. 'He says how dramatic that someone is asking his father to buy Simon back for some millions.'

Ben sobered slightly. 'How did *he* know that?'

Her hand inched higher. 'It is known from Gerhardt Wolf, of course. He is friend and business associate of Sir Chetwin.'

Ben frowned. 'But I understood the whole affair was being kept under wraps.'

'Under what, *Liebchen*?' she asked with a soft giggle. 'Is that some more of your funny army talk?'

As he began to respond to her wandering hand, he decided it was time for action. He got to his feet, pulling her up to stand beside him, and said in her ear, 'I was out on a gruelling exercise from dawn until just before you turned up. I'm desperate for something to eat and I might start on you if I have to wait much longer.'

Brushing her lips against his, she said, 'Why did you not say this before? You will need to be strong for what will happen later.' She rounded on her friends. 'Come, my sexy-eyed soldier must have food before he eats me instead.' It was said in German, but Ben translated it well enough. This girl really was the limit. She was also the most exciting one that had crossed his path.

Due to that fact and to the amount of alcohol he had downed at the end of a very tiring day, Ben headed for the toilets before joining them in the restaurant. Once there he tried to steady himself by taking deep breaths. A hearty meal would set him up for the remainder of the evening – whatever it may hold. So what if Herr Meikel paid for it? It would be a drop in the ocean for a man like him and, with a daughter like Sonja, he must expect her escorts to be in prime condition for 'what will happen later'.

Pushing open the door, he walked the thickly carpeted corridor, dwelling with anticipation on the culmination of this amazing evening. On the verge of crossing the foyer to reach the restaurant, he slowed to a stunned halt. A couple had just entered the club and begun climbing stairs leading, according to signs on the wall, to the private committee rooms. The deep breathing had done the trick, but Ben now felt distinctly bemused again. He recognized Gerhardt Wolf from his visit to the Ferrari Club – Sonja had pointed him out. But what was Tara Kington doing here when she should be at home anxiously waiting for news that her husband had been released unharmed?

As Max drove from the main gate to the CO's house he was startled from his thoughts by a silver missile hurtling towards him. He instinctively hugged the kerb as it roared past, and swore under his breath, but it was going too fast for him to read the registration in his rear mirror. The corporal who had just checked him in would have it on record, so the bastard would be reported and admonished.

The Commanding Officer's quarter was easy to find. He pulled on to the flagged driveway hoping Colonel Trelawney was a more relaxed character than Roger Kennedy. After leaving Tara Kington he and Tom had called on the 2IC. The meeting had been chilly. Kennedy felt justified in his opinion that the Kington affair should never have been taken up by SIB; claimed their interference had made far too many people aware of the abduction, which had put Mrs Kington through untold distress and might very well endanger the negotiations for his release.

'It was a regimental matter which we would have handled more discreetly. Now the entire base is aware of what's developed in the UK,' he had maintained. 'Too many phone calls and e-mails back and forth between your people and those most closely concerned. Not good. Not good at all!'

Keeping their theories to themselves, Max and Tom said only that they were intensifying their investigation of the murders, and hoped to have a breakthrough soon. At which point Kennedy revealed that Colonel Trelawney had cut short his trip to the World War 1 battlefields at Gallipoli and was flying in that afternoon. With some irascibility he added that the CO had asked that Max should call on him at around half past seven to put him fully in the picture.

As Max locked his car he wished he had a more positive picture for this man who felt concerned enough to resume command at a time of regimental unrest. That was in Trelawney's favour and boded well for what Max hoped to achieve here.

As he crossed to the door of the double-fronted house his mobile rang. It was Tom calling. Oh, let it be good news. Something that would make this meeting run more smoothly.

'Yes, Tom?'

'Good time to speak?'

Max grunted a laugh. 'I'm two feet from his door. You couldn't have gauged it better. Tell me they've identified the toxin, they've discovered who broke in to the Reinhardt Klinik, they've found Simon Kington in a hotel in Paris with a NATO secretary. Any of those'll do.'

'I wish! Thought you should know Klaus Krenkel called in. His guys found someone who saw a car parked on the heath on the night White's body was dumped there. Seems the witness and his girlfriend were indulging in sexual athletics in the back of his van. Saw the other vehicle when they arrived there around ten minutes after twenty-two hundred hours. No one in or near it. They supposed it was another couple gone to cover for their activities.'

'And?' prompted Max hopefully.

'The witness claimed he heard it drive off while he was heavily occupied. Reckons it was some time later. Didn't see who was in it, for obvious reasons. But he's earned Brownie points. The suspect vehicle was the saloon version of his van – only a few hundred made before the model was withdrawn. The witness is an auto nut. He wrote down the registration when he first arrived intending to trace the owner and beg a thorough look over it.'

'The *Polizei* traced the owner?'

'The vehicle was stolen from the driveway of a house in Bergdorf some time during Sunday evening, when Brian New was killed. The owner informed the *Polizei*, but it was back on their forecourt on Tuesday morning, when White's body was found. Krenkel's men have taken it in for forensic examination, but the owner's been using it in the interim.'

Max's hopes dwindled. 'It's a bit of a long shot.'

'I agree, but if they find fibres that match those on White's clothes we'll know the killers definitely used it. Maybe also to drive to the Golden Key to murder New.'

'If they find matching fibres it'll shoot down our belief that it's an inside job.'

'Not necessarily. The killers could have taken the car to do the Golden Key murder, then hidden it somewhere until they drove out to the Reinhardt Klinik to get White.'

Max sighed with frustration. 'Possible, but I hope this is a false lead, Tom. It'll complicate things further if they prove some law-abiding burgher's car was involved in White's murder.'

'Klaus has sent men to the clinic to seek matching tyre prints, and to ask staff if they happened to see a car of that description in the vicinity.'

'Huh! From what you told me the staff at that place are like the three monkeys. I'll check in with you after this meeting.'

Max stood for a moment reviewing what Tom had said. Could they be completely and dangerously wrong in dismissing the possibility of local civilian complicity in these deaths? And in suspecting what had really happened to Simon Kington? If so, they'd be back where they started.

Sighing once more, Max rang the bell. John Trelawney opened the door and shook his hand, inviting him in. 'Thank you for coming.'

'I'm sorry we're meeting under these circumstances, sir.'

'Yes. Nasty business.'

Trelawney was a tall, graceful man with crisp brown hair and alert eyes. A scar ran down his right cheek. There were others on the backs of his hands. He wore a pearl grey shirt and charcoal slacks, with a regimental tie. He looked what he was – a man with heavy responsibilities. Max warmed to him.

They walked to a large, elegant sitting-room where the CO offered Max a drink. As he poured two whiskies, he explained that his wife and family were still in Greece.

'No point in their cutting short the holiday. My profession disrupts their lives enough as it is, but this business has grown so serious I knew I should be here. Roger Kennedy has put me more in the picture, but I'd like you to fill in the remaining blanks so I can better deal with the question of morale, which is being affected by these bizarre attacks on members of the regiment.'

Bringing the glasses over he waved at one of the matching chairs each side of an ornate fireplace, where an electric fire with artificial glowing coals gave an air of cosiness the central heating did not. They sat and sipped their drinks in relaxed manner. Max sensed that he was now dealing with a different kind of man from Roger Kennedy. The CO aptly fitted the description officer and gentleman.

Trelawney looked across at Max. 'I'm sure you have a theory on what's behind these two deaths, Captain Rydal. If you'll outline it I maybe can add to it. I knew the victims reasonably well. Aside from a year and nine months on loan to the Sultan of Oman's army, I've been with the battalion since they both joined our ranks.'

Max gave a wry smile. 'We've had several theories during the course of the week, most of which we've discarded because we failed to find a link between the three victims.'

'Three?' he asked sharply. 'There's been another murder?'

'Not that we're aware of, sir. We had to consider Major Kington as a possible third.'

'Yes, I see.' Trelawney spoke frankly. 'I have to say that case must concern me the most, simply because the crime was committed on-base. In this present era of terrorist activities I have been scrupulous over security. It's highly daunting to be given evidence that this establishment can be penetrated so easily.'

'We initially shared your dismay, but we think it more than likely the abduction was carried out by military or civilian personnel working here.'

'As were the two killings?'

Max elaborated on the results of their investigation so far, highlighting the fact that the victims' movements were so well known. 'Only one or two of Sergeant New's friends were aware of his date with the woman he wanted to marry. They have solid alibis. We've so far not found anyone who was party to Captain White's medical decision, but some-one must have been. And whoever snatched Simon Kington had to have been waiting outside his office or his quarter that evening.'

'I agree on that. But are you still linking the kidnap to the murders, despite the ransom demand sent to Simon's father?'

'We are, yes.'

'I see.' Trelawney drank some more whisky thoughtfully. 'I rang Tara Kington just before you arrived. She wasn't there. She's probably being supported by friends while this sus-pense lasts.'

Max said nothing. The lady was able to cope unaided with the situation, as he and Tom had seen earlier today.

'Does SIB have evidence that the ransom

demand isn't genuine?' the CO asked with sudden bluntness.

'No, sir, none whatever. It's more a gut feeling from past experience.'

'You believe he's already dead?'

Leaning forward Max gave this shrewd commander a complete rundown of his and Tom's thinking, knowing as he did so that it would prove invalid if Kington were shortly released unharmed.

Trelawney nodded several times when Max had finished. 'There's a great deal of logic in that. The twins, or Lady Kington would certainly be easier targets, but I sincerely hope you're wrong. Simon is a top rate Defence Liaison Officer, a credit to the regiment and a very nice chap. If his body is discovered, as you fear, morale will really plummet. He's one of our most popular officers.'

That gave Max the perfect cue. Outlining the fact that Kington, White and New apparently changed their personalities at some point in their careers, he asked if Trelawney could think of a traumatic experience the three men had suffered that might explain it.

'I know the battalion served in Bosnia, and tales of how that tragedy affected UN peace-keepers are legion. Were the victims involved in some particularly horrific situation there? Is there any other action or duty they undertook together that might have brought about a sobering of their high spirits?'

'That's a difficult surmise to answer.'

Max nodded. 'Of course. I've several times been under fire in my career, but by individual gunmen we've cornered. You must be more aware of the effects danger, battle fatigue and the gruesome aftermath of military action have on fighting men.'

The CO spread his hands in a negative gesture. 'Over the years we've been in some sticky areas. Northern Ireland, Afghanistan, Kuwait, Bosnia. None of those tours were easy on the regiment. Leave it with me. I'll give it some thought. And I'll check the regimental records to see if they jog my memory. It has to be an action involving all three victims?'

'Yes. That should narrow the field, because I believe there could be a fourth person who was with them; someone now driven to destroy his colleagues who became better men after an experience that actually *dehumanized* him.'

'I see. Most soldiers emerge from battle changed men. Warfare tends to make us adjust our priorities, recognize the shallower aspects of our present society, understand the meaning of life and death. For some it's a turning point, showing them they want no further part in soldiering. For others, the suffering and inhumanity they witness is comparable to a religious experience. They see the world in a new light.'

He got to his feet, signalling the end of the meeting. 'Of course, there are always a few who emerge brutalized, having relished the

190

sense of power with an SA80 in their hands; having been exhilarated by bloody mayhem. In extreme cases a regiment has to rid itself of them. For the rest, their commanders have to keep tight control of them in action.'

Max was on his feet ready to leave. 'It could well be a man like that who is reacting to a long spell away from the violence that hypes him up. Someone who needs armed aggression the way an addict needs drugs.' As they walked to the door, Max added drily, 'Captain White's father-in-law, a man willing to take on all-comers as I found to my cost, reckons soldiers are just trained killing machines who, if there's no war, start knocking each other off. Could be he's right, in this instance.'

They paused on the doorstep illuminated by a security light. 'I'll have a word with my officers first thing,' Trelawney promised. 'Get from them the names of any men they have to keep a rein on. You'll have a list by lunchtime, along with any info I can find on dangerous forays the three victims might have carried out in unison.'

'That'll be a valuable addition to what we already have.' Max stepped towards his car, then turned. 'We'll find the killer as swiftly and with as little disruption as possible. Goodnight, sir.'

It was one of the grey periods. Grey as opposed to black. They came, then went again before paling into full dawn. It was frustrating, yet he hoped this time the fog would clear enough to make sense of what was happening to him. He was still in the bare room overlooking a considerable stretch of water, although he could not at this moment summon the energy to crawl to the window and pull himself up to peer through it. He was lying on the same mattress alongside the same wall.

The paper on it hung down in strips here and there where it had peeled away. There was a pattern of strange animals on it. Recognition hung tantalizingly near. Black ones, brown ones. They had extended noses, pointed ears and long, bushy tails. Yet they had no feet, just the arc of a large wheel on the ends of their four legs. Somehow familiar, yet not.

If he could only gain an identity surely the rest would fall in to place. He was a sturdy man; muscular. Tall, because when he lay full-length his heels jutted over the end of the mattress. There was thick growth on his chin. The hairs on his arms were dark, so it must be a brown infant beard. Dark-haired and brown eyed? So what? Without a name, without a personality, without a history he was nothing.

He lay in these few moments of vague clarity pondering what he knew of this curious existence. There was no ill treatment, just enforced isolation in a room minus furniture. A mattress with blankets on the floor; a basic toilet in the corner. Ventilation was provided through an open louvre high in the window. There was silence, apart from the regular thud of footfalls when 'the person' came with food and water.

This shadowy visitor in hooded black top and trousers could be male or female and never spoke, yet exuded no malice. 'The person' fed him as if he were an invalid, helped him to use the toilet, then washed him, gave him a long drink of honey-scented water and silently departed. These mealtimes were most welcome. The hot, tasty food warmed his body and produced a sense of calmness and peace once more.

He forced his fuzzy thoughts back to the worrying lack of identity. He had no personal possessions with him as clues; his only clothes basic dark underpants similar to those worn by men all over the world. Why was he kept almost naked in a locked room? Was he a dangerous lunatic? Surely he would then be in a padded cell, not in this dilapidated nursery.

Yes, of course. A *nursery*! The wallpaper was covered with pictures of toys. Children sat on those animals and rolled back and forth. He had sat on one many times. Many, *many* times. But he had not rolled back and forth. He had raced headlong. Others chased him. They must not catch up with him.

Perspiration broke on his face and body as an image hung so very, very near and he strained to reach out and grab it. Make sense of it. But there came the familiar sound of heavy footfalls approaching and the flimsy image shattered.

It happened as always. He ate hungrily, was made comfortable and drank the refreshing water. Soon, the grey period darkened to another black one, his arduously formed questions left unanswered.

Eight

Saturday, thank God! Despite the usual hearty morning exchanges and door slamming beyond the walls of his room, Ben managed to remain in his pleasant half awake state. He had returned with the milk after an unbelievable night with Sonja Meikel. He wanted to wallow in that memory within the warm cocoon of his duvet, keeping all else at bay for as long as possible. In truth, he was physically drained and needed to recoup some energy before attempting to face anything that lay beyond his bed.

He grinned into his pillow. How many of his fellows presently clattering and galumphing around in the corridor could have performed as well as he after a gruelling all-day exercise? So maybe he had flagged once or twice, but not seriously enough to earn the derision of the girl who did everything in the fast lane. Sonja had managed to keep him active for as long as her desire lasted, and his grin broadened at the thought of the surprise she would get when he *hadn't* spent the previous fourteen hours on all-out, hard soldiering.

It was mid-morning by the time Ben rose, still yawning. At that hour the showers were deserted, so he savoured the pummelling hot spray on his lethargic muscles. Then he completed the revival process by turning the tap to cold and enduring it until he was gasping. The shock had done the trick, dispelling the lazy aftermath of lust.

As he towelled down, his thoughts returned to the unexpected sighting of Tara Kington in company with Sir Chetwin's German rival. It was perfectly conceivable that she might know Gerhardt Wolf socially – she and Simon moved in higher circles than Ben – but his admiration for her had instantly faded.

Sir Chetwin had just received a ransom demand to secure Simon's release; maybe even to buy his life. Why wasn't Tara sitting in agonizing suspense beside her telephone at home, waiting for news? Ben had been awed by her self-possession and courage after her husband's disappearance, but last night she had been dressed to the nines clearly enjoying the company of the silver-haired business giant. Ben was unaccountably disturbed by what he had seen. It didn't fit the image he had had of the accomplished, intellectual major's wife. He had at one time actually envied Simon earning her devotion.

He pursued these troubled thoughts while he shaved, then dressed in chinos and a soft wool shirt. Came a return of his earlier doubts over the way Simon had vanished. Was it, after all, a cover story for a highly secret mission? Was even the ransom demand a mere fabrication to bring about SIB's withdrawal from the investigation? If Tara was in on the deception it would explain her behaviour last night.

Ben made a mug of black coffee and raided his biscuit tin. Within the hour he could go down for a huge lunch. Digestives would keep him going until then. While he munched he reluctantly accepted that there was another possibility to be considered. It was wild, way-out, preposterous, but...! He had been drawn in on this bizarre affair by the ill fortune of being Duty Officer that night. His rating with the 2IC had been badly damaged because of it, and had not yet been repaired. Had they all used him like a puppet on a string?

An alien passion suddenly burned in his breast, giving birth to a resolution both daring and determined. He delved into the pocket of last night's trousers; found the elaborately printed card he had taken from the pile in the silver holder on Sonja's coffee table before slipping away.

Switching on his computer he rapidly keyed an affectionate message of thanks for a wonderful evening, making no secret of his admiration for her physical attributes and the devastating way she used them. His lusty fluency surprised him – he had never been silver-tongued – but typing words on a screen made overt flirtation relatively easy, he discovered. Then he unashamedly claimed he was on fire for her and would be totally consumed by the flames unless they met again tonight or tomorrow.

Reading it through, Ben was very pleased with his wordy flamboyance. It was over the top enough to appeal to her and would surely bring the response he needed. He sent it, telling himself there was no reason why gumshoe activity couldn't have a sexy sideline.

For the next few minutes his thoughts dwelled on his additional purpose in urging another rendezvous with this gorgeous, unconventional German girl. She knew the main players in Ben's speculative scenario and could facilitate access to places otherwise out of bounds to him. Sonja Meikel's passing fascination with her 'sexy-eyed soldier' would be a godsend in his bid to dance on his own string, not one pulled by others who knew the truth about Simon Kington.

One by one, members of the team gave their reports at the Saturday morning briefing. They had been working flat out, all determinedly seeking the elusive breakthrough. Connie Bush had failed to find anyone at the regional *Krankenhaus* with links to staff at the Reinhardt Klinik. She was disappointed that her bright idea had come to nothing.

'I questioned Vera Maitland's friends once more, hoping they had remembered something useful,' she added. 'A nurse called Grobler gave the victim a lift to the Golden Key on the way to meet her boyfriend – a local computer salesman she's since ditched, hence why she was prepared now to offer the info. He knew about the rendezvous at the Golden Key, but was with Grobler when the murder took place, of course. I checked with the guy whether he'd mentioned the meeting at the restaurant to anyone else.' She pulled a face. 'He was an obnoxious bastard. Sneeringly suggested, in impeccable English, that the British Military Police were clutching at straws to cover their ineptitude.

'I interviewed the Golden Key staff again. Nothing new. Local police tracked down the other diners present when New and Maitland were. No one saw anything suspicious. Dead end on both counts, sir. Sorry.'

Piercey and Beeny were still checking the accounts of all personnel who had been off-base last weekend. They had nothing to report, so far. Even the volatile Piercey was showing signs of dejection over lack of progress.

Staff Sergeant Melly, with Heather Johnson, had discreetly questioned RCR officers about Colin White and had discovered someone who was aware of the victim's wish to have a vasectomy.

'We thought we'd struck lucky,' said Pete Melly. 'Seems White mentioned having the op to his neighbour, Luke Maybury.'

'But Captain Maybury said it was only in the heat of the moment when he heard his wife's family had invited themselves over to see the latest babies,' Heather Johnson put in. 'Apparently, White muttered something like "I'll bloody get myself sterilized or they'll be with us permanently". Maybury didn't take him seriously at the time, but was concerned about his friend's obvious stress during the last week of his life. That White had taken the plunge didn't really surprise Maybury, but he didn't understand why he went to the Reinhardt. Said White didn't have that kind of money to spare.'

'He's right,' affirmed Tom. 'We've checked his finances. What about Captain Luke Maybury?'

Pete Melly shook his head. 'He was Duty Officer last Sunday, when Brian New was killed. Perfect alibi. Was at a meeting of the Mess Committee next evening. It went on until twenty-two hundred hours. He couldn't have done for his neighbour and dumped him on the heath.'

The level-headed female sergeant summed up their interviews. 'Unless one of the officers is a consummate liar, their stories all stand up even at our second check.' She gave a wry smile. 'And they all *liked* Colin White. Said he was an all-round nice guy.'

'Yeah, bloody perfect,' growled Tom. 'Like everyone else in that sodding regiment. That's how one of them managed to commit two perfect murders.'

Piercey couldn't resist muttering under his breath, 'Three, if you count Kington's body in a shallow grave on-base.'

Max then reviewed the report he had received from Klaus Krenkel. 'Our German colleagues have made extensive inquiries along the route between the Reinhardt and the heath where the body was found. Several witnesses claimed to have seen a car, similar to the one stolen from outside the house in Bergdorf, being driven at speed in the direction of the heath late on Monday evening. One elderly woman said there had been four large men in dark overcoats and sunglasses in it, but the *Polizei* are discounting her statement.

'A garage attendant mentioned a sale at around nine that evening. Said the driver paid in cash and never spoke during the transaction; thought he was probably a foreigner with no German. There was a man in the passenger seat, and a third in the back wrapped in a rug and apparently asleep. The witness couldn't swear to the colour of the vehicle – could be dark green, dark blue or even black – but he noticed it was an unusual model. No reg details, of course. The men who took his statement reckon he was watching TV. Simply took the cash and concentrated on the box. However, the car was heading in the right direction at the right time, and a sleeping man in a rug could be significant.'

'It's a needle in a haystack, sir,' protested Connie Bush.

'I agree, Sergeant, but it's their needle, not ours. Once they have proof that the stolen car was used to transport Colin White's body, they'll tear the haystack apart, believe me.'

Max drove out to the base after telling his

team to go home for the remainder of the weekend. A message from Klaus Krenkel had put paid to even that vague lead. There was no forensic evidence linking the murdered officer with the stolen car. The *Polizei* were now treating it as a case of youths 'borrowing' it for a spree.

Deeply frustrated, *angry*, over the deviousness of the killer, and of their own inability to find even a tiny crack in the seemingly perfect execution of the crimes, Max was too restless to stay in his digs at *Frau* Hahn's. Colonel Trelawney had promised to have information for him by lunchtime, so Max satisfied his need for action by going to collect it rather than waiting for an e-mail.

As he drove, he brooded on his theory of a military action that had changed the personalities of four men. Three had grown sober and responsible. The fourth had become brutalized. It was feasible, Max felt, yet surely the killer would have *shot* his victims. Used the weapon that had caused the carnage they had participated in and which had turned his mind. Murder by injection didn't fit the hypothesis.

He had telephoned his intention before setting out, and now received a message on his mobile that the CO would see him in his office at noon when he would have collated the information SIB wanted. To fill the spare half-hour Max decided to have another confrontation with Jim Slater, Christine White's bombastic father, in an effort to talk to the widow.

There was a military ambulance outside the house, parked behind a car Max recognized as the MO's. The front door was open, so Max didn't think twice about walking in. The room was full of people. Christine White was strapped to a stretcher, wrapped tightly in a blanket. Her face was ashen; she appeared to be unconscious. Major Clarkson was giving quiet instructions to the paramedics readying to take her out.

Jim Slater stood staring pop-eyed at his daughter. Beside him, a brawny, hard-faced woman was wiping her hands on a damp overall. Next to her was a bottle blonde in her twenties, equally hard-faced, who watched the scene with overt anger. The Slater family closing ranks? From upstairs came a chorus of crying and screaming barely deadened by closed doors.

The MO turned and saw Max. 'What the hell are you doing here?' he snapped, indicating that he should move aside to allow the stretcher through.

'What happened?' he asked.

Clarkson ignored his question, focussed instead on Mrs Slater. 'She needs complete rest, so no visitors for at least forty-eight hours. The number of the hospital is on that form I gave you. You can check on your daughter's progress by phone. If you change your mind about having someone to help with the children, call me.' He waved a hand towards the stairs. 'Pacify those babies before they make themselves ill,' he ordered harshly.

Picking up his medical bag, he followed the stretcher-bearers down the path to his car. Max caught him before he could get in it.

'What happened?' he repeated, pressing his hand against the door to prevent the man from opening it.

The MO said, stony-faced, 'She slit her wrists. I've no doubt that bloody family drove her to it. She'll be admitted to the Psychiatric Wing. After they receive my report I hope they'll keep that overbearing mob from her for as long as possible. They've refused help with the kids, but I'll make regular checks on them.'

'They won't let you in,' advised Max from experience.

'Oh yes, they will,' Clarkson retorted with force, 'or I'll threaten to have their grand-children taken in to care.' He looked pointedly at Max's hand. 'I need to get that report underway.'

He stood away from the car. 'And I need to find whoever killed those children's father.'

'You're at a dead end here.' Clarkson dumped his bag and sat behind the wheel. 'Christine's had a total breakdown. It'll be months before she can function fully, and unless she can break away from those mon-sters she probably never will.'

Max watched him drive away behind the ambulance round the curve in the road. The murder of Colin White had set in motion a tragedy with little hope of an eventual happy ending. Christine's bid for freedom had lasted too short a time to make her independent. Her children were almost certain to grow up as bigoted and aggressive as the Slaters. For a moment or two he dwelled morbidly on the legacy of sudden death. He knew about the shock and grief, but couldn't begin to imagine what state of mind trying also to deal with four babies and a bullying family would induce.

His meeting with Colonel Trelawney was brief. The CO was clearly busy dealing with the backlog from his absence, but he greeted Max courteously and handed him two sheets of paper.

'The top one gives details of missions that Major Kington, Captain White and Sergeant New took part in together. Quite a few, you'll see. All of them were large-scale operations involving a considerable force. There was no special op in which they and maybe only one or two others embarked on, I'm afraid.

'The second sheet has a short list of those men considered by their commanders to have maverick tendencies, or who need to be kept on a tight rein. I spoke to as many of my officers and sergeants as were available this morning. I'll tackle the rest on Monday. I hope this will be of some help to you.'

Leaving the office, Max faced a heavy downpour, so he decided to use his temporary membership of the Officers' Mess to get some lunch. Over coffee he could study the pages he had been given. Being Saturday there were very few diners in the long, high-ceilinged room. A young man and woman deep in conversation, a grey-haired captain in uniform who was Duty Officer that day, the Padre with a visiting civilian cleric, and Lieutenant Ben Steele tucking into an enormous plateful of steak pie and vegetables.

The latter smiled at Max and waved him across. Sensing that the young subaltern's errant boot was about to land heavily where it was not wanted, Max reluctantly joined him at the table.

'Thought you'd have been off enjoying yourself for the weekend,' he said. 'Don't tell me the 2IC has landed you with some "volunteer" duty because you're still under a cloud.'

Ben grimaced. 'Well, I am, as a matter of fact, but I'm on-base because I led a cross-country exercise yesterday so slept in late. I was going to call your headquarters, but I can now tell you first hand an intriguing bit of info I found this morning. I'm sure it's quite significant.'

'Oh yes?'

Growing pink with enthusiasm, Ben said, 'My lazy morning gave me a chance to catch up on my e-mails. There was one from Mitch Donnegan, a friend from Sandhurst days. We both opted for the RCR, but were posted to different battalions. He's with Number One Battalion in the UK.'

'Oh?' Wanting lunch, Max wished Ben would get to the point.

'I'd given him the news of what's been going on here, of course, and his response has really set me thinking.'

Oh dear, he's doing his Miss Marple thing again, thought Max. 'Thinking about what?'

The large, expressive brown eyes glowed with fervour. 'Mitch commented on our murders and said it looked as if the Cumberlands were being spooked. One of their officers recently went on terminal leave to Hong Kong, where he was mugged and died of a massive heart attack on the Star Ferry. The Honkers police had no idea who he was until one of them recognized Barker's regimental tie. Seems a relative had married one of our blokes way back. Mitch said everyone was taken aback because Barker was only in his mid-thirties and apparently one hundred percent fit. Bizarre, don't you think?'

The kaleidoscope of facts suddenly spun around in Max's head and fell into a recognizable pattern. Brian New had married in Hong Kong and sobered down. Colin White had been a malevolent prankster until he returned from Hong Kong and swiftly impregnated then married his Christine. Simon Kington's personal wildness had been tamed into a love of legitimate, daring pastimes, and he had been with the battalion wherever it had served. The tingle that invariably accompanied a breakthrough fizzed through Max's body. Here was the link they had been searching for!

'So do you think it's significant?'

Max returned from interpreting the kaleidoscope pattern to see the eager young man across the table watching him closely. 'Very significant. You're shrewd enough to be one of us,' Max told him expansively, getting to his feet and abandoning any idea of lunch.

Breakthrough it might be, but that death on a Hong Kong ferry threatened to broaden and deepen this multiple murder case. Max's guts told him that that healthy, mid-thirties, ex-RCR officer's heart attack had been induced by an injection of an as yet unidentified toxin.

Tom was in his garden playing badminton with his daughters when the heavens suddenly opened. They all rushed indoors to where Nora was about to make the gravy for their lunch. She glanced up as they shook the rain from their hair.

'Can't you do anything without *squealing*?' she complained.

'*I* didn't squeal,' Tom asserted virtuously. 'I *never* squeal.'

'Oh yes, you do,' Beth, Gina and Maggie cried in chorus, turning on him to tickle, pinch and gently pull his ears and nose.

'Ooh, ouch, eee!' he uttered in a falsetto, loving this affectionate attack and playing along with it until they stopped.

'See!' Gina said smugly.

'He *does* squeal,' claimed Beth with satisfaction.

'He's supposed to be a super-tough policeman,' crowed Maggie, who had held back a little during the concerted assault.

From the recent onset of her menstruation there had been a slight change in the easy father-daughter relationship. Both Tom and Maggie were now hesitant when it came to touching. Nora told Tom he'd soon get over the shock of one of his little girls turning into a fledgeling woman, but he had dealt with cases of parental abuse often enough to make him wary of his child with swelling breasts who was biologically capable of having a baby. A father had only these days to kiss or hug his daughter in public to set people speculating. It worried him. Boys would have been easier. They'd have been mates. He would have understood sons better.

'Come on, you lot. This is ready,' said Nora. 'Have you washed your hands?'

There was a concerted scramble for the sink, where the soap was fought over with more squealing. It was amazing that Tom heard the telephone above the noise. He maintained that his ears were permanently tuned-in to that sound above all others, which was why he had no fancy jingle for his mobile. A shrill ringing tone always caught his attention.

'Tom, the link we searched for is Hong Kong,' Max's voice announced vibrantly. 'Ben Steele provided it a moment ago.' He recounted what he had just been told. 'The pattern fits. Young, healthy bloke has a sudden fatal heart attack. Add the fact that he's in the RCR – well, he was until a month ago – and coincidence has to go out of the window. Luckily, there was a burial. I'm about to contact Colonel Simpson in the UK and ask him to apply for an exhumation order.'

Tom frowned. 'But the regiment was out there in the run up to 1997. If these men are being taken out because of something that happened then, why the long wait for reprisals?'

'It's just a hunch, but if we find this latest heart attack *was* induced by a lethal injection instead, it could be that the victim's visit to Hong Kong set the killing spree in motion.'

Tom swore. 'If you're right, it blows our theory wide apart. We're not dealing with a single rifleman who has a grudge against his colleagues out here. Just what kind of Pandora's box has been opened?'

'Exactly! I've booked myself a flight home with the RAF early this evening. I want to attend the exhumation, talk to friends of the victim, find out why he quit the Army and why he would go directly to Hong Kong.'

'Probably kept that to himself,' murmured Tom, finding it hard to assimilate this wide-reaching development.

'He could have taken someone into his confidence if he knew he was about to play with fire. I've checked Harold Barker out on WAMI. He was with the Second Battalion until six months after their return from Honkers. He transferred on compassionate grounds. I'll pursue that. It might give us a lead.'

'Yeah, deeper into this bloody complex business,' Tom grunted.

'Call in as many of the team as you can raise and get over to the RCR. Set them questioning all members who're on-base today about any event in Hong Kong that involved all *four* victims.'

'You're still counting Simon Kington as one?'

'Until he turns up, alive or dead, yes. And Tom, tackle Colonel Trelawney or the 2IC on that same subject. I'll fax across the lists I was given by the CO. I'm not sure they're now relevant, but you might pick up something from them.'

'Will do, sir.'

'Sorry about your weekend.'

'What's a weekend?' asked Tom in mock innocence.

Max chuckled. 'I've also forgotten what it is, but I think we're getting to the heart of this business now and it's all systems go. By the way, while I'm in the UK I'll set guys questioning the School of Oriental Medicine and all Chinese practitioners to see if they can throw some light on our mystery toxin. The answer to that could also lie in the East.'

Tom stood for several moments assessing the import of what had been revealed. What if Harold Barker really had died after a heart attack? What if he'd flown back to Hong Kong to visit friends he'd met there years ago? Was Max jumping the gun on this in a bid to unravel the tangle? He gazed from the small window beside the front door, deeply uncertain. Had all their careful investigating been no more than a drop in a worldwide ocean? All the same, what other leads did they have? He had better run with this.

While he was punching out the mobile numbers of all the team, he heard the girls calling that his lunch was on the table getting cold. He could only raise Connie Bush and Derek Beeny. Briefing them, he then left text messages for the rest to call him soonest.

Nora glanced up as he entered the kitchen. 'Don't tell me, let me guess.'

He sat at the table where a helping of cheese-topped shepherd's pie was set for him. 'I'll have this before I go.'

Eight-year-old Beth flung down her knife and fork dramatically. 'Not again! Other dads are *always* home on Saturdays ... and you *promised* to take me to the display at the Falconry Centre this afternoon.'

Tom fixed her with a straight look. 'I've told you before that when I make a promise I mean it, but duty overrides everything. Those other dads have jobs that end each Friday teatime. Mine is different. I'm really sorry about the Falconry Centre. I was looking forward to it, too, but what I have to do instead is extremely important, Beth.'

Nora said in her no-nonsense voice, 'Pick up your cutlery and finish your meal. It's not the end of the world. There's ice-cream cake for pudding, and if you take that grumpy look from your face you can join our shopping spree. *Demoiselle* is opening a branch in town today and promise half-price bargains.'

Gina and Maggie cried accusingly, 'You never told us!'

Nora smiled. 'I was keeping it a secret because Beth would have wanted to come with us instead of watching the birds of prey. Dad would have been bitterly disappointed.'

'I still am,' he said, playing along with his wife's peace-making. 'But Beth at least has an exciting alternative. I have *work*.'

His youngest, sunny again, said dismissively, 'You wouldn't like *Demoiselle*. It's full of girls' things. And they play pop music ever so *loud*,' she added slyly, knowing he avoided trendy boutiques like the plague. Then she relented and patted his hand. 'I'll give you two spoonfuls of my ice-cream cake to make up for missing the falcons.'

He left his womenfolk stacking the dishwasher and predicting exactly what they might buy at *Demoiselle*. He actually was disappointed about missing the falcons. It was a unisex kind of entertainment rather than the more usual girly outings they chose. He had told Nora to expect him whenever – a message she understood all too well.

Out in the driveway he was about to set his car in motion when his mobile rang. It was the pathologist who had examined the bodies of Brian New and Colin White. He got straight to the point.

'Heard on the grapevine your murdered officer had been snatched from a vasectomy clinic several hours after receiving the treatment. The corpse I examined hadn't had a vasectomy. It would have been noted in my initial report, but I've now taken another look at it just to be certain. They either lied to you at that clinic, or their patient was there masquerading as Colin White for some reason.'

Nine

Browning got it right, thought Max as the driver took the car through lanes bordered by trees hung with lambs-tails, past thatched villages rioting with spring flowers. It *was* good to be in England in April. Pushing to the back of his mind the reason for his visit he sat enjoying the bleats of lambs and the song of larks ascending. He travelled the world but was always happy to be home again. In his native land, that was. He had no actual home.

Philip Simpson had last night greeted Max warmly but, after the usual news exchanged by servicemen meeting again after a few years, switched to the matter in hand.

'Weird business you've got caught up in. I had to do a hell of a lot of fast talking to set up this exhumation; persuade the authorities a death in Hong Kong might be related to two in Germany. Our involvement was heavily questioned, but I convinced them that Barker was still on the regimental strength until his terminal leave expired.'

'Unfortunately, he expired first, and I'm damn certain he was murdered by lethal injection like the others.'

'If you're wrong, there'll be some extremely

penetrating questions asked all round.'

Max was well aware of the gamble he was taking. Until the exhumed body had been examined SIB had no definite link to investigate, and even if his suspicions proved correct Barker had been killed in Hong Kong so the case would be handled by the Home Office and the Chinese police. Yet such proof would raise the portcullis blocking the solution to the mystifying killings in Germany.

Barker was buried at a small village church served, along with two similar small, ancient places of worship, by a travelling cleric. There was no service there that Sunday, so the early morning opening of the recent grave would not disconcert members of the congregation.

'The faithful who keep these lovely old churches going probably amount to no more than ten dear old ladies in flowered hats and white gloves,' observed Philip Simpson as their driver pulled up in the lane beside a heavy wooden gate.

Max grunted. 'They're the backbone of this country. The more I see of modern family life – or lack of it – the more I appreciate dear old ladies and their moral code.'

They trod up five mossy steps leading to the small burial ground at the rear of the church, where canvas screens had been erected around two men already tackling the task of uncovering the coffin. It was then possible to see the discreet dark van and two cars parked in the lane on the far side of the graveyard. The officials overseeing proceedings, and the

216

soberly dressed pair who would accompany the body to where it would be examined, stood around talking desultorily.

They gave brief nods as Max and Colonel Simpson joined them, making the military men well aware of their unpopularity over this action. Their presence was, however, necessary to check with the others that the correct coffin was lifted from the earth.

The diggers soon uncovered the brass-trimmed box and made ready to lift it. Philip had just commented that the recent dry spell had thankfully made the business relatively easy, when the sound of sobbing caused everyone to turn. Beside the gate some fifty yards away a thin, grey-haired woman was being comforted by another as they gazed at the activity beneath the small tent.

'Barker's widowed mother,' Philip murmured. 'She lives in the village with her spinster sister. We had to inform her of this and why it was necessary, but I didn't expect her to turn out at the crack of dawn to witness something certain to be stressful. I'd better have a word.'

Max watched him walk across to the two women and talk to them, making a point of standing so that he blocked their view of the coffin now resting on the ground. Within a few minutes, Mrs Barker and her elderly sister turned away and descended the steps to the lane. Philip returned in time to check the brass plate that named Harold Barker as the deceased person who should rightly be beneath the lid.

'We now have to wait for the result of the examination,' the senior man said as they watched the coffin being loaded in the hearse-like van and the civilian officials settling in their cars ready to move off. 'If you're right, Max, I don't look forward to telling that woman her son was murdered. She doesn't look strong enough to take any more emotional pain.'

Feeling culpable, Max recounted the facts of Christine White's breakdown and the possible future for her and her young family. 'I'm sorry to put Mrs Barker through this, but I'm determined to get whoever condemned them to that, and who probably watched an innocent young nurse get in to a car with a man about to die at the wheel. That also rates as murder in my book.'

'In mine, too, Max. Let's attack those flasks of coffee and ham rolls in the car *en route* to this meeting with two of Barker's friends that I've set up. Talking to them now will save you another trip over here if your theory's proved right in a day or two.'

Four hours later they arrived outside a thatched country pub eight miles from the RCR's home base, where they would meet two men for an informal talk over pre-lunch drinks. After the business of early morning, Max wished he had simply come for a social get-together in convivial company. Laughing families were at bench tables in the colourful garden; children were playing Pooh-sticks on the ornamental bridge crossing a narrow

218

stream. Unbidden came the thought of whether Alexander Rydal might have played the game with his friends if there had not been a thunderstorm on that fatal day. What would the boy have been like? Would he have attracted a large number of friends, or be rather more reserved – like one boy who now stood slightly aside watching the rest have fun?

'Max! Something wrong?'

Philip's question brought him from maudlin introspection, and he forced a smile. 'I take back what I said about modern families. Just look at these having fun.'

It was not difficult to pick out the men they had come to meet. Soldiers, like policemen, were easily recognized. Don Jackman and Mitch Donnegan introduced themselves and accepted Max's offer of a refill. He studied them while waiting for the drinks at the bar.

Jackman, who had supported Barker's mother when the body was flown home, and at the funeral, had bright red hair, pale eyes and an air of melancholy. His companion, blond with startlingly green eyes, was the friend whose e-mail to Ben Steele had given rise to this development. Quite the opposite in appearance, Mitch nevertheless reminded Max of that other subaltern. Young, energetic and eager to participate in a murder investigation. It was he who broached the subject as Max put the tray of drinks on their table.

'You really believe Harry's death is linked to those in Germany?'

'It's possible,' Max replied guardedly. 'We'll have more evidence to support that tomorrow.'

'Or otherwise,' put in Don Jackman. 'I met Colin White on a course several years ago. As I recall he talked almost non-stop about mountains, but not enough to inspire murderous urges. Apart from his hobby-horse, he was pleasant enough. Certainly not a natural target for a killer, any more than Harry was.'

'Or Sergeant New,' agreed Max. 'General consensus is that the victims were popular, thoroughly nice men. I suspect you'll say the same about Harry Barker.'

'I didn't know him intimately,' offered Mitch. 'I've only been with the battalion a couple of years. Harry had a house in Amesbury so he was rarely in the Mess, apart from dining-in nights. When I joined he was in the throes of marital warfare. Discovered his wife had a lover on the other side of town. Took it badly.'

Unaware of the feelings he was rousing in Max, he continued with energy. 'There were two kids he doted on. He took compassionate leave to try to sort it, but there was a divorce last summer. Hit him hard. It was obvious even to those of us on the sidelines.'

Don Jackman nodded. 'Harry and I were reasonably close. Had a mutual interest in rugby and watersports. I know there are two sides to every situation, but I reckon he was the injured party. He made a number of concessions, but she wasn't prepared to meet him even halfway.'

He took a long drink from his pint, then sighed. 'He transferred from Second Battalion six months after they got back from Hong Kong because Marge wanted to be near her mother in Amesbury. The woman had had a severe attack of pneumonia shortly after being widowed, and claimed she needed caring for. Harry said she was a tough old bird perfectly able to manage on her own. He wasn't blind to the way Marge seized the opportunity to have a baby-sitting granny handy.' He gave Max a dark glance. 'That's how come she met her new husband. Granny collected the kids from school while Marge was at the local leisure centre flirting with the muscle-bound gym instructors.'

'Had she always been a flirt?' asked Max struggling with visions of a muscle-bound corporal with designs on his own wife.

'I heard she was very fond of a good time,' offered Mitch, eager to contribute. 'Always partying. Bought so many clothes the wardrobe wouldn't shut. Liked spending money. His money, of course.' He smiled wryly. 'Mess gossip.'

Philip Simpson, who had been quietly drinking, tackled Don Jackman at that point. 'You weren't in Hong Kong with Barker?'

'No, sir, I've always served with the First Battalion. But I believe the trouble between Harry and his wife began out there.'

'In what way?'

He sucked his lips reflectively. 'The life

221

suited Marge down to the ground. Clubs, dances, beach and tennis parties, shops overflowing with luxury goods, an *amah* to cook and clean. They'd only been married a year when they went out there. She was in seventh heaven until she realized the party was over.'

'Why was that?' Philip prompted.

'Harry saw how wild Marge was getting and put his foot down. Tightened the purse-strings, I guess.'

'Her behaviour wouldn't have done his prospects much good, either. Wives can often make or break a man's career.'

Don nodded. 'Harry once hinted that he'd been warned on the quiet on that subject. He should have got his majority a year ago, but Marge's affair was no secret and Harry was stressed to the hilt.'

Max frowned. 'Men have survived worse and gone on to reach a high rank.'

'Harry had become disenchanted with life; with the army. He was deeply depressed during those final months. I suppose that's why I managed to believe in his death from a massive heart attack. It happens to people younger than he who appear to be perfectly fit. It's murder I find hard to accept.'

'You may not have to,' said Max quickly. 'Our thinking might prove to be totally wrong.'

Jackman was clearly sceptical. 'He was mugged in Hong Kong – the final act to push his stress level over the top. Two men are murdered in Germany, one during a night out and the other after a nip and tuck at a private clinic. What's to link them?'

'How do you know those details?' challenged Max with a touch of acid.

Mitch explained that he and Ben Steele had been discussing the subject by e-mail. 'There was a four day gap between Harry's murder and the two in Germany. Long enough for the killer to fly from Honkers to carry them out. We haven't yet deduced the link between our man and your pair, but there must be one.'

Philip asked, 'Did Captain Barker make generally known his intention to spend some of his terminal leave in Hong Kong?'

'I knew he was, sir, so I think it was general knowledge that he had decided to revisit old haunts before settling down in a new life.'

'I thought it was a strange decision as that time in Hong Kong had apparently put a strain on his marriage and career,' said Don Jackman. 'He didn't have any definite plans for his future aside from that return to the East. In retrospect it seems as if some premonition told him his future would end there, doesn't it?'

Growing tense, Max said, 'Did you never question why he was going back?'

'Never got a satisfactory answer. Something he *had* to do, he said. He was in a very volatile mood during those last weeks. Acted completely out of character.'

Max sensed clarity within reach and urged the man to explain.

'He was hyped-up, restless, couldn't concentrate. He had a calendar in his office with each day crossed through with thick red pencil. Like a small kid counting off the days to Christmas. And he began drinking heavily.'

'That was unusual?' Philip asked.

'Very. Harry was no toper.'

Max's guts were receiving very clear messages now. Here was a perfect soldier who had begun going to the dogs. Because he was about to return to Hong Kong? Certain the answer lay in that former colony, Max pressed Jackman further.

'Are you sure your friend gave no hint of this thing he had to do in Hong Kong? Please think carefully. It could be important.'

The young captain shook his head. 'He came out with a lot of wild things while under the influence. About Marge and the gym instructor. Slanderous stuff, really. Claimed he could have shown Marge a thing or two never seen inside a gym, if *they* hadn't stopped him. As I said, it was the drink doing the talking. Didn't make much sense, on the whole. We gave him the usual mess send-off. I got him home in a taxi and put him to bed. He was rambling about becoming a free man at last. Said they couldn't shut him up any longer because he was out of it. Said he would go to Fanling to sort out what really happened on that border patrol.'

Max gave a long sigh of revelation. A border patrol in the New Territories. A small number in rough terrain, alert for signs of illegal

224

entrants and suspicious behaviour by the Communist soldiers within grenade-throwing distance. Harold Barker, Simon Kington, Colin White and Brian New together on such a patrol. Find the fifth man and all would fall into place.

Spring has sprung, thought Jack Fanshawe, MI5 Operative, admiring the wall of red and pink rhododendrons, the floral 'parasols' of almond blossoms, the rioting clematis and the vivid yellow daffodils growing wild all along the grassy bank sloping to tailored lawns. On a warm sunny day like this surveillance duty was a pleasure. Much better than nocturnal stake-outs in a steamed-up car in mid-winter. Nice and peaceful, clean air, and freshly baked currant buns with mugs of real coffee from the Kingtons' cook.

Passing a huge shrub covered in blue flowers he didn't know the name of, and taking the narrow red-brick path towards the front entrance on his third circular tour of the grounds, Fanshawe grew immediately alert. Someone was moving around just ahead.

Putting his radio close to his mouth he said very quietly, 'Jeff, movement by the gates. Could be a diversion. Keep an eye on the other areas.'

'Got it,' came the reply from his colleague taking a tea break in the room with six screens showing most aspects of the extensive grounds.

Edging cautiously towards the ornate

remote-controlled gates, weapon hand at the ready, Fanshawe's line of vision dropped to a small face pressed to a gap between the gilded bars.

'There's no handle on them,' the small boy complained.

'Do the people here know you?'

'Well, not really. Their boys sometimes play cricket with the village team.'

'So what're you doing here?' Fanshawe demanded, geared up for anything from a gang swarming over the wall to a van crashing through the gates.

The boy thrust a large brown envelope between the bars. 'An old lady asked me to bring this. She was on the old river bridge sort of panting, like Rosie when she's been chasing rabbits. Said this letter was urgent, but she couldn't come all the way up here with that terrible pain in her side. I said should I get Doc Meyer from his cottage, but she said no. Gave me two pounds and told me to hurry.' He waggled the envelope. 'Here it is.'

Fanshawe relaxed as he took it. He understood this now.

The boy's freckled face turned slightly pink. 'Mum'll say I shouldn't have taken her money.'

'I shouldn't worry, son,' said the father of two boys, with a smile. 'Old ladies like that often have more than they let on. I'll see this is delivered up at the house.'

'Useless going after the old lady, Jeff,' he

said after handing the envelope to his boss. 'She/he would have legged it as soon as the kid turned the corner. This lot are tricky. Nothing we could trace with our technology gismos, just an old-fashioned fake pensioner and a gullible small boy.'

'Sherlock Holmes would approve,' Trivett mumbled through a mouthful of currant bun.

Sir Chetwin was obliged to open the missive in the presence of Senior MI5 operative Ralph Robbins. Once again it contained a single A4 sheet and a photograph of Simon backed by a pair of hands holding a copy of that day's *Sunday Telegraph*. The letter was uncompromizing.

Put the cash in a wheeled travel bag like those used by air crew. Take it to Heathrow Terminal 2 Arrivals Hall tomorrow (Monday) at 10:45. Stand holding a board with the name HEREWARD printed on it. Keep your eyes on the arriving passengers. DON'T LOOK ROUND AT ANYONE. Once we've checked the money, the passenger you want will arrive.

We are not fools. If you do anything stupid, bring anyone with you, fail to follow these instructions to the letter, the deal is off and the passenger will suffer. We're sure you fully understand that threat. So will that man Robbins and his tame poodles.

Sir Chetwin glanced up tight-lipped after reading the message aloud. 'So much for your "low profile" presence! They even know your identity. I want you all off my property and out of these vital negotiations right now. My wife and I *will* have our son back unharmed *whatever it costs*! I've promised Tara he'll be safe; my grandsons need their father. This is a family concern only. I'll not tolerate your interference.'

Ralph Robbins remained implacably un-ruffled by this commanding managing-directorial speech. 'We've been through this before, sir. When a British officer privvy to confidential and restricted military data is abducted, national security is threatened. Our remit is to protect it by removing the threat. Your son will certainly understand that.'

Lady Kington was gazing fixedly at the photograph. 'I remember this picture of Simon,' she said slowly. 'It was taken a few months ago in Hamburg. All the delegates had to be snapped for identity purposes.' She gripped her husband's arm. 'He sent us a copy, Chet, remember? I ticked him off. Said he looked too stern, and he said...' Her voice faltered momentarily. 'He said he'd put on his "important" look to impress the other dele-gates.' She held the photograph out to Robbins. 'That wasn't taken today.'

Shaken by Molly's distress and by the guilt of not remembering having seen the picture before, Sir Chetwin lost some of his bombast and sank on a chair.

The Inspector studied the photograph. 'I

expect, ma'am, we'll find this one is another computer-fit using an old picture of your son and superimposing the headlines.' He addressed Sir Chetwin. 'This has to be carried through as we agreed. The notes have all been marked. We'll place a tracker in the travel bag. Our men are expert at blending with a crowd. They won't be spotted, I promise you.'

'Huh!'

'We have done this before, sir,' he reminded his host. 'Armed sieges, hijacked aircraft. We know how to handle far more complex situations than this successfully.'

Lady Kington looked Robbins in the eye. 'There's no guarantee Simon is alive.'

'No, ma'am, or that he'll be released in exchange for this one-off payment. That's why it's essential to follow whoever collects the bag. They'll do that openly, knowing we won't move in then. They'll have devised a slick getaway plan, but we'll be ready for it. If they're smart they'll ditch the bag in the hope that we'll follow the tracker.' He gave one of his pale smiles. 'We have back-up methods known only to us. You *must* let us deal with this.'

She walked across to lay her hand on her husband's shoulder. 'For once you must delegate, Chet. Let the experts do the job. For Simon's sake.' Then she glanced back at Robbins. 'Hereward is our son's third name.'

Tom went in fighting mood, and with a

photograph of Colin White, to meet Boris Mann at the Reinhardt Klinik that Saturday afternoon. The rear car park was empty of other vehicles; the clinic looked closed up. The German policeman was not with his car, so Tom left his and walked round the building to the front entrance. He found Mann in the reception hall talking to an attractive brunette in a cream wool dress.

Greetings were exchanged, Tom courteously speaking in German, Mann courteously replying in English. 'This is *Fräulein* Adler, Mr Black. She is here to answer the telephone only.'

Tom shook the girl's limp hand. 'I wish to speak to the Reinhardts,' he said in his best German.

'They are away for the weekend. I have just explained this to *Herr* Mann,' she said in barely accented English. 'We do not have patients on Saturday or Sunday.'

'Never?'

'It is usual not to do so. I cannot help you.'

'You can give me a contact number for your employers.'

A wary light appeared in her dark eyes. 'I cannot help you.'

Boris Mann spoke swiftly in German, and she replied in similar manner. Tom understood the gist of it. Mann said she must have a means of contacting the Reinhards in an emergency; she denied this was an emergency. He insisted they were there on official police business. *Fräulein* Adler argued that as

230

she was the only person there, and she had done nothing wrong, she did not see any reason for the presence of policemen.

Mann took Tom aside. 'We cannot force her to give us a contact number. I will tell you we are conducting an investigation into the business here, and could have much information on this soon. I suggest you return on Monday.'

Tom said forcibly, 'By Monday they could have destroyed any useful evidence. I don't believe that girl. I suspect the Reinhardts are up there in their apartment, lying low.'

The young German shrugged. 'I cannot burst in without a warrant. It is not a matter of life or death.'

'That's where you're wrong, chum,' Tom snapped, all courtesy abandoned. 'One of our officers is dead, and the Reinhardts lied in their teeth about him. That girl can't see any reason for the presence of police? Our man was either murdered on these premises, or someone came here masquerading as him. I need to know the truth about it. That's the reason for *my* presence. What's yours?'

Mann looked curious. 'You think now your victim was not at the clinic?'

'That's what I'm bloody trying to check.' Fighting his frustration, Tom lowered his voice. 'The Reinhardts told us Captain White booked in here at ten a.m. on Monday last, and they performed the minor op that same afternoon.'

'That is correct.'

'Wrong! The corpse had not had a vasectomy. When we received the initial path. report his car hadn't been discovered here. We weren't at that time looking for that kind of proof. It now throws a huge cloak of suspicion over this place. There are two suppositions to consider. The patient who received the treatment and occupied the room we were shown earlier had, for some unknown reason, passed himself off as a British officer named Colin White. The Reinhardts were very casual in their dealings with him, by their own admission, if you recall. That's why I need to look at those files the secretary has supposedly locked away before vanishing for a long weekend.'

'We have already taken away the locked cabinets,' Mann said swiftly. 'The contents are being examined closely. There seems to be much that is not in order.'

Tom was furious. 'When were you proposing to bring *us* in on that? This is a combined investigation.'

The tall German's eyes glinted coldly. 'The presence of his automobile is not proof that your officer was ever inside this clinic as you have already admitted. We have suspicions of a major crime taking place here. That is our priority.'

'And mine is to get to the bottom of the lies I was told about a murdered man whose widow has just tried to kill herself through grief,' Tom replied, his equally cold glinting eyes level with Mann's.

Somewhat stiffly, the other man changed direction. 'You said there are two suppositions to consider. You have said only one.'

Tom silently counted to five. 'The second is that Captain White did come here, was killed before the op could take place, and the Reinhardts are involved up to their necks in the killing.'

Mann nodded enigmatically. 'When our investigation is completed it may become clear what really occurred. For now you should show *Fräulein* Adler the picture you said me you would bring today.'

In his anger the German's English had suffered slightly. Tom controlled his own. SIB policy was to maintain cordial relations with their local counterparts. However, he vowed to tackle Klaus Krenkel when he got back to Section Headquarters about the major crime Mann was hinting at. To hell with cordiality.

Tight-lipped, Tom walked back to re-enter the reception hall. The hostile Adler was sitting behind the glossy white desk flipping through a glamour magazine. She did not glance up as Tom arrived by the desk. How could a woman look so inviting yet behave so frigidly?

Lowering the photograph of Colin White over the page she was so deliberately studying, Tom asked coldly, 'Have you ever seen this man here at the clinic?'

She nodded, not raising her face to look at him. 'I put him in room twenty-seven.'

'Do you remember his name?'

233

She kept her eyes on the magazine. 'Mr White.'

After lengthy silent inner battling, Tom turned and walked away. The woman's body language suggested she was nervous. Afraid, even. He felt instinctively that she was innocently caught up in whatever her employers were up to behind their legitimate facade, and was uncertain what to do in this worrying situation.

Standing on the forecourt, gazing across lawns to the tall trees screening the building from the road, Tom's thoughts ran riot. Did White die because he inadvertently discovered something that the Reinhardts would kill to keep secret; discovered it before the scheduled op was performed? It was one explanation, but it would make the investigation even more complex. Dear God, it was like an octopus with tentacles stretching out in so many directions.

Max was now all-fired over a Hong Kong link between the two murders and Kington's uncertain fate, yet how could that possibly tie in with criminal activity in a medical clinic in Germany? And who could possibly be behind it? Only an octopus itself, able to reach out wherever it wished simultaneously.

After a few stilted words with Boris Mann, Tom drove away in a dark mood convinced they were totally up the creek with everything. Brian New had most probably fallen foul of a local drug dealer, Colin White had poked his nose into something he shouldn't have, and Simon Kington would shortly be exchanged, dead or alive, for one million pounds. Oh yes, and Harold Barker had simply succumbed to a heart attack in Hong Kong. There you are, cases solved!

He abandoned his intention of confronting Klaus Krenkel. He would only stonewall like Mann. To hell with the *Polizei*! It was Saturday, when men with nine to five jobs were relaxing at home. He found the girls and Nora were still out. Buying up *Demoiselle*, no doubt. Having fun, he told himself morosely. Certainly not thinking about him having to do this rotten, stinking job day after day, night after night.

By the time his womenfolk returned festooned with carrier bags and glowing with satisfaction, Tom had sunk quite a few cans from their drinks store. Nora gave him an assessing once-over, but said nothing. She heeded the look that told her silence was her best policy.

Ten

The Arrivals Hall at Heathrow's Terminal 2 at 10:45 that Monday morning was teeming with flight-weary passengers and eager greeters. The atmosphere was hot, clamorous and heavy with the staleness of stressed humanity.

On his frequent journeys by air Sir Chetwin either used his private jet or was driven to the airport in the Daimler, swiftly checked in and fast-tracked to the first class or VIP lounge. To stand now in this jostling, malodorous mêlée holding up a board bearing his son's third name, alongside hired drivers and firms' reps who did this regularly, added to the emotion building in him.

Over the past four days he had faced many truths, the major one being parental affection for his son – his and Molly's only child. She would have liked more, but he had been wholly concerned with creating a business empire. If Simon should be lost, that all-con-suming drive would become meaningless. If Simon should be lost, Molly would need his support as never before and he would give it. She was presently summoning up that strength that had enabled him to rise to the top in his career, but this terrible crisis had penetrated his selfishness to allow him to see the distress beneath her outward calm. They had both long ago acknowledged the risks and dangers of their son's chosen profession. His death in action would be a dreadful blow, but an honourable passing they would eventually accept. Murder at the hands of mercenary thugs would haunt them forever.

The marked banknotes in the bugged black luggage were there beside him, but he kept his gaze on the stream of arriving passengers, as instructed. He had several times been jostled by people eager to identify and welcome friends or family, yet slight movements with his right foot told him it was still there. His mouth was dry, his heartbeat so heightened it created a nagging pain in his chest. Ralph Robbins had sworn his men would not be spotted, but Sir Chetwin had little faith in his assurances. He should have insisted on their non-participation. A business giant who could tame international rivals had allowed these shadowy men from a secret organization to dictate to him over this most vital issue. That last communication showed the devils knew their demand to keep the authorities out of the negotiations had not been heeded. They would also know that men were watching that bag beside him; watching for whoever came for it.

What would they do to Simon because their rules had not been observed? He had endangered his boy's life through lack of resolution when it was most needed. The pain in his chest was getting worse. Slipping a hand inside his jacket he pressed it against the starched shirt in an attempt to ease it. Time was dragging past and the bag was still there near his feet. The pick-up must have been aborted; they would punish Simon for his father's bungling of the opportunity to release him. *Dear God, forgive me for failing my son, as I've failed him all his life.*

He was suddenly surrounded by a group of screaming girls in garish clothes with hair dyed in rainbow shades who clutched enormous puce, heart-shaped balloons declaring everlasting love for someone named Dino. The screams increased to piercing volume as they surged forward, ducking beneath the tapes marking a clear corridor for arriving passengers. The onward thrust knocked the board Sir Chetwin was now holding with one hand. It fell to the ground and was kicked several feet from where he stood by a stampede of brightly coloured trainers.

Panicking, he bent to grope for it. They would think he wasn't there with the money if they couldn't see the board with HERE-WARD printed on it. As he reached out, a shaft of pain ran up his left arm causing him to gasp and double up. The floor now only inches from his face appeared to be undulating violently. The female screams had multiplied. Perspiration broke out on his body and brow as he fought against collapsing on to that heaving surface.

A hand gripped his left arm, another slipped beneath his right armpit. A voice said, 'Let me help you up, sir.'

In a daze he allowed himself to be eased upright despite sensing that any movement would worsen the pain. He turned blurred eyes up to see a black man in smart chauffeur's uniform. He had been nearby with a card bearing a crest and the legend SILVER-LAKE HOLDINGS. He looked concerned as he held Sir Chetwin steady.

'Are you all right?'

'Just a little ... the *board*,' he panted in distress. 'Must have the board.'

'I'll get it. Don't worry. Can you stand on your own?'

'Yes ... yes. The board!'

The chauffeur left him to walk the several feet to where the board lay face down. There now appeared to be twice as many people, all indistinct and swaying. A mass of puce balloons floated above him. The balloons were all screaming. He felt desperately ill.

Then he realized the money had gone. Fear rushed through him. They had taken the marked notes in the tagged bag. What, in God's name, must he do now? Think. Think! *They* had told him to watch for the passenger he wanted to see. Robbins had told him something different. What should he do?

The black man gave him the board; began speaking. Sir Chetwin heard nothing but the screaming balloons. His torso was filling with pain; perspiration coursed down his face.

Watch for the passenger you want. They had the money. They would release his son. Hold up the board so Simon would see it and come straight to him. He couldn't lift his arms. *He couldn't lift his arms!*

Through his fear and pain the distressed father heard a booming, echoing voice above the screaming balloons.

'This is a security announcement. You are asked to leave this building immediately. This is a security announcement. Everybody must leave the terminal immediately.'

Sir Chetwin's legs folded as the pain dominated all else. He fell beneath the multicultural swarm heading for the doors.

Monday promised to be a heavy day. At the morning briefing Max offered evidence for his belief that the motive for the murders of Brian New and Colin White lay in events surrounding a border patrol in the New Territories.

'I'm confident we'll hear today, tomorrow at the latest, that Harold Barker was killed by lethal injection. I've arranged for details of the toxin to be distributed to the School of Oriental Medicine and to purveyors of Chinese and other Eastern remedies. If we get it identified that could give us the source. I'd say it's unlikely to be Germany. Possibly the UK. More probably Hong Kong. Which would then suggest that after disposing of Barker, whom his colleague Don Jackman told me was "going to find out what *really*

240

happened on that border patrol", our killer flew here to silence the rest.'

'So the killer was also on the suspect patrol?' asked Connie Bush, her scepticism very apparent.

Max gave her a shrewd look. 'Or he found out what they'd been up to and held that over them to make them toe the line, become model soldiers.'

Piercey smirked. 'That's a bit far-fetched, isn't it, sir? Even supposing this patrol took place only a matter of weeks before the handover, that's a hell of a long time to maintain a hold over several others.'

'Yes, it is a hell of a long time, and that hold was about to be broken because Barker had done what he intended and uncovered the truth. We have to find out what that is,' Max insisted. 'You've been in this job long enough to know nothing's too far-fetched where human nature is concerned, Sergeant.'

Heather Johnson was frowning. 'Are we still regarding Major Kington as a third victim?'

Max sighed heavily. He honestly did not know. 'Until we have evidence that he's turned up safe and well, I believe we must.'

'He's in a shallow grave on-base,' murmured Piercey. 'Soon as the ransom's paid he'll be dug up and left somewhere obvious.'

'As I indicated, nothing's too far-fetched,' agreed Max, beginning to believe Piercey could be right. 'Mr Black has received notification through channels he prefers to keep to himself that negotiations for Simon Kington's return are going ahead today.'

'So we're waiting on three vital pieces of info,' concluded Connie Bush, counting them off on her fingers. 'Report on exhumed body of Barker, identification of the toxin by some Oriental apothecary, and the release, or otherwise, of the missing Major.'

'Make that four,' put in Tom sharply. 'The *Polizei* are hinting there's something deeply dodgy about the Reinhardt Klinik.'

'As if we didn't already know,' said Heather Johnson in disgust.

'We'll be chasing them today,' he promised, giving her a quelling look. 'Colin White had not had the op they claimed to have performed on him, so there's no proof he was there for medical treatment. Forensic evidence shows he had occupied that room, but he could have been held there before being killed.'

'The Reinhardts surely won't in any way tie in with the Hong Kong theory, if we're really going with that,' Beeny pointed out heavily, looking thoroughly unconvinced.

Piercey was still wearing an expression of incredulity. 'So our killer is ex-RCR and living in Honkers. Harold Barker goes on terminal leave and the first thing he does is fly out there to drag from a former colleague what threat he's been holding over the members of a years-old patrol. Is that the scenario, sir?'

'More or less,' said Max tautly.

'Why? What's in it for Barker? He's finished

242

with the army. Why risk his life by opening up old wounds?'

'If we consulted a medium we could get the answers from beyond the grave,' Max snapped, having asked himself that many times over the past thirty-six hours. 'As it is, we have to do it the hard way. I want you all to question anyone who was with the RCR in Hong Kong. That'll exclude those who joined after ninety-seven. Find out who had ever been on a border patrol with the murder victims. Check out anything interesting or dangerous. Did they apprehend smugglers or illegal immigrants? Were they attacked by Red troops? The evidence will be there. Keep digging until you find it.'

Back in his office with Tom prior to setting out for the Cumberlands' base, Max pulled a wry face. 'I hope to God I'm right on this.' When Tom said nothing, he asked, 'Are you among the doubters?'

'I don't know what to think and, to be honest, our chances of discovering if there'd ever been a patrol comprising Kington, Barker, White and New, and the man who's killing them off, are slim to the point of non-existence. By your reasoning, the killer is now a civilian living in Hong Kong. After your call yesterday I spent a couple of hours checking everyone who'd been discharged in the last six, seven years. They all had registered home addresses in the UK or Ireland. Any one of them could have moved on to Honkers. Trying to trace them will take days, possibly weeks.

'Another point. If Barker went out there to discover what went on during a patrol, it means *he* wasn't a member of it. In 1997 Simon Kington had just got his captaincy, Colin White was a raw subaltern and Brian New a lance-corporal. It would be unusual to have two officers on a routine border patrol, wouldn't it?'

'Not if it was a covert operation. Kington might have been involved in confidential activity even then.'

'Confidential activity that changed a pack of men into paragons, sir?' he asked with a touch of scepticism.

Max straightened from his perch on the corner of his desk and buttoned his jacket ready to depart. 'Unless Harry Potter waved a magic wand over them one dark night, that's the best explanation I can come up with right now. I bloody know the truth lies with the Cumberland Riflemen. Or Rifle *persons*, as Piercey would insist we call them. Who knows, Tom, it might be a case of *cherchez la femme*.'

It was a pleasant evening, sunny with a light breeze and the scent of flowers wafting on the air. Ben wished he could be driving Sonja's silver Ferrari – better still one of his own, scarlet probably – rather than the Ford he planned to swap for something jazzy soon. He'd also have liked to have Sonja beside him, except that this was a journey he had to make on his own.

She had met him again last night in response to his sexy e-mail, and thoughts of her had flitted in and out of his regimental duties today, disconcerting him at the most inappropriate times. Luckily, Roger Kennedy had not crossed his path to catch him smiling into space when he should be concentrating. Now the CO was back at the helm minor boot putting-in might be forgotten. This evening's adventure could not be counted as such. Could it?

As he turned on to a quiet road running through farmland and bordered on the right by a silky-smooth canal, Ben's spirits rose. His detecting prowess was surely equal to anyone in SIB. He had easily got from Sonya the info he needed. Admittedly, he had been naked in her bed at the time, which method SIB could hardly employ, but he had been cunning enough not to arouse her suspicion. He smiled in to space again at the memory of what he *had* aroused in her.

He was so lost in erotic reverie his destination loomed up to take him by surprise as he raced past the entrance to a tree-lined driveway. He pulled up a hundred metres beyond this and reviewed his options. There was certain to be some form of security, but more likely only activated after dark. The house probably stood well clear of trees so anyone approaching in daylight would be seen. Anyone save a soldier trained to creep up on the enemy!

He got out, locked his car and began walking back to the anonymous entrance. There was no wall, fence or railing enclosing the grounds to advertise the presence of a large property, just the coppice that had lined the road for the last two or three miles. Seeing a gap twenty-five metres from the driveway, Ben slipped through it and trod carefully over the tangled floor beneath trees sprouting new foliage. He had not gone as far as camouflaging his face, but his working uniform should blend well with this area not reached by the dying sun.

The house appeared sooner than he expected. In the old Germanic style it had two small turrets rising from the east and west walls. Ben's imagination ran riot, visualizing an attacking horde in chain mail on armoured horses, and the local baron's men waiting to pour burning oil from the parapet while flaming arrows rained down from the turrets. He grinned. Wolf was only a pharmaceutical baron and the attacking horde consisted of one junior officer.

He halted at the edge of the trees, pondering that thought. He was not attacking, of course, just reconnoitring. He was not really sure why, other than to satisfy curiosity over the evident closeness with its owner of a woman who should rightly be anxious, distraught, sitting beside the telephone waiting to hear the fate of her husband. Tara Kington had been altogether too relaxed and confident at the *Kaninchenstall* two nights ago.

And Gerhardt Wolf had been altogether too possessive of another man's wife. It had added up to something significant for Ben.

Crouching within the dappled shade, he studied the mansion. A wide gravelled forecourt gave an austere first impression. No bordering lawns, no shrubs, no ornamental fountain, but there were wide grassy walks alongside the eastern wall nearest to him and he could glimpse what looked like a lake at the rear of the house. The low sun gleamed on water stretching away for a considerable distance.

Ben remained there assessing all the aspects of Wolf's lair, growing ever more afraid he was on the right track. That Tara had arranged for Simon to be abducted and held here made sense of every angle save one. Why? The Kingtons were extremely wealthy, so it could not be for money, if it was Tara demanding the ransom. Of course, that could be the act of any shrewd operator seizing the main chance. If she and Wolf wanted to get together divorce was easy enough. Why stage this elaborate charade? Ben's brow furrowed. Could there be some legal impediment to a straightforward divorce; some financial penalty?

His thoughts darkened unacceptably. Staring at the distant view of the lake, Ben imagined Simon's weighted body lying at the bottom of it some distance out where it would never be found. Surely they had not!

He stood, unable to banish that image

however much he wanted to. To drop a body in that lake they would need a boat. If there was a boat-house on its banks it became a real possibility. Right now it was too light for covert surveillance. He decided to return to his car, wait for dusk, then make a recce. He had invariably earned top marks at Sandhurst for stealthy, undetected approaches. Wolf would never know he had been there.

Picking his way through the undergrowth to reach the road he had a sudden reversal of intent; wished he had left well alone. For some months he had lecherously admired Tara Kington; envied Simon. They had presented a picture of a glamorous, talented, devoted couple with an exciting future. How could he have been so wrong about her? Surely his judgement of Simon was correct. He was, after all, the victim here.

Lost in introspection Ben stepped out on to the road too late to notice a car approaching. He waited to let it pass before crossing, but it slowed then drew up beside him. A dark green Ferrari like Simon's. Tara was at the wheel.

'Ben! Whatever are you doing here?' she demanded sharply.

Even now he was slightly awed by her. 'Ran out of juice.'

'What about your spare can?'

'Used it last week and forgot to fill it again. Went up to the house to call a garage,' he invented swiftly.

She studied him closely. 'On a duty run, Ben?'

'Er...'

'You're in uniform.'

'Ah! Yes.'

'No mobile with you?'

'This is a dead area. No signal.'

'Which garage did you call?'

Tricky that. 'I didn't. No one at home.'

Her scrutiny this time made him even more uncomfortable. He must have been mad to think what he had. She was cultured, intelligent, the perfect army wife.

'Jump in!'

He stared at her.

'I'm about to visit the owners. They're friends of ours. They couldn't have heard your knock. I'll take you to the house and introduce you. They'll be only too delighted to let you call a garage. Jump in!'

Tell one lie, tell a dozen! Ben slid on to the seat beside her, feeling all kinds of a fool. Hordes of attackers, burning oil from the parapet, weighted body in the lake! How soon could he get back to his car and slink away?

Gerhardt Wolf appeared at the heavy oak door as Tara halted the car several feet from it. He made to come towards her, then pulled up when he saw Ben emerge from the passenger seat. His expression was a mix of puzzlement and concern. He spoke in German, which Ben easily understood.

'This terrible news you have. Does it concern this soldier?'

Tara ignored that, spoke in English. 'This is Lieutenant Steele, one of Simon's colleagues, Gerhardt. Poor lad has run out of petrol and his mobile isn't working. It was fortunate that I came along and saw him beside the road. He came up here to ask for use of your telephone, but says no one answered his knock.' She turned to Ben. 'Herr Wolf is the head of a pharmaceutical empire the size of Sir Chetwin's. The link behind our friendship.'

Wolf shook hands, said courteously, 'Please come inside. I'm sorry I did not hear your first arrival. You are, of course, very welcome to use the telephone.'

As they all entered the huge panelled hall, Tara said, 'Do give Ben a drink before he gets on to the garage. He's been on a duty run and looks about ready for one. And so am I. One of your special cocktails should do the trick.'

'Of course, my dear. Go through to the garden room. I will bring the drinks.'

On the point of demurring, Ben decided his story would hold more water if he went along with the offer. It would give him an opportunity to see more of the house. After the drink he would pretend to call a garage, then leave as nonchalantly as possible. The garden room gave a wonderful aspect of the lake bordered by pines and firs perfectly reflected in the still water now turning faintly pink in the westering sun. The garden was little more than large stone pedestal containers filled with flowers that stood like sentinels along a broad stone terrace. The owners clearly had no interest in lawns, shrubs and herbaceous borders. There was no sign of a boat-house, which deepened Ben's chagrin over his ridiculously fertile imagination.

Unable to think of suitable small talk, Ben silently gazed from the large square bay, once again wishing he had not embarked on this childish sleuthing. Tara could easily check whether or not he had been on a duty run, and here he was in battledress and hefty boots in an extremely elegant room having to live out a lie while accepting drinks from a high-flying German businessman.

Their host returned with three beautiful gold and ruby glasses on a tray. Tara said rather sharply, 'Do sit, Ben! You're not in a pub.'

He swung round, flushing at her reprimand, to find her sitting on a ruby velvet love-seat decorated with heavy tassels. Only then did he notice how pale she was, how strained her expression. The black trouser suit she wore was relieved only by a silver camisole and a diamond bar on the lapel.

'Yes, do please be comfortable,' said Gerhardt, handing a glass to Tara then to Ben. 'It is the cocktail hour so we must enjoy.'

Feeling out of place on the dainty chair, Ben forced a smile and sipped. The drink reminded him of the potent cocktails at the Ferrari Club. This man was a member so probably knew the ingredients to use. Wolf chatted lightly about his daughter's forth-coming performance of Bruch's violin concerto in a competition for young musicians, while Ben emptied his glass as fast as was socially acceptable without being obliged to participate in the conversation.

The cocktail was *extremely* potent. The effects were already creeping up on him. He would have to drive carefully after this, and if Tara intended returning tonight in the Ferrari she would have to stop at one drink. Ben stared goggle-eyed at the stone flower containers. They were starting to move around, dance up and down. Sudden nausea flooded over him, making him very giddy. Hot and unsteady. Wolf's voice sounded as if he were talking inside a barrel. Then it fell silent as the mobile in Ben's pocket rang.

Tara's voice floated to him, cold and brittle. 'Someone has managed to call you in this *dead area*, Ben.'

He tried to speak. Tried to stand. Night descended fast.

It had been a fruitless day. There had been no call from Philip Simpson with news of the exhumation of Harold Barker's body, and interviews with the RCR officers and other ranks who had known Barker had led nowhere. The summation of evidence suggested he had been an adequate rather than exceptional officer, neither disliked nor unduly admired by the men and women he served with. The one consistent comment was that he had a wife who caused him ongoing problems that had stunted his career, but he was too lovestruck to rid himself of her. All in all, a somewhat colourless character. Certainly not a man suddenly turned into a near saint. Very disappointing.

One question nagged Max as he walked in the cool of the evening. Why would such an easy-going man fly to Hong Kong the moment he left the army, for the sole purpose of investigating the truth about a patrol from ten years or so back? It seemed totally out of character. He frowned. Did that signify a change comparable to that which had overcome New, Colin White and the gifted Simon Kington?

His musing turned to that mystifying affair. The ransom was to have been paid this morning, but there had been no news on that, either. Tom had an old acquaintance at MI5 who was keeping him briefed on the situation, but contact was spasmodic. Max still believed Kington was a third victim. A fourth if Barker had died from a lethal injection. He wished to God the verdict on that would come through. The entire complex case was in limbo because he was so set on his Hong Kong theory. The only member of the team who was!

His frown deepened as he turned on to the path that ran alongside the brook. One of his favourite walks. This evening a number of local residents were taking the air so his deliberations were frequently interrupted by greetings from people used to meeting the tall, dark British soldier-policeman strolling alone in all weathers.

Restlessness and niggling doubts drove Max to push ahead beyond his usual turning point to where the path narrowed and few walkers ventured. Foliage closed in blocking his view of the water, but the swift passage of the brook could still be heard. The green dimness further lowered Max's spirits but he doggedly marched on.

Tom was not behind him right now. He was going along with it, displaying loyalty in front of the rest, but privately he thought it was moonshine. Tom was far more interested in events at the Reinhardt Klinik; questioning why Colin White had gone there. The two Germans were surely involved in something other than their surgical operations. White had possibly got unwittingly caught up in it. Yet it seemed unlikely the Reinhardts would have transported White's body back to the heath after killing him, leaving his car on their premises as red hot evidence.

Surprisingly, the path Max was following broke through to an attractive flower-dotted meadow across which, in the evening light, there looked to be a large house. He was curious. He thought he knew the area well enough, but that place must be well set back from the road. He must ask *Frau* Hahn about it.

Gazing at its pleasing lines and the stone walls mellowed by the pre-sunset golden glow, Max felt the usual stab of pain over the idyll in a cottage that he had shared with

Susan, ended so tragically. In that home across the meadow husband and wife, maybe children, would be sitting down to dinner or playing games before the infants' bedtime.

Would he and Susan be doing that if a corporal with bedroom eyes and a smooth tongue had not stopped to help when her car broke down? He sighed deeply. His job precluded a cosy domestic routine. He had often been called away at inopportune moments, had not arrived when expected, had stayed away all night at times that had been important to her. And, like now, his mind had more often than not been occupied with complex problems when she had hoped for a romantic evening.

He turned away from the charming vision of the house of impossible dreams and began retracing his steps. It was now quite dark beneath the narrow canopy of leaves so he trod carefully, still making fast progress towards the open area free of brambles. He had almost broken through to it when his mobile rang. He snatched it from his pocket in the hope that it would be Philip Simpson with the verdict on Barker he so much wanted.

'Rydal,' he said curtly.

'I've just heard from my contact with the Spooks,' said Tom with more enthusiasm than he had betrayed all day. 'The Kington affair grows ever more curious. Sir Chetwin complied with instructions; stood with the cash in a bag at his feet, watching the arrivals. The agents watching him saw a group of pop fans with balloons surge round him at zero hour, knocking to the ground the board he was holding. He stumbled and nearly fell, but was caught by a black guy in some kind of uniform.'

'Military uniform?' Max asked swiftly.

'Chauffeur. He'd been beside Kington for some time. They've taken him in for questioning, but he appears genuine. High-flying employers vouch for him. Someone grabbed the suitcase when Sir Chetwin stumbled. At that moment there was an urgent security announcement telling everyone to leave the terminal at once. There was a concerted rush for the doors.

'Airport Security say an anonymous call advised that a bomb had been left in the female toilets to explode in ten minutes. They had to take it seriously. A bag was found there by the bomb squad, but it was a child's backpack filled with crayons and a colouring book.'

'Did they follow the pick-up guy?' Max asked impatiently.

'To a squat in Islington. He's one of an opportunist gang who hang around airports and rail stations. They grab bags, scarves, leather gloves – anything they can sell on at market, including teddy bears or dolls temporarily neglected by kids. The airport police know most of them, but they're quick and usually get a good haul.' Tom chuckled. 'The guy had no idea the bag was bugged. He was gobsmacked when two uniforms from the Met collared him. He'd have been even more so if he'd had time to open the case and see what was in there.'

Totally intrigued, Max sat on one of the benches along the path as darkness slowly gathered. 'What conclusion have the Spooks reached?'

'A ransom drop fouled-up by a petty thief. They reckon the bomb warning was designed to cause chaos to ease their getaway.'

Max wagged his head. 'None of it adds up, Tom. They were already aware MI5 were on the case, so they'd know of their wide-ranging methods of tracking vehicles.'

'Fits our own theory of an amateur cashing in on Kington's disappearance, but they don't agree. They think it could be some kind of diversion, or a tightening of the screw. "We haven't got the money and we're getting impatient enough to turn nasty" could be their next message, upping the ante.'

'I don't buy that. I have a horrible feeling Piercey's right about a shallow grave on-base.'

'Snatch Lady Kington or the twins for cash, yes. A British officer engaged in defence plans, no. That's the mark of terrorists or some brand of obsessed looneys.'

'Either way he ends up dead.'

'Looks like his father might. Sir Chetwin's in Intensive Care on the critical list. He had a heart attack and was badly trampled by the crowd. It's touch and go.'

'His poor wife!'

'I understand she's the stoical type.'

'Maybe, but the pain and grief go just as deep.' He paused, gazing at the clear, fast-flowing brook now pewter in the half-light. 'There are times when I hate the work I do. This is one of them.'

'Where are you? I can hear water.'

'On the way back from a walk. I can hear girlish laughter where you are.'

'They help to keep me sane. Get outside a good hot meal followed by a whisky or two. The outlook'll seem much brighter. Good-night, sir.'

'Goodnight, old friend.'

Eleven

There was a distinctive sound. It reminded Ben of his aunt's kitchen clock. As a small boy he had waited expectantly every hour for the little doors to open, and the wooden bird to pop out. This cuckoo he could hear was calling too infrequently to be telling the time. It was also too chilly and uncomfortable for him to be in Aunt Rose's kitchen.

With a great effort he opened his eyes to slits and saw a different kind of clock. It showed the hour of six. Must be morning because it was a twenty-four hour clock. He knew that well enough, but why he was slumped in his car at dawn he had no idea. Further forcing up his eyelids he saw a rosy horizon at the end of a long, empty road bordered by flat farming country. He did not recognize the area.

A spurt of panic chilled him further. Where the hell was he, and how had he got here? A few minutes of racing pulse and hovering nausea while he tried to get to grips with the facts he had. He was wearing uniform early in the morning on a lonely road somewhere in Germany. Long experience of military life told him he had not showered or changed his clothes recently. He must have been on the road for a long stint and decided to sleep in the car. His bursting bladder supported that theory and sent him out to the roadside to relieve himself. His legs immediately folded, forcing him to urinate in a kneeling position supported by one outstretched hand on the rough verge.

Real fear now assailed Ben. What was happening to him? Where was he going, where had he been? He did not feel ill exactly, just lethargic and floppy. As if he had no bones or muscles. He was thirsty and very heavy-headed. Trying to zip his fly one-handed took too much effort, so he left it open while he clambered heavily back behind the wheel. He sat there for some time trying to think what to do.

He then spotted his mobile phone in the hands-free holder. Good idea to call a couple of friends for assistance. Trouble was, he could not remember the names of any friends. Dear God, his condition must be serious. Leaning from the car he vomited several times, then lay back riding out his pulse-racing sense of dread.

Fifteen minutes later he had recovered enough of his natural assurance to make a firm decision. The only way to discover where he was was to follow this road until he reached a village, even a house or pub where he could ask for directions back to base. Pushing aside the truth that he was uncertain where his base was, he turned the key in the ignition and heard the satisfying roar of an engine. Thankfully, the tank appeared to be three-quarters full.

It was instantly apparent that he was not fit to drive. The car made a kangaroo hop and stalled. Ben restarted it and tried to co-ordinate brain and limbs until, after two more false starts he moved off smoothly. Steering remained a problem after bumping over the verge several times, but the road was deserted and Ben determinedly pursued this hope of getting help in this frightening situation. It was essential to reach some place of human habitation,

Max decided on the lengthy walk to his office from *Frau* Hahn's. He badly needed an intake of fresh air after a night of weird dreams that had left him sweating and restless. Breakfast had been black coffee. He had not wanted anything to eat; he was too weighed down by doubts and a sense of drowning in very murky waters.

Before Susan's death he had been able to hold aloof from cases he investigated. Perhaps he was losing his grip. Last February he had become caught up in the bizarre death of Major Leo Bekov; had empathized too closely with the man's beautiful ex-wife. Now, he could not rid his mind of Christine White's tragic breakdown and her four infants facing a repressive future. Or of Lady Kington pre-sently in danger of losing her husband as well as her only son. Max felt burdened by his failure to move forward along any tentacle of the octopus he was wrestling with.

Drawn from introspection by a squeal of brakes, Max turned to see a blue Ford thumping back on the road after its nearside wheels had mounted the pavement. It continued erratically before stalling at an angle in the centre of the road. He strode over to the vehicle whose plates identified it as having a British military owner.

'I'll have him for this,' Max thought grimly, approaching the driver wearing lieutenant's pips on his uniform. He was nonplussed to see Ben Steele gazing at him with hugely dilated eyes. A jolt of dismay shot through Max. Another RCR victim.

Ordering the goggling subaltern to move over, Max forced his way behind the wheel knowing it might already be too late to save the likeable young officer. Ben had fallen across the passenger seat like a rag doll, his legs tangled in the gears. Shoving him into a half-reclining crouch, Max drove hell for leather to Section Headquarters fully expecting Ben to be dead on arrival there.

He was very much alive, however, when Max fetched Tom to help carry the afflicted man to his office and on to the worn leather couch for which SIB had been unable to find an alternative home. Efficient as ever, Tom then went to find Staff Sergeant Melly, who had had advanced first aid training. Max's dread of another murder victim faded as Ben embarked stumblingly on a long, seemingly far-fetched tale about a lost day and night.

'I'm glad to see you, even if you bang me up for this,' he eventually confessed in wobbly tones, 'It was bloody scary; like something from a sci-fi film.'

'When Staff Melly has looked you over we'll get you back to Major Clarkson, who'll make a more thorough examination. Meantime, we'll check your recent movements; when you left the base and why. You're in uniform so it must have been a duty run logged on your company records.' He summoned a smile. 'How are you feeling now?'

'Happier because I'm in a situation I can identify with, but I'm still worried about those lost hours.' The smooth brow furrowed. 'D'you reckon I had a slight stroke and blacked out?'

Max thought an attempt could have been made on his life and failed, but he kept that to himself. 'I'm not a medical expert. The MO will be able to give you a better idea of what happened.'

'I hope to God he can sort the problem out easily enough; assure me it's not likely to happen again.'

'*That* will probably be up to you.' Max had now had time to sort his reasoning and decided Ben Steele was too young to be a potential victim of their killer. The known victims were in their thirties; had been with the RCR at least ten years. And Ben had not been in Hong Kong. Max sighed inwardly, no longer sure that fact was at all significant. It seemed most likely that the young officer had taken some kind of knock-out substance potent enough to remove from his memory the events of the previous twenty-four to thirty-six hours. Possibly something akin to the date rape drug Rohypnol. Instinct told Max it had been given without Ben's knowledge, and Clarkson would automatically look for signs of sexual assault.

Of course, Ben might remember all too well being set upon by a group of thugs determined to debase someone they saw as an upholder of military suppression. An ordeal he might choose to deny for several reasons. Yet, if that had been done to him he was remarkably neatly dressed, apart from an open fly, and there were no obvious signs of his having been beaten up. They would have to get to the bottom of this intriguing development.

Tom returned with Pete Melly and the large glass of water Ben had asked for. While Melly carried out basic physical tests and assessed the patient's mental stability, Max and Tom exchanged views on the other side of the office.

'That lad's too open and above board to have drugged himself, Tom.'

'I agree. Someone dosed him and left him out in the sticks. Could have been a prank, or something more sinister. I'd say it stands alone, however. Nothing to do with our case.'

'Thank God! If he'd been DOA just now it would have blown sky-high our thinking on it.'

'*Your* thinking,' Tom corrected. 'We've no evidence to support the Hong Kong connection so far. I've alerted Corporals Trent and Adcock to drive Mr Steele back to base and directly to the Medical Centre. They're right now impounding his car for forensic tests. We'll be investigating suspected rape or the administration of an obnoxious substance against a person's will, I guess. Either way Krenkel's boys will probably have to be brought in on it.'

'Messy. Bound to be.'

'As if we haven't enough to be getting on with, sir.'

'Mmm,' agreed Max thoughtfully. 'Coincidental that he happens to be with the Cumberlands, though. If he's been fed a drug that blots out recent memory, he'll not know the circumstances that enabled someone to approach him, render him incapable of resistance, take him to some lonely spot and leave him there for several hours if not all night.'

'And?'

'What if Simon Kington was treated the same way, but given a stronger dose and dumped much further away? Across a border somewhere. So he wouldn't reappear for quite a time.'

'And, if and when he did, he'd have no idea who'd drugged him or where he'd been,' added Tom with a nod. 'But what's the motive?'

'Get him nicely out of the way over a vital period.' Max gave a tight smile. 'Maybe Tara Kington was right. Hubby overheard some skullduggery being planned to rig an important vote, so they gave him the treatment until they get what they want.'

Tom looked askance at him. 'Yesterday the shallow grave on-base was favourite. And who would want to keep Ben Steele out of the way overnight ... apart from a jealous rival?'

'That may become clear when we've investigated his activities over the last few days.' He pursed his lips. 'I'm wandering in the realms of moonshine, Tom, but I do think it's significant that out of thousands of servicemen in the area this happens to a Cumberland Rifleman.'

'Rifle*person*,' corrected Tom with a grin, hoping to soften his earlier snide comment about Max's Hong Kong theory.

As if by ESP Phil Piercey knocked lightly on the open door, then walked in holding several computer printouts and wearing an unreadable expression. 'Just came through, sir.' He handed them to Max and waited expectantly.

A sensation of quiet triumph assailed Max as he handed them sheet by sheet to Tom. Harold Barker *had* been killed by a lethal injection of the same unidentified toxin as Brian New and Colin White. The Hong Kong link was now undeniable.

At the end of that day they were no nearer to getting the vital information needed to

266

progress their investigation. They again rigorously questioned everyone who had been with the regiment in Hong Kong. The answers were all similar. It was too long ago The border was patrolled every day and night. How could they possibly recall who had gone out with whom each time?

Pursuing Harold Barker's words to Don Jackman that he was going to find out what really happened on that patrol, Beeny was slightly more successful than the rest. A sergeant cook said he remembered Second Lieutenant Barker laying into the mess kitchen staff when he went down with food poisoning.

'Got very stroppy with Staff Perkins, he did. Blamed us. Seeing he was the only officer affected, stands to reason it was something he ate elsewhere. Always very short-tempered, he was. You'd hear him sounding off in the Mess. When the senior officers weren't around, of course. Got a terrible load of grief from his wife, he did. Constantly on a short fuse because she was spending their money faster than he earned it. Could sort out everyone but her. Nothing special about the bitch that we could see, but she had him dancing to her tune.'

'What has this to do with border patrols?' asked Beeny.

'The reason he let rip at Staff Perkins! Due to the food poisoning he missed going on a night patrol. Had to be replaced, didn't he?'

'He *complained* because he was excused

patrolling the New Territories border at night?'

'Yeah. Beggars belief, don't it? That's why I particularly remember it. Steam almost came from his nostrils.'

'Who took his place?'

'How do I know? I just cooked their bloody meals.'

At Section Headquarters this snippet of information was met with dour expressions. Heather Johnson spoke for them all when she said they had already known Barker wasn't on that patrol, and if Beeny hadn't found out who went in his stead they weren't any wiser.

Piercey objected. 'Yes, we are. We now know Barker was desperate to go on that patrol; almost did his nut because he couldn't. That strengthens our theory that the motive behind the killings is what happened along the border that night.'

'Barker's determination to uncover the truth suggests he suspects those who did go on it lied about the outcome. Which was why he rushed out to Honkers bent on a showdown,' said Tom.

'So Barker and the rest were engaged in illicit dealings of some kind, and he lost out on his share because he was ill,' Heather Johnson concluded. 'So who's killing them all off?'

'The guy who set up the business and made a pile out of it. Enough to leave the army and live in style out there,' put in Beeny quietly. 'Life's wonderful until Barker turns up on his doorstep. He silences Barker on the Star Ferry, then gets nervous and decides to take out the rest as a precaution.'

'If this Mr Big has done so well out of his illegal activities, why haven't the rest followed his example, left the army and become entrepreneurs?' challenged Heather Johnson.

'Because he tricked them out of their rightful shares, and had such a hold over them they had to take it on the chin.'

Connie Bush, who had been silent throughout these comments, now offered her thoughts. 'So Mr Big has a supply of some obscure Oriental poison. That's reasonable. He feels so endangered he comes to Germany to kill off everyone who could expose him. That's also reasonable, if the crime was serious enough. But how did he know the movements of his victims? Even White's wife wasn't aware he was going to the Reinhardt.'

Beeny nodded. 'But a lot of his colleagues knew – or thought they did – that he was off on a walking tour that morning. Our killer stations himself outside the base and follows when White leaves through the main gate.'

'Then waits until that evening to kill him? Why?'

'We'll ask him when we catch him,' Beeny responded.

'My point is that he had to have an informant within the regiment,' she persisted. 'Someone also in on the illegal dealing but who somehow doesn't represent a threat.'

Tom interrupted at that point. 'It's been apparent from the start our killer had to have known Colin White's and New's movements, which pointed to someone in the RCR. Barker's death in Hong Kong either disproves that or poses the possibility of *two* murderers. I tend to believe our man took out Barker then flew here to silence the rest. Sergeant Bush is right. There's an informant on that base; an accomplice to multiple murder. A person the killer trusts implicitly.

'Beeny and Piercey, go through all the interview statements looking for one person who would know where New and Captain White were at the time of their death. It hasn't been apparent this far, but it's there. Must be. If the statements don't throw it up, go out there in the morning and interview everyone again. *Stringently*.

'I don't go along with the idea of the killer tagging on behind White's car, following him to the Reinhardt, then kicking his heels until the evening before killing him. I suspect the informant only discovered where the Captain had actually gone a short while before the murder. Which, on the evidence we have so far, is bloody impossible. So we need new evidence. Go out and find it,' he instructed the whole team.

Max then addressed them. 'We're slowly peeling away the layers of this Chinese puzzle. Two victims were murdered here on successive days a week ago. Harold Barker was found dead in Hong Kong three days earlier. Until we discover who formed the members of that patrol we can't be absolutely sure, but I'm fairly confident that the killing has stopped. On our patch, anyway. Time may bring to light another victim, two even, who quit the RCR way back but who also needed to be silenced. That's for the future. Right now our priority is to find the informant. Through him – or *her*,' he added with a glance at Piercey, 'we'll get the killer, who could be anywhere in the world now.'

'Are we completely discounting Major Kington as a murder victim?' asked Connie Bush, gnawing away at her pet theory.

Max avoided a direct answer. 'I want you and Sergeant Johnson to continue your investigation of Lieutenant Steele's activities over the last few days. Major Clarkson intends to keep him in Sick Bay under observation for forty-eight hours. Find out if he's remembered anything about that lost night yet. If he hasn't—'

Connie Bush interrupted him. 'Sir, we did get one piece of info we haven't followed up yet because it concerns his love life.' She grinned. 'She must be some woman to have that effect on a man!'

'Go on,' Max invited, smothering a smile.

'On Sunday evening he had a hot date with a German girl he's recently taken up with. According to his friends she's very sexy and very rich. Called to pick him up on Friday evening in a silver Ferrari.'

'Ah! It passed me at breakneck speed when

271

I visited the CO. Did you discover who she is?'

'Sonja Meikel. Daughter of a distinguished publisher of medical tomes. She's a member of the Ferrari club Simon Kington joined. Heather and I pursued the military angle today because Lieutenant Steele was in uniform. Not what a swinging young guy would wear for a date with a girl like that. We know he left the base at seventeen thirty, but there's no record of a duty run that evening. Only conclusion was that he was late for a meeting and hadn't had time to change. We plan to interview *Fräulein* Meikel tomorrow morning.'

'Good. He was drugged and abandoned off military premises, so she might provide some clue to who he was meeting. Pursue the Ferrari Club link, and check the girl out for any signs of drug abuse, and so on. I want to get to the bottom of this assault before we bring in the *Polizei*, as we'll have to.'

He was about to round off his input when a telephone rang. Pete Melly was nearest to it and picked it up, listened briefly, then drew Max's attention.

'Sir, they've been ringing your office number. Lieutenant Sanders, who climbed with Captain White, is on the line.'

Max nodded, hoping another layer of the puzzle was about to be lifted. 'I'll take it in my office.'

He crossed the room leaving Tom to send the team off cognizant with separate investigations. Lifting the receiver he said, 'Captain Rydal.'

'Kevin Sanders here. I got back from leave Sunday night. Had no idea Colin had been murdered until Mark Lang rang me a moment ago. It's terrible! Poor Christine! And all those kids. However will she manage?'

'She's had a total breakdown. Her parents are looking after the children.'

'Oh God!' There was a slight pause. 'I feel partly to blame.'

'What?'

'Look, can we meet? It isn't something I can – I want – to discuss over the phone.'

'Come to Section Headquarters.'

'Christ no! I haven't done anything ... A private chat, that's all. There's a bar in town called the Crazy Parrot.'

'I'm not going there to discuss a murder case,' Max told him sharply. 'I'll be at the Golden Lion in Frühberg in an hour. Should give you time to drive over. I'll listen to what you have to say then.' He cut the connection, took up his car keys and walked out to inform Tom.

'Think it's a lead?' he asked.

'It'd better be. I need my dinner and a few hours' sleep ready for a long day tomorrow. He sounded rather spineless.'

'Isn't he one of the climbing foursome?'

'Maybe he comes in to his own dealing with mountains.' Max smiled. 'Get off home, Tom. We're almost there. The next few days should reveal answers to most questions, and I've a

273

gut feeling we're in for some shocks.'

'You mean the Royal Cumberlands are. It takes a lot to shock us. Give me a call later?'

'No, Sanders won't be identifying the killer. It'll wait until morning.' He made his way to the main double doors. 'Enjoy your evening with Nora and the girls.'

Tom grinned. 'The sitting-room is festooned with ivory satin and bridal veiling; the bedrooms are festooned with posters of some guy dressed as a Trojan, who makes girls squeal. I think I'll have a quiet session with my model steam engine collection. Male stuff! Goodnight, sir.'

It was one of the lighter periods, yet it was somehow different. The pale greyness was all around him, not just from the square of glass in the wall.

For some while lethargy prevented him from recognizing the other differences. It slowly dawned on him that there was no square of glass; no walls covered with pictures of children's toys. The glittering expanse of water was stretching away to the distance, but he could see it from where he lay. It was as if the walls had crumbled and vanished.

The water fascinated and beckoned to him. He studied it with mounting pleasure until, emerging into focus, he saw the figures of children. Children floating small boats on the dancing surface while adults chatted together on nearby benches.

He felt wonderfully warm; had no urge to

curl against the rough blanket. He was lying full-length revelling in the blessing of the sun's rays on his body. It was then he realized he was fully clothed. A spurt of alarm disturbed his contentment. What was happening; what did it mean? Gone was the familiar room with paper peeling from the walls. He was lying on warm grass, not the bare mattress, and he was dressed in the kind of clothes soldiers wore. It worried him. Where was he? *Who* was he?

Sitting up induced nausea. He retched until the world stopped spinning and the sensation passed. Hovering fear began to push forward to further destroy his first contentment. Had he been abandoned by 'the person' who had given him food and honeyed water? He felt dangerously alone and helpless. Had the madness he suspected now taken another form to set him wandering in fantasy scenes?

His head drooped, his shoulders began to heave, great sobs shook his entire frame as he yearned for the room with rocking horses on the torn paper. He had been a prisoner, but *safe*. Now, the demon madness would possess him.

A soft, high-pitched voice broke through the rasp of his sobs. He heard it several times before he grew calmer and turned his wet face towards the sound. A small girl in a blue cotton dress stood a few yards away regarding him with concerned curiosity.

'*Haben Sie Angst?*' she asked again.

How did she know he was deeply afraid?

Was she part of his nightmare? Had she been sent to torment him? He stared at her silently and with great suspicion for so long she suddenly turned and ran to a woman hurrying across the grass. Half-sheltering behind the adult's skirt, the child pointed at him, chattering non-stop. The woman swept the girl into her arms and hastened back to where a group of excited boys watched a race between their boats. These youngsters were swiftly ushered away to their guardians already preparing to leave in response to the woman's words.

Within minutes the extensive waterway lay undisturbed, the surrounding grass and benches deserted. He then knew utter terror and desolation. His cheeks grew wet again as he began to crawl towards the area where, until a few moments ago, he had imagined parents and children behaving normally. His fantasy! Yet he was driven to rediscover it, be comforted by it, escape from this barren wilderness where he would lose the last of any sanity he might still hold on to.

Kevin Sanders might have sounded spineless, but he looked the reverse. Six four, at least, and broad shouldered. Only a flop of milk-fair hair and baby-blue eyes dispelled the first impression that he was a real bruiser. His grip was very firm when he shook Max's hand; his smile was apologetic.

'Sorry about this. It isn't something I wanted to discuss over the phone. Can I get you a drink?'

Max was tempted to order a snack to go with it, but resisted the urge. This was not a social occasion. He demonstrated that when they settled with their lagers at a small table near the door.

'You said you're partly responsible for Colin White's death.'

Sanders looked alarmed. 'Not for his death, no! I had nothing to do with that.'

'So explain your earlier comment.'

'Look, I refused to come to your head-quarters because I didn't want any kind of official interrogation. You're starting one here,' he accused edgily. 'I didn't have to come forward with this.'

'Calm it,' Max advised. 'When you see me produce a tape recorder it becomes official. Not until then ... and if you have evidence that throws light on Colin White's murder it's your duty to tell the people investigating the case.' He made an effort to soften his approach. 'Mark Lang gave you the bad news earlier today, you said. It prompted you to call me. Take it from there.'

Sanders drank deeply from his glass, then gave a sigh. 'We were all good friends from way back. Had some fantastic outings together on mountains in the UK and Europe. Colin was a great guy to be on a rope with. Knew what he was doing; never put a foot wrong. I trusted him completely.'

'With confidences as well as your life?'

'Well, we were at different bases. Easier to

talk over problems or grievances when you know it's not going to become general knowledge in your own workplace.'

'Colin discussed his in-laws with you?'

'God, yes! They're diabolical.'

Max gave a wry smile. 'I've encountered them. What other problems did he share with you?'

'Money. His lack of it. They knew in advance Chris was carrying another pair of twins. They had deliberately tried for another kid, but the prospect of *two* more was daunting. Colin gave generous financial support to his sister who gave up her job to look after their mother with MS, so he'd find it a struggle to cope with four little ones.' He gave a harsh laugh. 'Told me he'd either have to put Chris in a chastity belt or tie a knot in his tackle, because they couldn't keep their hands off each other in bed.'

'He went instead to the Reinhardt Klinik for a vasectomy.'

'No.' After a moment of hesitant contemplation, during which several noisy couples arrived and greeted friends waiting at an adjoining table, Sanders looked across at Max with pain in his eyes.

'It was meant as a joke. I mean, I never dreamed he would ... I underestimated his concern over his bank balance, that's obvious. I thought he'd have a good laugh and send back a rude message.'

Max knew better than to prompt him at this point. Sanders was clearly very upset. He must be allowed to confess in his own time and in his own way. Signalling a waiter to bring more drinks, Max suspected that he was about to learn something Tom would find most interesting. It was he who had dealt with the Reinhardts and their clinic; he who was certain of their involvement with dodgy practices.

'I forgot Colin's affairs while I was back home in the UK. I met a girl.' Sanders forced a smile. 'Confirmed bachelor me, until I went to a friend's party and saw his cousin. Took all the joy out of me when Mark told me about Colin.'

The waiter set down the two lagers and Max paid him before taking a long drink from the chilled glass. Sanders ignored his.

'I do a bit of body-building in the gym, and one of the instructors passed on a German magazine. Said to do some of the non-equipment exercises shown in it while on leave. Keep the muscles in shape. Those mags always have ads at the back. You know the kind of thing. Gays seeking partners; clubs to enjoy the company of others keen on creating the male body beautiful. Semi-porno stuff.'

Max nodded. 'Perfectly legal these days.'

'I saw an ad that targeted super-virile men. The wording was obscure and designed to flatter, but no one would mistake the idea behind it. Men with really high sperm counts were urgently needed to help with scientific research into infertility in males. All donors would receive generous payment. Confidentiality guaranteed. There was a number to ring for an initial consultation.

'It was pretty obvious there was more to it than the normal business of going into a cubicle with a pot and wanking, out of the goodness of one's heart. Something very iffy about getting "generous payment" for doing it.' He gave Max a level look. 'I sent the ad to Colin. Suggested he'd be their prime client. Told him to ejaculate for payment instead of pleasure. It was meant as a joke, for God's sake!' he said bitterly.

'How d'you know he didn't take it that way?'

'Because after Mark told me where Colin was killed, I checked the phone number of the Reinhardt Klinik. It's the same as the one on that ad. I'm responsible for sending him there.'

Tom was sitting in the large alcove beneath the stairs their landlord had furnished with a narrow desk, two power points and some shelves to form an office. The shelves now held a collection of top quality models of famous steam engines. They were protected by glass cases Tom had made, and illuminated by spotlights. The desk drawers contained files in which he had catalogued the history of each engine along with photographs and press cuttings about these wonderful old examples of engineering inspiration at its peak.

The latest edition of the collectors' magazine his father sent out each month had arrived that morning, and Tom was so engrossed in studying the items for sale or exchange in the hope of enlarging his collection, he visibly started when a hand fell on his shoulder.

Nora ruffled his hair affectionately. 'Come quietly, chum, or I'll have to use the cuffs.'

Tom stretched and yawned. 'You've finished for tonight?'

'Yes. Sergeant Dean's dress was simple enough, it's the multi-flounced train she wants that's taking so much fiddling to get right.'

'Talking of trains,' he said, getting wearily to his feet, 'there's a model of—'

'No, Tom, don't say any more! Your dad put a private note to me in with that magazine. Said to stop you from sending away for anything until after your birthday.'

He smiled. 'Good on him! He knows which ones I'm after.' They walked past the half-finished bridal gown on its hanger and covered with a sheet, in to the kitchen-diner. 'What are you giving me for my birthday, woman?'

'As well as the usual?' she countered. 'That should be enough for any man.'

'I'm not any man. I'm special.'

Nora shook her head. 'You have to be a Trojan to be special these days. The girls have convinced me.'

He watched her taking mugs from the cupboard and reaching for the biscuit tin, knowing *she* was special and always would be to him. 'When this case is over, how about I take the deferred leave I'm due? Should be five or six weeks. Have some fun with the girls, then leave them with our parents while we go off on a luxury jaunt. Anywhere you like.'

She turned cautiously. 'Is that a serious offer?'

'Sure it is. We both deserve some fun.'

'And I can choose?'

'That's what I said.'

Her smile warmed him through and through. 'Then we'll go to—'

The telephone on the counter beside him rang and he picked it up automatically. 'Sar'nt Major Black.'

'Tom, here is Klaus Krenkel. Good evening. This is very late, but it is that I have a duty to tell you immediately. It was reported to us that a man, a British soldier, is behaving with menace in the Zoopark. We have him here being examined by our doctor, because he has certainly taken drugs in large amounts. He is in great distress, has much fright of what is happening. He does not give identification, but I have checked with the photograph you sent out and I am sure we have with us your missing Major Kington.'

Twelve

Although their phone call requesting an interview had very obviously woken Sonja Meikel, the German girl was beautifully made-up and dressed in a lemon crop-top and silk palazzo pants when Connie Bush and Heather Johnson arrived thirty minutes later. She seemed amused by their business-like dark suits and neat hairstyles as she invited them in and offered coffee. Her own crowning glory flowed past her shoulders in an expensively contrived designer tangle of the kind worn by women who never washed their own hair.

Connie and Heather exchanged covert glances as they registered the glossy décor of the large apartment of which she appeared to be the sole occupant. Caramel carpet, cream leather furniture, great swathes of semi-transparent curtains highlighting floor to ceiling windows offering views of open country, combined to give an air of serenity not apparent in the young woman they had come to question. Sonja Meikel was fizzing with energy. She was also extremely conscious of her physical allure and her social status. It was apparent in every graceful movement; in the expansive small talk about her world of which her guests saw only the seamy side.

Coffee was brought and poured by a stout woman who was probably the daily help. It was rare for them to enjoy luxury in the course of their work, so the detectives made no move to hurry things along. The coffee was excellent, the biscuits mouth-watering. Sitting in that elegant, sun-filled room they were momentarily filled with envy.

Sonja ate biscuits at an amazing rate, eventually brushing crumbs from her lap to the floor. 'So you wish to talk to me about Ben with the so-sexy eyes? Is it that he has been a naughty boy?' Her smile suggested pleasure at the prospect.

Keeping her voice neutral, Connie said, 'We understand Lieutenant Steele arranged to meet you last Sunday evening. Did he keep the appointment?'

'But yes, he is very eager, that boy.' She took another biscuit and nibbled it like a rabbit.

Heather watched her closely. 'Would you mind telling us what you did that evening?'

'We went to a club. Met friends of mine for a race.'

'A race?'

Sonja waved at a silver car ornament on a glass-topped table against a wall. 'We all are members of the Ferrari Club. We like to race. Who wins is given every wish for that evening.' Her eyes opened theatrically. 'You are to punish Ben for this race?'

Heather shook her head. 'That would be for

the *Polizei* to decide.'

'Then what is it you are here for?' she demanded, scooping up the last chocolate biscuit.

'We'd like you to describe Lieutenant Steele's mood that evening,' Connie told her. 'Was he quiet, thoughtful? Perhaps a little abstracted? Not his usual self?'

'This was just the third time we meet. How do I know his usual self?' She grinned. 'He was *very* good in bed. Is that usual?'

'We'll ask around,' returned Connie, poker-faced. 'So you had a car race, then probably celebrated in someone's apartment?'

'Here. I won the race, so we came here. It was one of my wishes, you see.'

'And Mr Steele was with you all the time?'

'Of course.'

'Did you take drugs that evening?'

The lovely face hardened. 'I think that is not for the British Army to ask me.'

Heather said swiftly, 'We meant you collectively. We are entitled to ask if one of our officers took drugs in your company.'

Sonja thought that over, then nodded. 'Yes, that is so. Your *Lieutenant* would not. He said it was forbidden him.'

'And as far as you're aware no one slipped him anything without his knowledge?'

'That would not be done. My friends would not.' She grew cautious. 'Is it that something has harmed Ben?'

'He's perfectly all right,' Connie assured her. 'He'll doubtless contact you soon. We're just checking on his movements over the last few days. So, from your point of view, he behaved normally on Sunday night?'

She shrugged. 'He laughed, he drank, he ate a large steak. That is normal man behaviour. He enjoyed the race. He wants very much a Ferrari. That is also normal man, no?' Her smile was surprisingly fond as she added, 'Ben is very easy to understand. He does not hide emotions. On Sunday he is excited by the race. He is eager to buy one for himself. He asks about Gerhardt Wolf.'

That name set Connie's antennae buzzing. 'Isn't he the head of a large pharmaceutical company? What has he to do with buying a Ferrari?'

'Gerhardt is the president just now of the Ferrari Club. Ben thinks he will be a help in this. Even while we are having sex he is asking me where Gerhardt has his home; thinking all the time of the car he wants. Is that not normal man behaviour?'

The two detectives nodded heartily in agreement.

Simon Kington was installed in a room in a private clinic with a military guard outside his door. Max had strenuously fought his right to be present when Ralph Robbins, who had been in charge of the ransom fiasco in the UK, arrived to question the patient. Nothing had been gleaned from that interview. Kington's physical condition would return to normal when the residue of the drug he had

286

been given cleared from his system; the mental outcome was less clear-cut. At present he was deeply confused and suspicious of everyone approaching him, including his wife.

Analysts claimed he had been given, over the period of his absence, regular doses of a drug that induced memory loss. They could not absolutely identify it, but it fell into the same category as Rohypnol. Tests proved it to be similar to the substance found in Ben Steele's system.

Events moved fast then. Following the SIB interview with Sonja Meikel, Klaus Krenkel began an investigation into Gerhardt Wolf's current development programme. This revealed quantities of an experimental drug which was that used on Kington and Ben Steele. Wolf was subjected to questioning and a warrant to search his house was obtained. Simon Kington's ramblings about a lake, which had been interpreted as the one in the Zoopark, took on a more significant meaning when German investigators saw the body of water at Wolf's estate.

With that aspect of the case out of his hands, Max drove out to the base leaving Tom to contact Boris Mann about information on the Reinhardt Klinik given by Kevin Sanders. Tom had been eager to follow up on it, certain they would uncover something deeply unprofessional, if not illegal.

The bulk of the team were still endeavouring to find a lead on the Hong Kong border patrol link. Most of their work was pain-staking and often disheartening, but they were determined to get that elusive break-through. Deprived of his shallow grave on-base containing Simon Kington's body, Piercey needed to compensate with a success.

Max tracked Ben Steele down to his room. The young officer looked slightly alarmed when he saw his visitor, but he invited Max in with an apology.

'I'm sure I didn't thank you properly that morning. I was very woosy.'

'Back to normal now?' Max sat in the arm-chair Ben indicated while he occupied an upright one before his desk.

'The Doc says I can get back to work on Monday. I actually feel fine, but my mind's still a blank over what happened.'

Max nodded. 'We'll be able to fill that blank for you before long.'

'Good God, how?'

'Have you heard that Major Kington has turned up?'

'So it's true! There are all manner of rumours going round, most of them pretty bizarre.'

'It's a bizarre affair, Ben, and you've played a vital part in it.'

'Me!' He flushed. From embarrassment or pleasure Max was unsure.

'Simon had been drugged with the same substance he used on you, but for a much longer period.'

Eyes large with curiosity, Ben asked in text-speak, 'Who *he*?'

'My sergeants interviewed your girlfriend, who told them you'd been eager to discover the home address of Gerhardt Wolf. Knowing Wolf has a laboratory dedicated to developing new drugs I suggested the *Polizei* investigated. They found large quantities of the stuff you and Simon were given. It's still in the experimental stage, which means you were both involuntary guinea-pigs. That's a very serious crime.'

Ben was now a shade paler, and Max hastened to re-assure him. 'We think there'll be no side-effects other than possible permanent loss of memory for that period. Major Clarkson told us the amount in your system suggests just a single dose. Simon will have to be carefully monitored in the coming weeks, however.' He studied Ben's strained expression. 'Seek confirmation from the MO if you have doubts, and certainly report to him if you feel unwell during the next week or so.'

The young man seemed deeply unsettled by Max's words, but not because of possible side-effects, as he then revealed. 'What you said just now has nudged my memory. Sonja told your people I asked for Wolf's address. I don't recall doing that, but *why* I did it has just come back to me.'

Max prompted him as he hesitated. 'Go on.'

'On my first date with Sonja she took me to her club. *Das Kaninchenstall*. It was that day we heard of the ransom demand sent to Simon's father,' he added with a frown. 'I

289

came out of the cloakroom and spotted Tara Kington with a man I'd seen at the Ferrari Club two days before.'

'Gerhardt Wolf?'

'It was a shock. She was out on the town having fun when she should have been sitting by the phone in a state of acute anxiety.' His frown deepened as his memory cleared further. 'It then occurred to me that maybe Simon *did* arrive home that evening, and Tara knew where he was hiding. As a theory it made little sense except to explain why I could find no evidence during my comprehensive search in a downpour of how he could have left the base.'

'Because he hadn't,' finished Max, satisfaction flooding through him.

'Tara seemed genuinely upset and alarmed when she called me in just after midnight. I never for a moment suspected her of lying, despite the curious circumstances,' Ben said unhappily.

'She put on a convincing act for us, too,' Max added. 'The two murders suggested very strongly that Kington had either committed them, or was a third victim. That clouded the issue for us until the ransom note put the case in a different category and it was taken out of our hands.' He got to his feet. 'Your evidence has just put it firmly back in them. Thanks.' At the door he said, 'If you'd like to join us, apply for a transfer. Just don't try acting alone again. You might not get off so lightly next time.'

Tara Kington was in a small room designed for the privacy of relatives of seriously ill patients. She was gazing from the window and made no move when she heard someone enter. On the table were a plate of biscuits and a cup of coffee. Both were untouched.

Max crossed to her. 'I've just been told your husband is no longer in a state of fear, but still refuses to speak to anyone. Including you. The medics put this down to being the next stage in his emergence from a drug-induced torpor. What do you put it down to, Mrs Kington?'

There was a considerable pause before she said to the windowpane, 'It was supposed to be a brief, simple business doing him no harm.'

'Planned by you and Gerhardt Wolf?'

She swung round. 'I *trusted* him. He said nothing about an experimental drug.'

It was all Max needed to hear. 'Mrs Kington, I'm arresting you and taking you to Section Headquarters for questioning about the administration of a noxious substance to Major Simon Edwin Hereward Kington with intent to incapacitate, and his subsequent abduction.'

Tom was waiting with an Intelligence Corps captain named Frayle, who would sit in on the interview. Max read Tara Kington her rights and asked if she wanted a legal representative. She said no and waited with her usual composure while he repeated the basis for her arrest.

'Would I be right in suggesting that on the evening of Monday April fourth your husband returned from his office, parked his vehicle in the car port, then entered your house?'

'Yes.'

'Please tell us what happened next.'

'I had poured our usual drinks. Simon likes to sit for half an hour with a G and T when he comes in; a habit we formed in Hong Kong. Sat on the verandah there, of course. Gerhardt had given me a small bottle of knock-out drops. I'd put the prescribed amount in Simon's glass and waited for the drug to act.' She gave a faint sigh. 'It happened quicker than I'd bargained for. He keeled over within minutes. So there he was spreadeagled on the carpet, and I was supposed to call the Duty Officer at about midnight and say he hadn't come home. I couldn't lift him, of course, so I dragged him in stages through to the dining room and behind an old divan we keep there. I prayed Ben Steele would accept my story and not start searching the house, but I knew he was very susceptible. Pity he didn't remain that way,' she added, her expression hardening. 'I left all Simon's things on the table where he'd put them, but I hid the laptop behind the divan with him. That was a crucial part of the plan.'

'Why not drug your husband somewhere outside the base?' Max asked. 'Much easier, surely.'

'That would have involved the German police. We didn't want that.'

'Your husband is more than a normal regimental officer. You must have considered the possibility of Intelligence intervention in the case.'

'I believed that would be an advantage. It would support the idea of a political slant.' Her eyes grew cold. 'From the moment *you* came on the scene the plan became fraught with hazards. I was horrified by your news of a sergeant being murdered the night before, with your hints that Simon was a suspect. Then Colin White's body was found and I was being viewed as the wife of a double killer. I couldn't have that. I just couldn't. So I acted to bring the plan back on course.'

Max's eyes narrowed. 'Are you saying *you* sent that ransom note?'

'A friend was flying back to the States with a stopover in London, so I asked her to give a small package to a courier agency there. It removed the possibility that Simon had killed and run. It also shifted interest to the UK and got you off my back.'

'It caused your in-laws immense stress, culminating with Sir Chetwin's collapse at Heathrow,' Tom put in stonily.

'Gerhardt organized that second letter without consulting me,' she said swiftly. 'You were getting nowhere on the murders, which forced us to keep Simon longer than we intended. When we heard about the third murder in Hong Kong I knew we could go

293

ahead. That's when I was told about the second letter. Gerhardt had no intention of collecting the money, of course.' She frowned. 'I never dreamed Pa would get so worked up. He's ultra-sharp at handling complex negotiations.'

'Not one that had a man's life in the balance. He truly believed his son's survival lay in his hands,' Tom said.

Her response was to repeat that SIB pursuit of the possibility of Simon being the killer had forced them to strengthen the kidnap theory. 'It was the greatest ill luck that someone committed multiple murder at that precise time.'

Max had to force his mind from the thought of Christine White's mental breakdown and the dreary future for her four infants being regarded as ill luck by this calculating woman. He focussed on getting back to the start of the interview.

'So, when you called the Duty Officer at midnight on Monday April fourth, Major Kington was lying unconscious in an adjoining room. Please tell us what you did with him consequently.'

She seemed glad to return to that. 'I had to leave him on the floor all night, of course, but I set the alarm and rose early. Gerhardt said the drug would begin wearing off after about twelve hours. Simon was awake but not fully alert, which was perfect for what I had to do. I gave him a drink containing another dose of the stuff, then led him out to my car. He had no real idea of what was going on, so it was simple to get him on the back seat. Within minutes he was away again. I covered him with rugs and my tack I brought from the stables the day before. After eating breakfast I drove to the stables, as usual. The guard waved me through the gate; they know I go most mornings to ride or check on our horses. Halfway along the route I rendez-voused with Gerhardt and we transferred Simon to his car. I then continued with my routine visit.'

Tom leaned forward to fix his gaze on hers. 'So Major Kington was kept in a drugged state in *Herr* Wolf's house until he was found in the Zoopark three days ago? Who dumped him there?'

Tara looked at Max. 'I'd like a cup of tea.'

After slight hesitation Max nodded to Tom, who halted the recording. While the tea order was being fulfilled, Max had a quiet word with the I Corps officer outside the open door.

'She's a cool customer,' remarked Frayle. 'I'd like you to get from her where that laptop is. We want it.'

'I've already got the CO's permission to search her house. My staff are there at this moment. I'd say they'll find it in plain view in his office.'

'Did it *never* occur to you that he had enter-ed the house that evening?' came the abrasive question.

Max answered in kind. 'We went to investigate a murder and discovered an officer had vanished the day after the killing. We automatically focussed on his being either a suspect or a possible second victim. The highly respected major's wife was intelligent, cultured and clearly distressed. Then a second body was discovered while we were speaking to her about her husband and everyone believed it must be Kington's. It was another officer of the same regiment, so we fully expected Kington to be a third target of the killer.

'Before long, however, Mr Black and I sensed that the lady was feigning anxiety, but at that point Sir Chetwin received that ransom note and the case was taken out of our hands.'

'You must still have had your suspicions.'

'Of course we bloody did,' Max replied irritably, 'but evidence of an actual third victim kept our priorities on that, although we had a theory about an outside party trying to cash in on the Kington disappearance before his body was discovered. When he turned up alive in the Zoopark we really were confounded, but not for long.' He gave a smooth smile. 'Here's the tea. Is there anything else you specifically want us to ask her?'

'Yes. Was their motive in any way political?'

'Given that Kington's father and Wolf are rival business giants, I suspect industrial rather than international politics could be at the core.'

'Which would make her a treacherous cool customer.'

'We're about to find out,' said Max, turning back in to the room.

The preliminaries dealt with, the recorded interview continued.

'Mrs Kington, we've established that you gave your husband two drinks laced with a drug you knew was designed to render him helpless. You then hid him on the back seat of your car and drove through the main gate for a rendezvous with Gerhardt Wolf, where Major Kington was transferred to Wolf's car for the purpose of transporting him to your friend's country home. Is that correct?'

'Yes.'

'What happened there does not come under our jurisdiction. What does is whether or not you were fully aware of what *Herr* Wolf's treatment of your husband would be during that period, and whether you freely consented to it.'

'In principle, yes,' she replied calmly. 'The plan was to keep Simon in the disused nursery on the top floor in conditions suggestive of captivity, so that any vague recollections he might have later would support the theme of abduction. During that time Gerhardt would give him regular doses of a drug that induces memory loss.' She looked from Max to Tom and back again. 'There was no question of ill treatment or bondage, you understand. Simon was fed and tended to several times each day. He had a mattress, blankets and fresh air through louvres.'

Seeing their expressions her composure

slipped momentarily. 'He's suffered harsher privations on exercises.'

'But in full command of his senses and body,' Tom said coldly.

'He was under no stress,' she snapped, getting slightly rattled. 'And it was to be for a period of only a very few days. Those murders ruined everything. You had Simon marked as the killer, so I had to send the ransom note to divert attention. Pa and Molly should never have been involved. *You* forced me to make that move.' She accused them with a cold glare. 'I expected you to solve the case swiftly. Your ineptitude condemned my husband to a far longer spell of incarceration than was necessary.'

As Max prepared to ask the vital question, she continued her apportioning of blame. 'That prolongation allowed time for Ben Steele to grow dangerously curious. I found him outside Gerhardt's house, obviously there to spy. His clumsy lies told me he suspected something of the truth so I had to take him up to the house for Gerhardt to give him some drugged wine. He should have kept out of something that was no concern of his.'

'So you watched while Lieutenant Steele was given a substance that would remove all awareness of the previous twenty-four to forty-eight hours?' probed Tom for clarification on the tape.

'I had no choice. He couldn't be allowed to blab his suspicions to you. We didn't suspect that he had already done so.'

Both Max and Tom let her continue to believe that.

'That's when we realized we must release Simon as planned.' She sighed heavily. 'It should have been so simple. By the time serious investigation into his disappearance was underway, he would have been found in the Zoopark with faint, if any, recollections of a bare room and a person in black who brought food. No harm would have been done and the affair would have been an unsolved nine days wonder.'

Max controlled his dislike of this arrogant woman before saying, 'Medical tests suggest there is slight damage to your husband's brain cells which is irreversible. The drug *Herr* Wolf administered has so far only been successfully tested on volunteers. He unlawfully used Major Kington as a human guinea-pig, and unhesitatingly did the same to Lieutenant Steele. You allowed that to happen. Will you now tell us why?'

Tara Kington's eyes flashed with sudden passion. 'I repeat, with great emphasis, I was *at no time* aware that the drug given to my husband and Ben Steele has not yet been clinically approved. I accept *no blame* for anything that may have resulted from its application.'

Max and Tom said nothing, just continued to fix her with their steady gaze until she spoke again, with less fire.

'My husband's maternal grandmother doted on her only grandchild. Molly's brother was killed during the Berlin Airlift, and Simon looks remarkably like him. The old lady left her beautiful mansion in Cheshire and a considerable fortune to her beloved grandson. Together with the interest from a large block of shares in Grant Bonner Kington that Pa and Molly gave him on his coming of age, Simon was a very wealthy man when I met him at Cambridge. He was also lively, passionate and full of ambitions for an exciting future together.

'The early years were all he had promised. The twins added to our great happiness, and those years in Hong Kong were the icing on the cake for me. We made a large number of friends, many of them Chinese, and explored Eastern culture together with matching interest. I suppose we were regarded by others as a golden couple blessed with everything anyone could want.'

The light in her eyes slowly died. 'When the regiment returned to the UK everything changed. The buzz Simon used to get watching races at Happy Valley led him to try participating in the sport as a jockey as well as a punter. Like everything he attempts, he was a natural and soon acquired a couple of thoroughbreds for point-to-pointing. We'd always enjoyed riding, but our stable suddenly expanded.

'At about that time, Simon's talents were taken up by the army and he was offered an opportunity he seized with both hands. He was sent on a series of courses which refreshed and added to his range of European languages, and also groomed him in international politics. To a highly intelligent, gifted man these challenges fulfilled his professional ambition. Between studies there was the challenge of daredevil speed on the back of a superb horse. I saw very little of him during those two years, but a soldierwife has to be prepared for his long absences.'

Tara now spoke as if she were back in that time. 'It wasn't an absence in that sense because we could afford to rent a flat in whichever area he was working. It was absence in the sense that he was rarely in those rented places. There was always an excuse, of course. Classes went on late, a visiting VIP he *must* meet, he was too exhausted – or too inebriated – to drive home. Easier to stay in-mess overnight. Weekends were spent driving the horsebox to race meetings. He was never too exhausted for that.'

Her eyes focussed again on the two men facing her and she gave a faint, sour smile. 'The Ferrari appeared six months before our move to Germany. There had been no mention of it, no discussion. It just turned up with him in the driving seat wearing a huge smile. I thought it had taken over from the horses. Not a bit of it! If he wasn't behind the wheel, he was in the saddle.'

There was a quiet moment before she continued. 'I found things to do, cultivated my own interests. He barely noticed. I soon discovered why. He was negotiating a quarter share in a Learjet, and took to the air before I was even aware of the fact. A third risky pastime that could leave me a widow and the boys fatherless.' Again the sour smile. 'They think he's God personified, but of course, they're male, too.'

Max did not wonder at a man who could neglect such an elegant, intelligent woman. He had too often dealt with cases of errant husbands of beautiful women. It was the irresistible male urge to conquer. Normally, it was sexual, but Simon Kington's mistress was the drive to defy man's limitations by any available means. Had he thought himself God personified? No, he was popular with his fellows. But they were all male, too, of course.

'As you discovered, like Toad my husband couldn't resist buying a new machine. A microlight. As sole owner he could fly it whenever he had the time and inclination. And he did.'

Tom shifted in his chair, asked, 'Did you never offer to join him in these sports?'

'And risk the boys losing both parents in a crash? I love them too much for that.'

'Mrs Kington, is it because of what you've just told us that you drugged and hid your husband?' Max asked, unable to accept such reasoning.

She continued as if he had not spoken. 'The boys deserve to be given all the advantages Simon had. They're both bright and have set their sights on highly rewarding careers that require expensive training. Their education costs us a large sum annually, and they also naturally want the things teenage boys need to match their peers.' Her voice grew cold. 'Simon has run through his grandmother's inheritance and most of the capital in the bank. Sir Chetwin would block any attempt to sell the company shares, so Simon has just put the house in Cheshire in the hands of an agent.' The passion was back with a vengeance. 'It's our home; our *future*. I love it. The boys love it. His grandmother expected him to value and cherish it, see that it was passed down the generations. Simon ... he was preparing to sell it *to buy a new toy*!'

Her voice grew even thicker with emotion. 'You'll have read about the auction in the States of *Silver Flash*, the boat that took the water speed record to an all-time high six years ago. Simon was so determined to own it he was going to rob us of High Gables and any funds he could access, and bid for it. He was deaf to all my attempts to make him see reason, refused to face the certainty of having to remove the boys from Winchester, reduce our lifestyle, struggle to stay solvent, sign the death warrant to our marriage. He was like an addict being told not to have what he craved.'

She struggled for composure, then looked across the table with defiance. 'I *had* to stop him from committing this ultimate madness. I told Gerhardt the only way was to lock Simon away until the auction was over. He suggested how it could be done. It should have been so simple,' Tara said again. 'Three days, that's all. The danger would be averted and, hopefully, the belief that his mysterious abductors had meant him harm but were forced to change their intentions would bring Simon to his senses. Value what he had. Realize his true priorities. Understand his duty to me and the boys.' Her arrogance, her sophistication were replaced by basic frankness. 'It was an act of desperation, Captain Rydal. *Utter* desperation.'

Max walked by the stream in the early evening April hush. Sunset was now no more than an apricot glow behind the stand of trees, and late-roosting birds were racing soundlessly to the safety of high branches.

Frau Hahn had friends coming for dinner and cards, so Max intended to eat at a small restaurant he often used. Before heading to it he needed some exercise and fresh air to clear his mind of that day's revelations. The air was still and retained some of its earlier warmth as he walked on through the overgrown stretch to where the path widened once more. Once there he stood, as he always did, gazing at that house way off across the meadows and imagining the family within it having returned from their time in classroom or office. Children chattering, showing their school books to their parents, then settling to homework while mother and father enjoyed a predinner drink during an affectionate exchange of news on their individual working days. A cosy, appealing image Max invariably conjured up whenever he watched that distant manor until dusk gradually hazed its outline, and pinpoints of light twinkled at the windows. Then it was swallowed up by darkness as curtains were drawn and night descended.

Max now retraced his steps with the aid of a strong torch beam, feeling curiously chilled by the loss of that vision. He told himself it was impossible to know what really went on inside any house. People presented an image to the world that frequently cloaked a very different one. Simon Kington: handsome, gifted, admired, universally liked by his fellows, hero-worshipped by his sons, was a selfish, callous bastard prepared to destroy his family with his avarice.

Before parting today, Max and Tom had agreed to leave until tomorrow the difficult task of deciding how to report this unusual case to Colonel Trelawney, who must then consult the legal department. Tara Kington may well have been desperate, but she had committed a serious crime for which there could be no justification in law. When asked why she had not confided in Sir Chetwin, with whom she shared mutual affection, she had said she wished to spare him and Molly the truth about their son. Yet she had sent that ransom note surely knowing it would cause them great distress.

Max suspected her motive was more a desire to protect her own reputation than to spare others. She admitted to sending it because it was being whispered that she was married to a double murderer. Keeping up appearances!

Feeling the chill dampness rising from the stream, Max quickened his pace. He had lingered too long gazing at his fantasy house and family across the meadows, and he suddenly wanted his dinner.

Gerhardt Wolf was a German national and therefore beyond military justice, but he would have to be called as a witness. Without a doubt he would attest to doing only as directed by Tara; that she was the true perpetrator. Max was happy to leave the rest to the *Polizei*, who must investigate his use of an unaccredited drug. Thankfully, Ben Steele was given just a single dose and was A1 again. Time would reveal the full cost of the prolonged dosing of Kington. It did not augur well for him. Tara's act of desperation was likely to have an outcome far more tragic than her hope of getting her husband's priorities on the right lines.

Regaining the road, Max stepped out towards the restaurant. It was wise to sleep on this. His feelings about it were very mixed. Could Tara plead provocation? But she had let the trend continue for so long before seeking outside help from any direction. In the army there were many opportunities to seek a solution to problems. Why had she ignored them? Protecting the golden couple image, he supposed. How had they managed to hide the truth for so long in the confined society of a military base? Pride was an unacknowledged weakness, of course.

Approaching the restaurant and savouring the aromas wafting from the kitchen, Max thought about Tara's answer when he had asked why Wolf had been so willing to aid and abet such a risky plan.

'We are occasional lovers. His wife is forever in the US promoting her cosmetics range; Simon has his other life. It has nothing to do with adultery, just satisfying a need for affection. After all, I've had none from my husband since he fell in love with his own masculinity.'

Thirteen

The girls were in bed supposedly settling for sleep but more probably still reading pop or fashion magazines, chancing their arms until a stern parent told them to put out their lights, or else! They had eaten supper as a complete family tonight. Nora insisted on everyone sitting round the table and talking to each other, so the TV was switched off during meals bringing the usual grumbles from the sisters. They were good-natured protests, in the main, and conversation was lively although mostly what Tom called 'girl talk'. When he was able to join them, he did his best to broaden the subjects under discussion so that he at least understood some of what his daughters were talking about.

While Nora explained over the phone the finer points of a bridal train consisting of numerous flounces, Tom sat quietly trying to get to grips with the Simon Kington affair. They had been way off beam trying to link it with the murders Tara Kington had found so 'inconvenient'.

Sir Chetwin was still critically ill, although the news of his son's safety had brought a slight improvement in his condition. Neither he nor Molly Kington yet knew of their daughter-in-law's involvement, but they would have to be told of it and of Simon's uncertain mental state as a result of the drugging. Tara Kington's 'act of utter desperation' could well split that family asunder where a genuine kidnap would certainly have drawn them closer.

Taking the broad view, Simon Kington would surely have endangered his career with his passion for expensive playthings. Debts piling up, unpaid mess bills, refusal of further overdrafts at banks, the inability to return social invitations, the breakdown of family. Bad enough to ride those stormy seas in civilian life; almost impossible in the close military family here in Germany. A senior army officer was expected to maintain a certain standard, set an example. Tara Kington might have saved the inherited manor she loved from being sold, but would she ever live in it once her husband learned the truth?

Nora came to sit beside him, holding out her glass for a refill. 'Hope you've left some in the bottle for me.'

He grinned. 'Would I dare drink it all?'

''Course you would!' She stared at the small amount he poured into her glass. 'Got here just in time, didn't I?'

'You should have cut short the flounce gossip. Ten minutes you've been rabbiting about them. Surely one flounce is much like another. How can there be so much to say about them?'

'I often wonder how you can spend so long gazing at a model engine,' she returned smartly. 'They don't change from day to day, yet you study them as if it's the first time you've set eyes on them.' She snuggled against him, sipping her wine contentedly. 'So long as it's model engines, not other women, you're in the clear, chum.'

He slipped his arm around her and kissed the top of her head, knowing she knew there would never be other women. After a moment or two, he said, 'About this birthday of mine. You said Dad dropped a hint they're getting me the one I'm after. It's pricey. Can you offer to go halves with them?'

'No, they'd be offended.' She angled her face up to his. 'What brought that on?'

'That collection I have is worth a bit. Have you ever resented what I've spent on it?'

She sat up and faced him. 'You mean because the girls have had to go without shoes, and I have to go out scrubbing floors so we can afford to eat?'

'You do all that dressmaking and flounces,' he pointed out with a frown, unable to match her mood.

'Because I love doing it.' She punched him gently on the arm. 'It's not because we'd starve if I didn't. What's come over you?'

He looked deep in to her eyes. 'What if that were true? What if each of those models cost thousands and I kept buying them until we were bankrupt? Wouldn't listen to anything you said, made those engines my main reason

310

for living. What would you do?'

Sensing that he was serious, she pursed her lips and thought for some seconds. 'I'd never let it get to that stage. Early on I'd stop your dad sending the magazines to tempt you to buy another model. I'd have a quiet word with Max and ask him to talk some sense into you. If that failed, I'd approach one of the padres for the same reason. As a last desperate shot, I'd draw most of the money from our joint account and put it in one in my sole name where you couldn't get at it, because our three daughters and I need you to support and care for us.'

Tom nodded. 'I thought you'd say something along those lines. In a nutshell, you'd do something constructive before I ruined all our lives.'

'Tom, whoever this has happened to has a serious problem. If you made those model engines your whole reason for living it would be because you had nothing else to live for. The girls and I make sure you have, because we all love you dearly. I suspect your man has been starved of it, so he compensates by having passionate feelings for things he can buy. They never let him down.'

'You should have been a psychologist,' he murmured, seeing a new angle to the case.

'I know, but who'd do all those bloody flounces?' She kissed him. 'Let's open another bottle of wine. I didn't get my fair share of the last one.'

Tom selected a bottle from the cabinet and

was drawing the cork when the phone rang. He picked up the receiver beside him. 'Tom Black.'

'Piercey, sir. I think I've cracked it,' said the eager voice of his sergeant.

Tom put down the corkscrew, said slowly, 'Let's have it, then.'

'I've been going through all those statements yet again, and I've found someone who would have known where both Brian New and Colin White would be when they were killed.'

'Why wasn't it apparent before?'

'Because we didn't have that evidence from Lieutenant Sanders, White's climbing partner. It all now fits.'

'Convince me,' invited Tom, knowing Piercey's tendency to make mountains from molehills in the hope of pre-empting his colleagues with a solution.

'Lieutenant Sanders sent his friend the info about donating sperm. A joke, or not, as the case may be. We know all contact with the Reinhardts was by e-mail. There was chaos reigning at the White home – all those twins and the monster in-laws about to arrive – so I guess he did it all on the office computer, or a laptop he kept there. Probably the latter.'

'Fair enough,' agreed Tom, gazing blindly at the bottle as he digested this information.

'The bloke – Captain White – was stressed out, so it's likely he didn't delete everything immediately. Which means it could be accessed by someone without much difficulty when he vacated the office, and that person would know where he was really going for his leave.'

'Yes!' Tom was now listening more keenly.

'I've checked on the staff of Number One Company, but can find no strong link to Brian New. Certain I was on the right track I rang the company sarn't major and asked if there'd been any changes of staff over the past month ... and bingo!'

Piercey loved dramatic pauses and this one really irritated Tom. 'Get on with it, Piercey!'

'They had two sergeants off with that stomach bug that ran through the regiment, so Number Three Company let them have one of theirs pro tem.'

Pieces flew together to present Tom with a startling whole. 'Sam Dawkins, Brian New's best mate who had every last detail of the dinner date with the nurse! It's possible. More than possible, man.'

'I've just now contacted the base, sir. Dawkins has gone AWOL.'

Sergeant Samuel Arthur Dawkins was apprehended by Interpol in Holland after three days of freedom. During that period Max received confirmation from the School of Oriental Medicine that the killer toxin was of Eastern origin. Several stimulants used in Chinese medicines peddled by charlatans in the backstreets had been massively augmented by an hallucinatory substance that would induce panic, sending the heart into spasm followed by cardiac arrest. The School would like to be informed of the source, if it was revealed to SIB.

Connie Bush put forward one of her bright ideas at the morning briefing. 'We've been working on the premise that the killer silenced Barker in Hong Kong, then flew here to do the same with New and Colin White. We know Sam Dawkins wasn't in Honkers to murder Captain Barker, but it's more than possible he finished off the other two. If that's so, where did he get hold of the fatal cocktail of Oriental potions?'

'We'd like to liaise with the *Polizei* to suss out what connections back home the owners of local Chinese restaurants and take-aways have,' added Heather Johnson.

Tom shook his head. 'Not until we have Dawkins here and hear his evidence. If we get a confession, we'll get that, too. We've already landed Klaus Krenkel with investigations into the Reinhardt Klinik and Wolf Oberfeld Pharmaceuticals. He won't want to expend time and manpower on Chinese chefs without strong reasons.'

'Nothing to stop us doing it ourselves. They're not German nationals and it is our investigation,' persisted Connie Bush.

'*I'm* not prepared to expend time and manpower on it,' snapped Tom, irritated by Connie's description of 'finishing off' Brian New and Colin White. 'The Kington case is rounded off. So is the inquiry in to Lieutenant Steele's drugging. Until we have Dawkins' evidence to act on you can all get back to the tasks you abandoned to concentrate on these murders. Get to it!'

Waiting for the official processes necessary for the return of Sam Dawkins was annoying, but it gave Max and Tom time to discuss the tricky subject of their report on Tara Kington which must be submitted to Colonel Trelawney. Her husband's laptop had, indeed, been found lying openly in his home office so there was no question of divulgence of privileged information, but she had committed a number of chargeable offences that would earn her a prison sentence. SIB therefore had to present the evidence to the CO in a way that would enable him to ensure justice was done.

Punishing Tara would, however, not diminish the damage her 'act of utter desperation' had inflicted on Simon Kington, nor would it eliminate the toll it had taken of Sir Chetwin and his wife. The Kington twins would not only suffer the break-up of their family, but also the backwash from predictable media publicity. The wages of sin!

Tara Kington claimed she had suffered marital neglect. Nora Black maintained that any man who craved possessions was compensating for it. Having had no dealings with Simon, Max and Tom could only agree that the notion of the sophisticated, intelligent, coolly elegant woman he had married offering any man great passion was difficult to imagine. Immaculate support in her social role of wife to a high-powered senior officer, certainly, but unlikely to excite him in bed. Or on the kitchen table!

'He might be such a cold fish himself, he'd never think a kitchen table had any other uses,' grinned Tom, as a girl brought coffee for them both. He glanced up at her. 'Where'd these doughnuts come from, Corporal Hill?'

She pulled a face. 'Sergeant Piercey's handing them out like nobody's business. Says he's celebrating his great success.'

As she closed the door behind her, Tom muttered, 'Piercey sets my back up so often it's as well he picks up kudos now and again.'

Max chuckled. 'What with Piercey and my guts to contend with you cope very well, Tom. *Salut*!' he quoted comically, holding up his doughnut and taking a big bite.

Knowing Dawkins would be brought to Section Headquarters on Tuesday, the SIB team had a welcome free weekend. So Tom was mowing the grass prior to a trip to the river, where he would hire a boat to row to a favourite family picnic spot. Nora and the girls were busy packing a basket with enough food to feed the five hundred, as usual. When Tom was tapped on the back by Maggie, he switched off the mower guessing what she would say.

'*Telephone!* Might have known.' She stamped back to the kitchen door where the gloomy faces of his other two daughters watched his approach. He suspected his own expression was pretty gloomy. This family day was important to him.

He snatched up the receiver. 'Tom Black.'

'Here is Boris Mann. Good morning.' Typical German politeness.

'Good morning. What can I do for you?' Not quite so polite.

'It is for me to do something for you, I am glad to say. It is concerning your Captain White.'

Tom's heart sank. Bang goes the boat on the river! His last Saturday was taken up by meeting this officer at the Reinhardt and returning home deeply frustrated. What the hell was he chasing now?

'I told you some hint of our big investigation of the Reinhardt Klinik, and said that I would tell you of it soon.'

'Yes, that's right.'

'I have only this quick message for you now. A full report will be sent, as a courtesy, at a later time.'

'That's very good of you,' said Tom automatically, wishing Mann would get on with it.

'You have discovered that your Captain had not the operation, as they claimed, but he was at the Klinik for some other purpose. With that information from you we have discovered *Herr Doktor* Reinhardt and his wife have also patients who receive from volunteers as your Captain White the artificial fertilize. This is accepted if normal, but these women are chosen because they make certain mothers. Time and again. The babies are then given to clients who pay much money to have

317

them. Some is passed to the donors, some to the birth mothers, but most is kept by the Reinhardts.'

'They're running a *baby factory*?' demanded Tom, aghast.

'I fear, yes. We are with Interpol on this. It appears many of these babies are sold out of Germany. It is bad, you agree? It will take some weeks – perhaps months – before we have the full truth, but I wished to give you this much to inform your own investigation.'

'Much appreciated. Thanks.'

'We must work together, I think.'

'Absolutely. If I can be of help to you any time, call me.'

Although the picnic went ahead, Tom had to force himself to join in the family fun. His job habitually brought him in to contact with the sad, sordid and venal side of human life, yet Mann's revelation pushed through his ability to hold aloof and depressed him. Watching his three loving and deeply loved daughters he could not help thinking of babies being sold to the highest bidder anywhere in the world. Poor little devils with such uncertain, risky futures.

He also could not help dwelling on the tragedy of Colin White's innocent involvement, along with many other men, who were duped into believing their sperm would assist scientific research. White was beyond learning the truth, and his own four legitimate babies would at least have a stable home and family members during their childhood, untouched by this scandal.

When Sam Dawkins was brought in for questioning his hostility and contempt had faded. He looked a broken man and offered answers before any questions were put to him.

'I never had any inkling he meant to *kill* them,' he blurted out miserably. 'Brian and me were rookies together. Mates from day one. I just couldn't live with it any longer.'

'Absconding wouldn't remove your guilt,' Tom said grimly. 'Why imagine it would?'

'What were you intending to do in Holland?' asked Max.

'Dunno. I had to get away from all the reminders of him here. Every day that passed made what happened to Brian seem more terrible. I had to think, work out what to do. I've no idea where he is now. Might lie low somewhere for a spell before going back to Hong Kong.' Dawkins licked his lips nervously. 'Once I heard about Harry Barker I knew it was all up; knew you'd get around to me eventually. I just had the idea of getting back at him for what he did to Brian and that poor Maitland girl before you nabbed me.'

He thrust his hands through his hair and gripped his head in despair. Then he said in matching tones, 'He told me Barker had turned up on his doorstep demanding a large handout to help set himself up in civilian life. If I'd known how he really solved that problem I'd never have gone along with the rest, I swear only a bloody monster would put an end to them all. Christ, it's as if I did it myself.'

'Can you offer proof that you didn't?' demanded Tom.

Dawkins' brain shifted into gear and began to work cohesively. 'You checked my movements for the vital times on the second day of your investigation. I never left the base. A dozen or more of the lads vouched for me.'

'But you're now admitting to being an accessory to the murders of Sergeant Brian New and Captain Colin White?'

'No!' It was a vehement denial.

Max said tersely, 'A moment ago you stated that if you'd known how "he" resolved that problem – referring to the killing of Harold Barker in Hong Kong – you would never have gone along with the rest. Isn't that a confession to being an accessory?'

'No, sir, no! Not to murder.' Dawkins dragged his sleeve across his brow where sweat was now beading. 'He told me he wanted to talk to them on the q.t. Offer them compensation for their loyalty over the years, as he had to Barker. He could well afford it. He had some good deals going in Honkers.'

'So you passed that news to your best mate; told him to expect a possible financial bonus on its way?' When Dawkins avoided his eyes, said nothing, Tom accused him. 'You set your friend Brian up, let it be known he'd be at the Golden Key that evening. You must have known there'd be nothing above board about the so-called compensation. You then created a strong alibi for yourself and left your best mate to his fate, which was shared by a totally innocent young nurse.'

Speaking then to the top of Dawkins' head, buried in his hands again, Tom continued. 'You were helping out Number One Company when a gastric virus laid low half the battalion, and you read personal e-mails on Captain White's laptop. They told you where he was really heading on leave. You then also betrayed *him* without compunction.'

Max broke the ensuing silence. 'I want to talk about what happened on a certain night patrol along the New Territories border around ten years ago. That's behind the murders, isn't it?' Still silence. 'Dawkins, we've had enough of your histrionics. *Answer my question!*'

The soldier's instinctive reaction to an order brought the Sergeant's head up, and he squared his shoulders against the back of the chair. 'Yes, sir, that's behind it.'

'So give us the identity of the "he" you keep referring to.'

'Norrie Packman. A real wheeler dealer who latched on to the main chance wherever the battalion was stationed. Anyone wanted anything, he knew where to get it cheaper than at the legit outlets. Took his percentage, of course. Has a smooth tongue has Norrie. Never gets sussed.'

'He conducted dubious dealing in Hong

Kong without falling foul of the criminal brotherhoods operating there?'

Dawkins shook his head. 'It was only small-time. No kiddies, no porn, no drugs. He'd get stuff straight off the boats, or buy stall-holders' entire stock at knockdown prices. Watches, handbags, kids' games. Then he'd flog it at double what he paid to the lads to send home.'

Max exchanged a swift glance with Tom, who read it correctly. Where were the Red-caps while this was going on?

'He did this all the time he was out there?' asked Tom.

'Well, there were only so many watches and bags he could shift, so he took up a more profitable operation when it fell in his lap.'

'Go on.'

Dawkins shifted uneasily on his chair, wary of incriminating himself with what he must reveal. 'Norrie always had his eye to racking up his finances. He'd picked up a lot of their lingo from the Chinks he'd had dealings with, and he'd wander round the outlying settle-ments chatting up the old boys who more or less ran the small communities. Once or twice they politely showed him the door, in that frozen-faced way they have. But his silver tongue often won them over. Being twice their size helped.'

'He threatened them?' Max asked.

'No, nothing like that. It simply backed his spiel that he was a man of considerable in-fluence in the British Army.'

'Which led to the profitable operation that fell in his lap?' prompted Tom.

Dawkins nodded. 'He was approached in one of the small villages by a young bloke he rated a Sammy Sharp. By the name of Tang, this bloke was wanting to set up a regular run for illegals in cahoots with soldiers on patrol who would turn a blind eye. He saw Norrie as a hot candidate.'

Max leaned back in his chair now knowing this complex case concerned the purchase of perceived freedom. How curious that the separate development during these past days had involved the kidnap and abuse of a man for personal gain. Trade in human souls!

'So you were involved in Packman's criminal operation?' probed Tom.

Dawkins began to bluster. 'We didn't see it that way. They were desperate to escape persecution, poor devils. Family members had been murdered, they'd themselves been tortured. Hong Kong offered their only salvation.'

'Your motives were purely philanthropic, were they?' suggested Max dryly.

'Yeah, in a way. They'd been brutalized by the Commies.'

'So how did this illegal border crossing work?' demanded Tom.

Dawkins folded his arms and prepared to tell all, knowing he had little choice. He was suspected of killing two men here in Germany and he must prove his innocence of that crime, at least.

'You're aware of the routine out there at night. Observation posts every few hundred yards between the tall watchtowers, and a cycle patrol along the track. To make the op work Norrie had to rope in three others. A bloke with him at one post, and two in the next. The refugees would cross between them, avoiding the cyclist.'

'Name the three men,' Max commanded.

'Norrie already had a hold over a pretty-looking bloke called Coles. They manned one post. Brian and me were in the other.'

'Packman also had a hold over you two?'

'Not me. I just went along with Brian. He'd married Jacki. Mad about her, he was, and she knew it. Before long her relatives began turning up. Came over by boat after dark. Aunts, cousins, sisters-in-law, you name it. The Chinese are great family people. They had false papers but no money. They'd given it all to whoever owned the boats. Jacki threatened to leave Brian if he told the army authorities or the Hong Kong police, so he was struggling to feed and clothe them all on his lance-corporal's pay. He was in a real state when Norrie recruited him. See Norrie had discovered what was going on and knew Brian was ripe for earning something on the side.'

'Packman agreed to split between you whatever he got for the op?'

'After he'd taken his whack, yes. Had no option, did he?'

Tom frowned. 'So these illegal immigrants

were paying Tang sufficient for him to have the lion's share, yet leave enough for four soldiers to think it worth risking their careers and certain punishment?'

Dawkins shrugged. 'They were getting freedom from persecution and a new life under British rule. They believed it was worth selling everything they owned to reach Hong Kong, where friends or relatives would take them in.'

Max leaned forward, asked intently, 'How many times did you allow people in to the colony illegally?'

'Whenever Tang organized a big enough group. He'd let Norrie know, and Norrie then wangled the duty roster so we were on it together one night.'

'So how did the two officers become involved?'

Dawkins frowned. 'Barker was another victim of marriage. His wife was one of those women who run wild on an overseas posting. Party mad, spending money like it grows on trees, drinking too much. He was a wet-behind-the-ears subaltern who couldn't control her. Eventually, he was sent out to gain experience of night patrols and he bloody caught us sending a group across. Norrie wasn't fazed. He put pressure on Barker because he'd seen him frequenting banned backstreet money-lenders – the slippery path for any young officer. There was a stand-off, but Barker was desperate with loan sharks snapping at his heels and he pulled rank. Wanted in on the op in return for his silence. Only time Norrie was caught on the wrong foot. He agreed because there was no time to argue it out with the last of the Chinese moving across the border.'

'Harold Barker went out every time you operated?' asked Max.

'Checked the roster for when we were all on it. Little we could do. Barker would wangle a duty for himself those nights. No one ever questioned it, apparently, and he took his cut on three occasions.'

Max eased his back which was stiffening up on the uncomfortable chair. 'You've not so far revealed how Colin White became linked with your syndicate.'

'He was never part of it,' said Dawkins. 'He simply came out that night as a replacement for Barker, who was sick. It was his turn, anyway, to gain experience of night patrols. He'd only been with us a couple of months. It was his bad luck that the business collapsed before his eyes.' Letting out a deep sigh, he added hollowly, 'Each one of us has honoured the pact we made then; managed to put it behind us, get on with our lives, tread the straight and narrow from that time on.

'We were all professionals keen on a full-time career in the army. Except Norrie. He left at the first opportunity. Soldiering isn't in his blood. Wheeler-dealing is and he saw a profitable future in that cosmopolitan marketplace. It was a risk, but Norrie's a born gambler. He's done well. We've all also

326

achieved what we wanted. Promotion, regi-mental respect, combat experience, being one of a body of men and women ready to defend what we stand for in Britain.' Seeing cynicism in the eyes of the SIB men, he bridled. 'That night changed everything, believe me. We realized where we were heading and pulled up sharp.' He shook his head in disbelief. 'Why, for God's sake, did bloody Barker stir it up after so many years and drive Norrie to take them all out?'

Max said quietly. 'We know why. Barker wanted money in return for his silence. Greed is something Packman well under-stands, but can't accept in others.'

'Yet Barker wasn't there on that significant occasion,' Tom pointed out.

'No. He became a right pain in the arse because of it,' Dawkins countered. 'Wouldn't believe our word that the op had been cancelled by Tang, who wanted out of the whole deal because it had become too dicey. Barker swore we were double-dealing him and threatened to blow the gaff on what we'd been doing. We knew it was just wild talk because he was in it up to his neck, but he kept pestering Norrie for money. He also devised ways to punish us in the hope that we'd buy him off.'

'Details,' demanded Tom, who could guess much of it, anyway.

'Huh! He used his officer status to humili-ate and aggravate at every chance. Gave out extra duties, refused weekend passes, wrote unfavourable monthly reports, allocated low marks for regimental efficiency or firearms tests. He even went out unofficially on several night patrols to check us out. Thing was, Norrie never had to wangle duty rosters after that night, so we were rarely all out there together again.' He frowned. 'Barker's persecution really got to Brian; made him determined to get some pips on his shoulders. Real power, he called it.'

Max disagreed. 'Only if rank is used dishonestly. Presumably, Barker's transfer to the First Battalion put an end to all that.'

'Oh aye, and we thought his obsession would fade, that he'd calm down and concentrate on his career. We heard, of course, that his wife was still leading him a dog's life and then ran off with a muscle-bound git from a gym. We also heard about the divorce that left him paying maintenance for kids living with his ex and her toy boy, but we never dreamed he was still nursing the cockeyed conviction that we'd shut him out of the syndicate so we could each take a bigger cut.'

'Which was why he flew to Hong Kong on the brink of cutting his ties with the RCR, determined to get the truth from Packman,' prompted Max. 'We have to assume that he did, and attempted blackmail.'

'I can't see that,' responded Dawkins heavily. 'We covered our tracks so well there's no one would suss it out after ten years. Barker must have mounted one hell of a

328

mammoth bluff to put the serious frights on a man like Norrie.'

'Serious enough to take the lives of three men.' Max leaned back fixing the prisoner with a challenging stare. 'What occurred that night, Sergeant Dawkins, that Packman committed triple murder to conceal? Time to bring it out in the open.'

Sam Dawkins slumped in his seat as if the weight of that knowledge bowed him down. It seemed to the two detectives that he was looking beyond them at an alien scene in a faraway place as he conjured up a long-ago drama he had determinedly locked away in the recesses of his mind.

The darkness was broken only by a faint yellow haze hanging above the distant border post manned by Red Army guards. The silence was broken only by the maddening chorus of bullfrogs and the occasional splash from the fish-breeding ponds that abounded along this border with China. There was no moon, an asset on these nights. Shadowy figures materializing from the undergrowth to cross the tarmac and merge with the blackness of New Territories terrain. The lucky ones!

Sam felt the usual mix of excitement and gut-wrenching apprehension. He compared it to the tension while watching for the enemy to appear out of the night, except that the 'enemy' were his mates scattered along the border track. If any of them behaved unpredictably at the vital time the game could be up. Discovery would put them behind bars; a lengthy stretch. Dishonourable discharge. But they had worked this successfully before. No reason for a balls-up this time. He told himself they were giving some poor wretches a new lease of life, but in truth he did it for the wad of dollars it brought and for the buzz it gave him. After all, the Reds would be taking over this outpost colony and imposing their regime in sixteen months. Back to square one for the illegals then.

The telephone crackled before coming to vocal life. Sergeant Emms checking that all was quiet. Sam gave the affirmative and signed off.

Brian shifted nervously beside him. 'Corporal Symes should be going by on the bike soon. If he's late...'

'He won't be. Symsie's always on the dot. That's how he earned his stripes. Soon as he's passed we'll move off to meet Norrie at the crossing point. Tang should be waiting by now.'

'Sam ... I've been thinking. This is the last time I'm on this. It's too risky and I...'

'Shhh!' hissed Sam, deliberately breaking in to Brian's oft-repeated whinge. He was already in it up to his neck by supporting Jacki's assorted relatives. Allowing a few more illegals entry made little difference to his culpability.

'What is it?' Brian whispered tautly.

'Heard movement. Probably a snake, or one

330

of those bloody great lizards,' Sam replied inventively and shone his torch to illuminate the track. The powerful beam fell on Corporal Symes, rifle slung across his chest, slowly and silently peddling past. He pulled up and dismounted, unslinging his rifle.

'What's up? Heard something?' he demanded.

'Just a bit of rustling. Probably a couple of courting snakes,' Sam returned lightly. 'Tie themselves in knots to do it.'

'Can't stand the bloody things.' The wiry NCO pushed his cycle across, ready to chat.

Sam had to move him on fast. 'Better not hang about, Corp. Second Lieutenant White's on duty tonight "gaining experience". That's officer-speak for checking on us. He's hyper-keen to make his mark; needle sharp. He'll make a meal of catching you off that bike.'

'Actually need a pee.' Symes urinated noisily into the undergrowth. 'Gets rid of snakes does piss. They slide off quick. So you know what to do if you hear any more.' He swung his leg over the saddle and rode off noiselessly into the darkness, heading for the next post.

'He looked suspicious,' breathed Brian. 'What if he doubles back?'

'A bursting bladder puts that kind of grimace on any man's face. Stop being so bloody jumpy.' Sam counted to ten, then pushed Brian's arm. 'Get going!'

Leaving their post they crept silently in the direction Symes had come from. Norrie and

Gareth Coles would be coming cautiously to meet them. This was the high adrenalin time; the buzz factor. Sam's mouth was dry, his heart was racing, his face and body running with perspiration. These tingling moments on these vital nights he would remember all his life. The rasping croak of bullfrogs, the whine of mosquitoes, his own heavy breathing. The enveloping darkness; feeling his way forward tensed for an unwelcome command over the radio. Tensed even further for the sight of the dim shadows of Norrie and the lad he bullied into working with him.

There they were; dark against a paler darkness. Sam heard Brian's sharp indrawn breath, his murmured wish for it to be over and behind them. No word was exchanged. The four soldiers stood together listening for the bird call signifying that Tang was waiting with the extra large group he said he would have tonight. Without warning the young Chinese was there. Sam's heart bumped nervously.

Norrie closed with Tang, spoke in an urgent undertone. Although Sam was unable to catch what was said it was evident they were in verbal conflict. Serious conflict. Tang's voice rose in passion, clear in the surrounding quietness.

'You wicked! Disgusting! I report to Hong Kong police. I report to army authority. I tell newspaper.'

'Shut it, for Christ's sake!' hissed Norrie. 'You'll have all my mates along here, and who d'you think they'll believe, eh? You've no proof, and I'll say we caught you trying to cross. You'll be shunted over into Red territory before you know what's happened.'

'Are we doing it tonight, or aren't we?' whispered Brian stepping over to the pair.

'No!' cried Tang. 'You no do any more. I tell police. I tell newspaper.'

'Tell 'em what?' asked Coles, clearly edgy.

'You deal with bad men. You tell when people cross. They come take young girl, young boy to sex house. Take in one truck. Old people in other truck. Old people no see childs again. You sell them for dollars.'

'*What?*' exclaimed Brian. 'Where'd you get that crazy notion?'

'Keep it down,' urged Norrie. 'Sound travels a long way at night.' He concentrated on Tang. 'You've got it all wrong. We wouldn't be involved in anything like that.'

'Yes, *you*,' yelled Tang, pointing at Norrie. 'My cousin discover. Hear your name, have description. It you. And you and you and you,' he added wildly, pointing at each of them in turn.

Brian rounded on Norrie. 'Have you been double-dealing us; making arrangements on the side with one of the brothel-keepers? *Have you?*' he demanded in a voice shaking with anger.

Sam grabbed Brian's arm, drew him apart. 'Leave it, mate. Leave Norrie to calm the bastard down or we'll alert Johnson and Coyle, Palmer and Brace. They'll surely hear

333

our voices from their positions and report in. Then we'll be done for.'

'But he's accusing Norrie of selling some of these poor devils in to prostitution.' Brian was highly worked up. 'If he has, and I wouldn't bloody put it past him, we've been helping him do it. We're as guilty as him.'

Sam grew seriously worried. Brian was too ethical for his own good. He would worry at this like a dog with a bone. Admitting illegals was one thing. If the authorities got wind of the other lucrative deal...

Tang was still shouting at Norrie, and Sam was just deciding to get himself and Brian back to their own guard post away from the disturbance when the situation climaxed. The distressed Chinese pulled a knife on Norrie, but he was confronting a highly trained military man. Tang's accusations died out on a gurgle as he dropped to the ground. There was a brief moment of awed silence before they were suddenly bathed in light.

'What the hell's going on here?' snapped Colin White, who had arrived silently on a bicycle and switched on his torch.

Norrie was typically quick off the mark. 'Caught this man trying to cross, sir. Had a large group with him, but they all turned and ran for it. This bastard tried to stick me in the gut. In the struggle he got it instead.'

White laid the cycle on the ground and crossed to examine the inert body. Glancing up from the small pool of light in which he squatted, he said, 'He's dead. There were others, you said?'

'Three or four dozen, I'd say. That's why we met up to tackle them,' Norrie lied smoothly.

'Did you call in to report?'

'No time, sir.'

The officer stood upright again, reached for his telephone.

'I shouldn't do that, sir,' Norrie advised him quickly.

White frowned. His face looked as young and fresh as a senior schoolboy in the reflective light thrown by his torch. 'Why?'

'You haven't been out here long enough to know the consequences of something like this. You'll have to write a full report for the CO. Another for SIB, who'll grill us endlessly. Then there's the Reds. This guy's one of theirs who's ended up dead on our side of the border. Potential political aggro. Bad news for the Brit administrators. Particularly bad for the regiment. The CO won't be happy that you've stirred up a hornet's nest unnecessarily.'

Sam smiled in the darkness. Norrie had a silver tongue. He would get them out of this dangerous development.

'For God's sake, Packman, a potential infiltrator has been killed. It has to be reported.'

Norrie stepped nearer in threatening manner. 'Much more sensible to dump the body in one of the fish ponds and forget the whole thing. No come back on us that way, sir.'

'*What?* I can't believe you said that.'

'You'd better believe it, sonny,' Norrie hissed in the youthful subaltern's face, 'because that's what we're going to do. I won't ask you to carry out the deed, but you'll act as if you never saw or heard any of this. You see, I happen to know *you* were the rat who leaked details to the *South China Post* of Lieutenant Masters' little scam at Happy Valley racecourse. Got a pal on the inside there. Great embarrassment in government circles, egg on the CO's face, black mark against the regiment, and lasting damage to Masters' career. Sent home pronto, and *you* took over his job with acting rank. Dirty, underhand way to settle a personal score and climb the promotion ladder at the same time.'

Sam heard all this in amazement. How the hell had Norrie learned that bit of scandal? If made public it would damage White as badly as his colleague Masters, and his future would be strewn with obstacles to advancement. As Norrie said, more sensible for all of them to dump Tang's body in a fish pond and walk away from it.

Colin White stared at Norrie for long moments, his face a sickly yellow in the torchlight. Then he turned, pulled the cycle upright, and rode off into the night.

As Max listened to Sam Dawkins' account of past criminal acts he finally understood why these men had changed into solid, worthwhile members of their regiment and society. Also why they had kept silent about the murder that had been committed that night. Yet Harry Barker, who had not witnessed those events, must have persuaded Packman he had discovered the truth from those who had been there, and demanded hush money. In doing so, he had condemned two other men to death. A man like Packman would hold life cheaply. More blood on his hands would hardly register with him.

'So Packman silenced Brian New and Colin White as a precaution, but what about Coles, the lad bullied into participation?'

Dawkins blinked as if coming from a dream back to reality. 'He got sick. They gave him a medical discharge just before we left Hong Kong. He died of AIDS a year later.'

'That leaves you,' stated Tom with heavy inference. 'Why weren't you another victim?'

The perspiration on Dawkins' face increased and he refused to meet Tom's eyes. 'Norrie always trusted me. He knew I'd never rat on him.'

'But you just have,' Max said harshly. 'I think you were in on more of Packman's schemes than that one. I think you were his right hand man, listening at open windows, looking through keyholes, following colleagues and noting their off-duty activities, giving him much of the info he needed to run his dodgy affairs without hindrance.' Dawkins shook his head violently. 'Oh, I think I'm right. I also think you knew well enough that a man like Packman was unlikely to offer a financial gift of appreciation for their loyalty when you told him the movements of Colin White and your best mate, Brian. That makes you an accessory to double murder.'

Dawkins was now fighting back tears. 'No, I swear to God I ... I didn't know he'd put an end to Barker when I did as he asked. If I *had* known ... Brian *was* my best mate. No way would I have let that happen to him. And to that poor girl.' He fought for control. 'I've told you this now because I want him caught and put away for the rest of his life. I went AWOL with that idea. Everything's going to be made public now, so I'm past caring what happens to me. If I could stick a hypo full of poison in that bastard I'd feel I'd righted the balance.'

'Righting the balance is our job,' Tom said grimly. 'As the sole survivor, we'll bleed you dry of every detail of your activities in Hong Kong. Packman will get what he deserves, never fear.'

'And so will you,' added Max, thinking of Vera Maitland who had received an offer of marriage shortly before dying, and of Christine White languishing in a psychiatric ward because this man had broken a ten-year-old pact of silence and betrayed his colleagues.

Max took his usual walk beside the river that evening, but the sound of water chattering over stones failed to charm and relax him. He gazed at the dusk sky in a mood of dejection. Many layers of the Chinese puzzle had fallen away, but some remained and SIB could not reveal the whole. All they could do was present their evidence against Sam Dawkins. As the sole survivor his story would be open to dispute, and there was no dependence on his confirming it in a court of law.

Packman's crimes would be the pigeon of the Hong Kong police, including the triple murder. SIB would give reports on the two committed in Germany, of course, but the killer would be dealt with by the Chinese. It would be months, even years, before the ramifications of Packman's criminal activities resulted in a trial. By then SIB would have handled so many cases any sense of personal satisfaction would be lost. Small wonder he felt low-spirited.

Breaking through the overhanging greenery he stood gazing at the house across the meadow, where lights were starting to twinkle in the windows. He watched until the curtains were drawn and the signs of human presence vanished. Tonight it felt as if he were being denied, as if that unknown family was shutting from their lives an unwelcome stranger. It added to his curious sense of loss.

Remaining there in the darkness, watching the moon growing wonderfully luminous, a deep longing for a home, a place where he truly belonged suddenly assailed him. Somewhere he could return to now and find warmth to melt this present inner chill. The longing became an ache in his chest. How good it would be to go home to a loving partner: to kiss soft lips, run his hands over satiny, scented skin, bury his face in long hair perfumed by shampoo, hear sighs of surrender.

Studying the lunar shadows and highlights that men had conquered and explored, Max came to realize the past was finally behind him. Time to move on, live fully again, grab his future before it slipped away from him.

The house was unusually quiet when Tom let himself in. The bridal gown with every flounce complete hung on the wall awaiting collection. A mouth-watering aroma wafted from the kitchen as he headed there. Nora smiled warmly at him and gave him a lingering kiss.

'The girls have gone skating with the Fellowes boys. Mike said he'll fetch them and deliver them home. So we have the place to ourselves, lover. D'you want to eat first or afterwards?' Then she studied him. 'Just eat, I take it?'

'Sorry, love,' he said, putting an arm around her. 'Feeling a bit flat, as you do when something ends unsatisfactorily. Let's open a bottle of that Shiraz and sink it swiftly. I usually perform wonders when I'm sloshed.'

The wine certainly helped to dispel the blues. The beef strogonoff followed by cinnamon pears added the finishing touches. Yet they did not go to bed. Their love was the kind that can also be expressed by perfect understanding and generosity. As they sat together on the sofa, finishing off the wine, Tom began to accept that the complex case was virtually over for them, although a complete resolution was a long way off. He gave a wry smile before pushing thoughts of it aside. Max had mentioned getting rid of bad apples. They had dismissed that notion because the victims had all seemed so saintly. But that *had* been behind the three murders. Packman was a bad apple who had tainted the others ten years ago.

'About that holiday you mentioned,' murmured Nora against his shoulder. 'Can we now arrange a date with your parents to have the girls while we flit off?'

'Sure. Whenever it suits them.'

'And whenever we can secure a booking at short notice.'

He kissed the top of her head. 'They've usually got some very cheap offers at the last minute.'

'Skinflint!' She glanced up at him. 'You did say I could choose where we go, didn't you?'

He smiled. 'I did, and you can. Just so long as it's not Hong Kong.'

Fourteen

The ramifications of what SIB considered an unsatisfactory outcome slowly unfolded over the following months. Their case against Sam Dawkins was reduced to a simple charge of absence without leave. At the preliminary hearing he claimed to have been subjected to mental torture and bullied into saying he had allowed illegals to cross the border. He had never known a Chinese called Tang nor seen him knifed by a British soldier. Lack of evidence along with the fact that all possible witnesses were dead prevented further action being taken.

Norris Packman offered unshakeable proof that he had not left Hong Kong during April and therefore could not have committed the murders in Germany. The Chinese police put on their back burner a request to investigate the killing of Harold Barker. They had no manpower to spare for what they considered was a purely British military affair when the crime rate in Hong Kong was so high. Besides, local criminal gangs so often silenced or abducted potential witnesses before they could give evidence.

Believing Packman to have employed a

hitman for the three crimes, SIB made extensive inquiries among the owners of Chinese restaurants and take-aways in Germany but were unsuccessful. Verdicts of murder by person or persons unknown were inevitable. Unacceptable to the bereaved and leaving the investigators with an unwelcome sense of failure. To know yet be unable to prove and bring to justice was not a new situation for the military detectives. Telling themselves it was all part of the job, it nevertheless rankled and remained in the background as they dealt with the more routine cases of drug abuse, sexual harassment, theft and insubordination.

It was after collecting evidence following the theft of large amounts of beer and spirits from the Sergeants' Mess, during which a staff sergeant was badly beaten up, that Tom returned to Section Headquarters in the middle of July. In Max's office he outlined details of witness statements.

'It seems more than likely to be the work of a coupla thugs who're in to wheeler-dealing. They're pretty well-known on the base for being able to lay their hands on stuff the lads'll buy on the quiet.'

'Huh! A pair of Norrie Packmans.'

Tom scowled. 'Don't mention that bastard's name. I've put two men on stake-out. They must have stored the booze off-base. A rented garage, probably. Phipps and Mayhew will watch and follow when they next go for supplies. There'll be other stuff stashed there, you bet.'

'How's Staff Corby?'

'Looks a mess, but making progress.'

'We'll get them on ABH for that. Good work.'

'Haven't caught them red-handed yet. But we will.' He smiled. 'I bumped into the RCR's Miss Marple as I was leaving.'

A corporal entered with tea and biscuits for Max, who asked her to bring some for Mr Black.

'Take a seat, Tom. Nothing urgent on the cards and we've had little chance to catch up on the lighter side of this plaguey job since you and Nora returned from South Africa.'

Tom's tea was brought as he sighed with pleasant recollections of what had been almost a second honeymoon. 'You should do something like that. Take off to an exotic location and relax.'

'No fun on your own.'

'Find someone when you get there.'

'So how was Ben Steele?' Max asked pointedly.

Tom accepted the switch of subject. 'Full of news. His hero, Simon Kington, took a medical discharge two weeks ago. Seems the slight brain damage has slowed his physical reactions and reduced his former mental acuteness. It's generally understood he plans to work for Grant Bonner Kington part-time, translating and assisting his father to entertain foreign clients.'

Max frowned. 'Is Sir Chetwin already back

at the helm?'

'He sounds the kind of man who'll die at it. Didn't you get the impression of a personality who would refuse to be bested by anyone? Or anything?'

'Nearly perforated my eardrum during that telephone conversation,' Max agreed with a nod, 'but he's a fool if he ignores the medical warning.'

'Maybe he'll heed the next one.'

'If it doesn't kill him.'

Tom took a biscuit and bit into it. 'Mr Steele said Kington's selling the Ferrari, the microlight and his share in the Learjet to shore up his ailing bank balance. It's pretty well-known now that he was heading for financial ruin when his wife took those desperate measures to keep the house she loved. Kington has plans to make his home there with his sons, and open a riding-school.'

'Phoenix rising from the ashes, eh? Tara will never live in that mansion. The case against her is certain to result in a lengthy term in Holloway. I can't see that family ever forgiving and taking her back in to the fold, can you?'

Tom shook his head. 'Steele said divorce proceedings have already started. However, women of that type rarely stay defeated for long. Once she's served her term she'll set about snaring some other wealthy prey. She used to give talks on art appreciation. Wouldn't surprise me if she decamped to France or Italy and haunted the art scene until the right prize came along.'

'Wouldn't surprise me, either. She had Gerhardt Wolf in the palm of her hand. Klaus Krenkel called in this morning to tell us they're gathering enough evidence against him to bring charges within a week or two. The Reinhardts are indefinitely suspended from practising and their movements are still drastically curtailed during the complex international probe into their criminal natal sideline. Krenkel estimates it'll be months, even longer, before they have the full picture.'

'I guess they'll never get it,' Tom said heavily. 'There could be dozens of little kids in far-flung corners of the world who'll never be traced. Doesn't bear thinking about.'

Max nodded. 'Some might be living very happy lives.'

The father of three said, 'So might puppies from a pet shop. It's the whole concept of selling babies – small human beings – that I'll never accept.'

Max allowed a short silence before asking, 'How are Nora and your girls?'

That softened Tom's expression. 'Fine. Ganging up on me, as usual.'

'Female prerogative, Tom. I'm afraid you'll have to break some unwelcome news to them when you get home.'

'Oh?' It was said warily.

'Notification came through an hour ago. We're being moved to one of the bases. The MoD rules this building too expensive to maintain, so work is to be started on renovating two disused stores blocks for our use. You'll be allocated quarters on the base.'

'Oh Christ, another move! Nora will go spare. She and the girls love it where they are now.' Tom got to his feet restlessly, facing the prospect of moving home, family and workplace elsewhere. 'How soon?'

'When the new Section Headquarters are ready. Sod's Law puts the date around Christmas,' Max said with a sigh.

Tom rocked on his feet for several seconds, then swung round to say, 'Do you ever ask yourself why you stay with this flaming organization?'

'Frequently.' He gave a wry smile. 'The answer's always the same. As a boy I wanted to be either a soldier or a policeman. This flaming organization allows me to be both.'